*For My Friend Patrick, Whose Irrepressible Spirit
Inspired Max's Adventures,
and
for Gary & Teddy,
Who Share Max's Interest in the Unconventional*

FOREWORD

This book is a fictional memoir, written for my enjoyment, and to document my earliest days in Los Angeles. Like Max, in 1979, I was fortunate to be tossed in with a collection of charming originals, some who had arrived from Europe to enjoy the fresh spirit of LA, and others of purely domestic issue. As other writers have more eloquently admitted, I have chosen to enhance and embellish these events, even to the point of creating villains and heroes. To those early friends who are made villainous or too heroic, please forgive me. My imagination and the interests of storytelling shaped these digressions. Know that, in my true memory, I don't forget your indelible contributions to the fun and vivacity of those days.

Montecito, 2016

Alex at the Chateau Marmont

It was the time of Europeans coming to LA. Nineteen seventy-nine and I was twenty-six. That's when I met Alex des Prairies at the Chateau Marmont. Perhaps you were raised as I was in New England in the 1960s, accustomed to hotels that were clean, or new. At least not tattered, neglected, with the run-down ambiance of an Irish country estate sold for taxes.

The Chateau's lobby was dark. Beyond thick faded panels of silk and velvet, French doors led to the lawn, while tapestry scenes of lute-strumming dandies and precious coquettes covered the walls. Fat implacable sofas and baronial chairs had been there since Don Quixote's time, in the depths of which wizened screenwriters and New York actors had seated themselves and then disappeared.

"Maxwell Rider to see Alex des Prairies," I said. "The international filmmaker," I added importantly. Alex had acquired a minor reputation as Europe's bad-boy of cinema before Roman Polanski's dark presence swept everyone from the field.

"Count des Prairies," I repeated, only too glad to use a real title for a real Count. But the pea-headed man behind the desk had been carefully trained to ignore the guests. Visitors too. My companion and I were on our own. And that, as Hemingway might say, was good.

I guess I didn't understand old wealth at that time, although I admired it. The desire for ancient dust and aristocratic decay unknown to me, unknown in the States, seemed a matter of essential comfort to the Europeans.

Anyway, we were there, cooling our heels for Alex des Prairies, a Belgian count from an established family. Alex's distant cousin (from his great-uncle's marriage to an Austrian princess) brought me along on a Saturday morning with the idea I might find gainful employment consulting upon the reshoot of Alex's film, Danse du Sang.

We stumbled onto the house phone and Alex himself, sounding bluff and surprised, assured me forcefully of his imminent appearance. "Rider? Here already—Christian, too? Be right down."

We shuffled around the lobby a bit more. I found myself kicking the threadbare border of its Aubusson carpet. And Alex, in due time, another half hour or so, appeared from the hotel's obscure elevator and strode with great energy to us.

Alex's hair was dark, slicked back wet, streaked with treads from one of those sterling silver brushes that lie on lowboys in antique stores. His oxford-cloth shirt was starched so firmly even the frayed threads at the collar stood at attention. A paisley ascot ballooned at his throat, striking a dubious note of controversy against the dull green plaid of his jacket. His trousers were made of heavy worsted wool in brown tweed.

As a child, I'd followed the line of thinking of the Esquire man—navy blazer, gray flannels, regimental tie. But my eyes soon learned to keep their counsel because my European acquaintances, and Alex in particular, never gave up on a perfectly good suit or trousers even if it had seen better days at university.

Alex shook hands with me, and greeted Christian, then excused himself to use the public phone.

"My car took fire," he said into the receiver, after a brief interval in which his call was connected.

The pay phone that Alex addressed with precise arrogance was out of place among the other artifacts in the somber lobby, and barely ten feet from where we stood like bookends, uncertain how to disguise the fact we could hear every word and were obviously fascinated.

"My rental car," he said with impatience. "Ignited. Took fire. Burned up." I could only imagine the effect this statement had on the Hertz representative at the other end of the line.

"It's useless to ask me to drive it over there. Don't you understand? The machine is charred. A blackened crisp. My own car won't arrive for days. Please deliver another to the Chateau Marmont, that's where I'm staying."

He listened. "The burned one? You can collect it at 301 North Larchmont. Do I know who lives there? Well, not really. I can't really say I know her."

Alex returned to us smiling, rubbed his palms together. "There, that's finished," he said. "Let's take lunch, shall we Max? You'll have to drive."

We dined at the El Dorado, a place everyone goes and no one mentions. Located in a shack on Melrose, with no sign or other identity, it's packed with people who require the best flamed steak in town in an atmosphere that hasn't changed since Raymond Chandler breezed east from Westwood Village along Sunset Boulevard.

Slightly cold that morning in February. So we began with pink bisque and a claret that put us right there on the damp green turf of Waterloo. I don't know where he'd got them— this was 1979 in Los Angeles—but the chef served delicate emerald-headed sprouts like I'd only seen in the cafés of Amsterdam, and sheaves of endive unknown in California at that time. My entrée was a flame-seared entrecote, with the crispest pommes frites nine hours from Brussels.

I'd read of Alex's one and only film in the trades, they heralded his arrival in the States as if he were Fellini. Danse du Sang was a huge commercial success in Italy, due to one obvious marketing detail which evolved purely from luck and fortuitous timing. Gina Paloma, who played the lead became, by the time of the film's opening in Rome, an international film star, the Sophia Loren of her generation. And Alex had filmed her in the nude.

Another aspect of the film ensured its Roman triumph. In one scene Catholic priests leered at Gina's perfect form. Who cared? This was America. We enjoyed, theoretically, separation of church and state. But twenty years ago in Italy, a Catholic country, a film's denouncement by the Church assured its success.

As for Alex, Christian filled me in. The family enjoyed the kind of wealth only a few names conjure. Alex himself had a formal moniker that could fill two lines of gothic type. His mother was a stunning British beer heiress, his father titled nobility for whom diplomatic appointments stretched the limits of suitable work.

Twenty million dollars Alex had received on his thirty-third birthday from his grandmother, and was just about down to nothing, although no one suspected it, including Christian. And you couldn't tell it by the ease with which he'd pick up the check.

Through fromage and blush pears we lingered. The topic was philosophy. Over double espressos, Alex held forth eloquently concerning the nobility of inherited wealth.

"It allows man to reach for perfection," he said, while I wrestled Nietschean nuggets from faint recollections of my boarding school classes in Connecticut.

Dark eyes shining with European certitude, Alex listened intently to an occasional protest by Christian or me, then brushed our remarks aside cheerfully.

"You must be serious, Max, that is not how it is at all, not at all. It is the most aggravated bad taste to be accomplished at making money—one of man's most vulgar interests. Tons more vulgar than prurient sex."

He tossed two fingers in the direction of the gods. "Really not worthy of the basest man's attention."

Alex's manner conveyed a robust vitality, an assurance about his position in life that imprinted itself upon me more powerfully than any person I've ever met, with the exception of my father.

Alex, Christian and the other Europeans who included me in their society for that brief time, could afford to elevate wealth to the level of style. A luxury I coveted, while I played an American game—Monopoly. Roll the dice, buy up the board, try to stay out of jail if you can. Really not worthy of any but the basest man's attention.

As I struggled with forming my reply: 'Even Michelangelo accepted commissions,' Alex bolted upright, his dark eyes lit with fury.

"That blackguard owes me $10,000!"

Alex lunged immediately from his chair into a table of two men who had just been seated not three feet from us.

"You are—not—a gentleman!" he sputtered at one of them, an effete fellow I knew vaguely as one of Hollywood's A-list directors. I'd gathered from the trades he'd abruptly left Alex's picture after accepting a $10,000 fee.

Alex threw his strong torso onto the man, pinning him to the table. The white cloth slid to one side like a toupée off a domed pate. The man's neck strained with the effort to throw Alex off. His face burst red and his eyes bulged from his skull. But it was hopeless.

"Presumptuous scoundrel, conniving rat, you double-crossing crook, I'll kill you!" Alex said.

By this time the chef had rushed from the kitchen still in his apron and hopped about the periphery of the scene like an amphetamined frog.

"Count! Get hold of yourself!"

Christian and I stepped in, grappling with Alex's arms, which repulsed our hold like reptiles.

"There are other ways to settle this," I said, alarmed.

"You're absolutely right, Max," Alex panted. He abruptly raised himself from the trembling figure who lay half on, half off, the table.

Alex straightened his jacket. Then tucking his ascot and smoothing his hair, he resumed his seat with exaggerated dignity.

The director, who turned out to be so insignificant I can't recall his name, heaved onto one elbow and glowered at Alex. He was not given a chance to compose himself, for the chef, with an amusing series of Gallic gestures and shrugs, implied that he should leave.

"I think now," Alex said to the chef, "the cognac."

We lingered a bit more, the cause of Alex's grievance departed, and Alex offered a toast. "Let us drink to the re-shooting of Danse du Sang for Hollywood audiences," he said. He raised his glass toward me. "And to Max, captain of my American team."

A snapshot from that moment might have caught yours truly, slender, fair-haired man of medium height—his nose softened in a prep school scuffle—wearing an expression that bespoke anxiety. By the time of my meeting with Alex des Prairies, I'd traded law for filmmaking and squandered my savings on a couple low-budget releases of my own. Thrilling as it might seem to produce the American version of Alex's film, I had self-doubts. As Alex tipped his tumbler and smiled radiantly in my direction, a strange maxim sprang into my thoughts: beware of toasts.

Two hours later, we burst onto the street into dizzying sunlight like three Tom Sawyers released from school. Exuberant with wine and cognac, Alex taunted a male hooker on Santa Monica Boulevard and ran down an androgonyous young man in a ponytail to settle a gender bet.

I didn't see Alex for several months after that. He left for Italy the next day for a polo meet. And the pea-headed man at the Marmont—I assume it was he with whom I left my name and telephone number—expressed doubt as to the date when Alex would return.

I thought about his words concerning wealth. I didn't recognize it then, but our meeting kindled in me a spirit of keen longing, not for any person or thing, but for a coveted past.

It was Alex's childhood I envied, set among estates I later saw in photographs and mistook for Medici palaces, or viewed from Bentley automobiles of remote, heartbreaking perfection. With the yearning of a child I envied Alex—the ease of his philosophy, and the comfort of belonging to a lifestyle so rare it was, by the time of our meeting, extinct—although neither of us could know it.

2.

Irving at Le Dôme

Shortly after my meeting with Alex, Irving Fain offered me a position with his bank.

We dined at Le Dôme. From that elegant shelf along Sunset Boulevard we could see the lights of Bunker Hill thirteen miles east. The Coconut Grove, Brown Derby and LA's old dowager, Perino's, lit up Wilshire Boulevard directly below. But I wasn't really looking at the view. I listened to Irving, and the siren call of my destiny.

"Banking's regulated, Rider," Irving said over dinner, "Regulated industry. I got something in mind that's gonna blow your socks off. That's why I need a good partner—a lawyer."

Irving Fain and I met each other in kindergarten. We parted at age six when my mother moved us to Greenwich from Brooklyn, then linked up again after a law degree from Yale propelled me to a New York firm known for its entertainment clientele.

Employed as a dungeon associate in the firm's library, I looked up from my law-texts one morning to find the senior partner introducing me to our "client" Irving Fain.

I found it unnerving. Irving was making it in Hollywood while I tiptoed the hallowed halls checking pocket parts for the latest legal citations. Irving moved to LA and I followed. And once I was here, I found I couldn't practice law any more. The success of Irving's venture, though nothing highbrow, had aroused my ambition. His first feature, made for $15,000, was titled Hot Dawg: A Boy's Adventure—it grossed $10 million and made Irving's reputation among the studios.

The plan he proposed that night was heady. Perhaps you've heard of Filmland Credit. Not just a bank, Filmland became the ultimate source for film financing in the 1970s. Timing could not have been better. Tax write-offs for film investment had been revoked, money had dried up and Irving reckoned our venture would fill a niche, drawing players of global stature, from Francis Ford Coppola to Europe's top directors—Filmland would serve them all—for a price. Participations. Another word for sharing profits. For the first time in banking a lender would share in the up-side: The way Irving saw it Filmland would latch onto the producer's percentage of gross.

"But the government requires capital of $3 million to finance a lending institution. I don't have that kind of money to put up, Irving."

"No problemo. I put up the cash. Two million. Courtesy of Hot Dawg. All you need to do is sign the note for $1 million. Just sign a friggin' note."

Irving could talk and chew at the same time. I'm not saying it was pretty. He'd ordered la specialitè de la maison— rare sirloin the size of a heavyweight's fist.

My attention was riveted by his fork and knife, which he gripped so firmly his thumbs were pressed white. He literally savaged the steak into bloody clots, shoveling forkfuls into his mouth with the relentless stoking of the boilers of a freighter. Potatoes, peas, parsley, horseradish and meat—all transformed into a hulking gob of masticated grizzle. This hovered precipitously along his lower lip, suggesting at any moment to lurch onto his plate, while a delicate stream of spittle coursed toward his chin, forming perfect goblets of grease on the white linen napkin spread like a drop-cloth over his lap.

"We'll own the studios," he said around the sickening gray blob. "When they come to us at the back-end, run out of dough, we'll pillage them for profits. You just keep the government off our backs. And I promise you," he fixed me with shrewd black eyes, "we'll be the biggest player in Hollywood."

3

The Lloyd's Model

The plan Irving devised that night involved Monopoly. Not just Boardwalk and Park Place. Hollywood and Wall Street.

"What exactly do you have in mind?" I asked, over a glass of twenty-year-old Manzanilla.

"Think about it."

"Syndication? You'll set up partnerships for the films we want to finance. We'll offer units to investors, a share in profits. And the investors will share the risk."

"That's it," he crowed.

"Isn't that a security?"

"You asking me?"

"I'm an entertainment lawyer, Irving. I know nothing about bank regulations."

"Window dressing, Rider. That's all the government wants. Just friggin' window dressing."

This was before Credit Lyonnais, the French giant who financed films in the 1980s. Leveraging the assets of financial institutions was a novelty. At least on the scale we proposed. Michael Milken hadn't yet devised his mantra: greed is good. But we had only to glance across the Atlantic for the supernova of syndications, Lloyd's of London. We would apply its model to the financing of films.

In the late 1970s, few firms in the States equaled the cachet of Lloyd's Insurance Trusts, pools of private investors who put up letters of credit promising to contribute up to £700,000, for the prestige of backing the largest high-risk insurance company in the world.

Americans, in particular, felt honored to invest. No prospectus or anything. Just introduction through a friend, to some frock-coated phony from London's Lime Street, nervously checking his pocket watch as he guided his rented Rolls Royce to Ma Maison.

Outwardly respectable and sound, Lloyd's was a discreet whore who didn't disclose her johns, and demanded an almost absurd secrecy from them. Fellows I knew, passive scions of old money, turned coy as geishas at mention of Lloyd's partnerships.

I remember running into a guy from my days at Exeter, whose mouth lifted in a sly, silly smile when he spoke of his Lloyd's portfolio. He had, of course, been attracted to Lloyd's for the fact the company was old and associated with the upper class. I was impressed—and envious—for I would not have been solicited to join.

"Highly profitable, Rider," my school chum told me. "The first year I got a fat check."

The game Irving devised worked similarly.

"Before Filmland lays out one nickel, we pre-sell distribution rights to our investors for hard dollars. Brilliant? If the film's a dog, we're covered."

"Complicated," I said. "Investment vehicles like you're proposing are tightly scrutinized. And our participation in profits could suggest self-dealing."

"But the potential's fantastic! Filmland only loans 10%, while the other 90% comes from investor partnerships. Trust-fund babies—that's where you come in. They'll be lining up to fund our films."

"So Filmland will act as producer as well as lender?"

"Yeah. Right."

"I'm not sure bank charters permit that."

"What d'ya mean? It's safer than lending the bank's money."

"Irving," I said, feeling like a spoiler, "what do we need a bank for?"

His shrewd eyes widened and he shook his head in disbelief.

"Respectability, Rider. Friggin' prestige. And—" His eyes grew dark with the prospect. "We'll have more cash than the studios can dream about."

Shortly after our dinner at Le Dôme Irving set about attracting a slate of pictures worthy of our new venture, while I launched Filmland's plan to round up investors. The two events, meeting Alex and appointment to Filmland's board—drawing me into a world both alluring and strange.

4.

The Phantom Twins

Only three weeks had passed since Irving and I set up Filmland. News had spread of my proximity to capital and, in March, 1979, Marina Loge telephoned "renewing" our acquaintance. She let it drop she was a friend of Alex— "de votre connaisance, n'est-ce-pas?" Would I accept an invitation to a party of his friends? In this casual way I came to be swirled by a blustering wind twelve screaming stories above LA.

The setting was the rooftop of the old Wrigley building downtown. The street was vacant, except for the human inhabitants of newspaper tumbleweeds taking shelter from the night. Original setting for a party but strangely claustrophic for those of us who suffer a fear-attraction thing with heights.

Our host Christian Ruhl claimed my attention immediately. Tall, boyish, athletic, Alex's cousin had been a Silver medalist for Austria's ski team. Now he teetered on one leg at the rail-less edge, flashing a wicked grin at the acrophobia he produced among his guests. He had an athlete's grace, but it wasn't the kind of activity you ignore in a host, and I found myself glancing up anxiously every few seconds.

"I got a call from a woman I knew when I was presented in Spain," Marina said. I stood mum. Never knew she had been presented, in Spain or in Barstow, for that matter.

I confess I've always been drawn to dubious nobility. Anastasia, the alleged Romanoff princess, would have found a friend in me. Not phonies though. I distinguish them. The guy who forges his degree from Brown—he knows it's false. The people I mean are those who carry, like rubies in a Gucci bag, their own fantastic past. A sense of destiny—credits, if you will, which speak of opulent backgrounds and rarefied worlds.

In short, I sympathize with those fragile people like Marina, whose souls refuse to question their secret aristocracy.

She continued, "My friend Countess is an editor for an international lifestyle magazine—Madame Europe. She's offered to include me in a special issue: LA's Most Eligible Women Under Thirty.

I checked my expression at the door. Marina could have been a day or a decade over thirty but her affectations gave the concept of "eligible woman" an unnatural torque.

"They flew the jewels from Cartier in Spain—with two armed guards. Of course I don't get to keep them. But I'll do it for funsies. What do you think?"

Reserving my reaction to even the most incredulous pronouncements has always come naturally to me. "Quite the honor," I said.

Marina's hand, blue and white with chill, trembled from the nicotine of her cigarette.

"The girls have to be between fifteen and thirty. When the photographer asked me the year I was born I panicked. I didn't want to add ten years."

I could see Marina through the eyes of the cynical photographer, her under-used reckoner clicking up the numbers in her beautifully formed head. Trying to sell time, she took a chance. '1950,' she lied. Really? His dry smile, Marina's girlish dissembling. That would have put her at 29. 'Well—not really, I was really born in 1949.'

"Just a teensy white lie." Marina adjusted the gold strap

on her lizard bag, tried a teensy one on me. "I guess now I've turned thirty I should start using moisturizer."

Alex was scheduled to arrive around nine, Irving wasn't.

"Friggin' expatriates," Irving replied to my suggestion that he come along. "I wanna fraternize with Europhiles, I got Masterpiece Theatre."

At ten-thirty, the rooftop was packed. As if Christian's acrobatics weren't enough distraction, Sylvester Stallone was there, feigning indifference to his own celebrity. To my way of thinking, no one wearing sunglasses at night on a rooftop in the wind is really at ease. I noticed him because of the pair of giants attached to him as bodyguards.

I'm not big myself. Average size, I guess. A girl once branded me narcissistic and it surprised me. But pleased me too. Because it meant she noticed something about me. Something I didn't know myself.

I stayed fit. Swam laps three times a week. Occasional sailing, biking. And I could take a set from the pro at the Bay Club. Not because I love sports. It's all about vanity— looking good in my clothes, feeling attractive to women.

And they've always been drawn to me, although my nose was broken in the East and never set right. Softens my face, my mother claims. And she admires my skin.

"Maxwell," my mother once said. "You've a golden skin tone. Like your Corsican grandfather." So my skin is naturally tan without the chore of sunbathing. And my hair's fine but plentiful, and wavy, for light hair.

Marina drifted away. I looked at my watch and found it was midnight. Stallone had left with his entourage. Alex hadn't appeared. I felt he wasn't going to. Exposed on a rooftop among people I barely knew, I felt a vague unease. And I prepared to leave.

Just then a couple of elegant ghosts materialized among the guests, entering discreetly through the small door that led to the roof staircase. It was one of those occasions where everything stops and the silence is deafening, like a forest of creatures before a hurricane.

Two waiters scurried to these wan figures, whereupon people started talking again. I thought it a good time to slip out.

"Max." Christian clapped me heartily on the scapula. He'd abandoned his rooftop hi-jinks to welcome the ghosts. "Do you know Winton and Susie Grass?"

Twins. Tall, fair, intense, with a compelling strangeness that prickled. Winton Grass' posture bespoke English public school. Attired in the double-breasted blazer, cream slacks, white shoes of a guy flogging yachts to landlubbers, he wore an expression of fanatic geniality beneath rows of pale blond plantings that covered his scalp from crown to temples.

"How do you do?" he asked. But I didn't respond. I couldn't get used to the unblinking strangeness of his sister's erotic expression. Susie used eye contact like crazy glue, and extended a delicate hand in a gesture that recalled garden tea and satin gloves.

Fixed in the night, in the wind, in the spell of Christian's manic exuberance, I'm still struck by my first impression of Susie. Her dainty luminous face, like a Renaissance portrait, suggested a perfect shallowness of spirit. Wheat-colored hair, eyes the color of an El Greco sky. And she regarded me with fine, almost limpid sexuality that drew me toward her like a faint exclusive fragrance.

"Winton and Susie own a gold mine," Christian observed in the mocking manner he used with his guests.

Suddenly Grass ducked, pulled Christian and me to one

side in a lugubrious gesture of urgent secrecy.

No one paid us the slightest attention, but Grass dropped his voice, gripped our sleeves, murmured sibilantly of plots, coups, men for hire.

"Secret partners," Winton Grass said. "The records are false. False. The Shah is involved. We need to act fast."

I consider myself a pretty quick take, yet I couldn't follow Grass' whispered plot twists concerning this gold mine of his. Could be I was distracted by his sister standing prim as a draped statue, and just as mute.

I left the party strangely exhilarated. Alex never showed up. I talked to no one save Marina and Christian, and I'd been drawn warily into a tale of intrigue by Winton Grass. Yet it was Susie I remembered, that distant feminine spirit who barely acknowledged my existence.

5.

Rider's Parents in Paris

I realize, reviewing what I've written, I've given the impression I belonged to the privileged world of my new friends. But Alex and the others who formed his circle, were as disparate from me as Europe from America.

Although French, my mother arrived in New York in her eighth month. She planned it that way, ensuring my dual citizenship. American as apple pie. Or tarte tatin.

My parents met in Paris. She was dark-eyed, an actress, with a dark vitality that drew aristocratic men to her. My father, a British officer, and titled. It must have offended my father's sense of order when I was conceived. And I guess he knew, even then, I'd be a disappointment.

"Idealist," he would have said. "Bleeping romantic like his mother." That's how he'd describe my flawed character. If he granted an audience on the subject—at the law courts, or at his club. Cool, disapproving. And married, six months before my birth, to someone other than my mother.

My father was engaged to the "right girl" before Paris, a jaunty blonde with a narrow, set mouth. I like to think my mother softened him, lifted a window for his escape. But in the end, the old life summoned my father; its structure braced him. He pushed away the shadow side of passion, my mother and me.

You wonder how we lived? A small allowance, grudgingly paid. And my mother? English-speaking French governesses were valued on the large estates in the East, despite the nuisance of a child.

Sailor suits? Yes, the children of the rich really wore them in the 1950s. Precious little Harlans, Lindsays, Nelsons, in their stark and gloomy nurseries, passed their cast-offs on to me. Outsider. I knew how it felt to be one. And some would say the word explains something about me. Like a childhood bout with polio that leaves an invisible limp.

6.

Susie and Winton Grass

The Monday after Christian's party, an honest-to-God chauffeur came to our bank. A strange fellow in a vested suit and chauffeur's cap with braid across the front. With a kind of lurking formality, he delivered a package from Winton Grass.

Inside was a lengthy narrative of the education and accomplishments of Winton and Susie, which seemed to owe much to their grandfather, a geologist entrepreneur who'd put together a collection of oil and mining interests which, at some early point in the past six decades, had attained a value in excess of $20 million.

Clearly, Winton Grass saw me as a money pipeline. And I saw him as the man standing next to his sister. But the puff piece left out a few things, filled in by Christian over drinks the day he bought a smashing Jensen Interceptor off a Saudi Prince at a stop-light on Rodeo Drive.

"Fellow got out and walked away," Christian marveled. "Would have given him a ride home but he said he couldn't bear to view the interior from the second seat. Business transactions are so easy in the States," Christian mused, overlooking the fact he had offered the car's owner one and a half times its street value in cash.

"Tell me about Susie Grass," I said.

"There's a kind of rhythm to wealth in America," Christian began, ordering another round. "First generation acquires it. Second generation affects it. Third generation loses it. The Grass twins never saw it coming. Never saw it could ever run out. That gold mine in Bakersfield—it's all that remains of their grandfather's legacy."

Winton and Susie had taken degrees from Winchester College in Oxford, England. When I met them, they'd just been summoned back from Europe where they were living the high life.

Their father, T.E. "Tom" Junior, had plunged into mid-life crisis and there was no way he was getting out alive. Immersed in lies and lust, his days were corrupt with the sad pathology of drink. No man can admit he'd voluntarily undertake to wreck his family and pluck a twenty million-dollar golden goose. He had to blame it on something. And eighty proof makes a convenient goat. He had transferred 30% of the Inca Princess Mining Corp. to Winton and Susie earlier that year to skirt a technical issue with the SEC. And Susie, even amid her European dalliance, had enough savvy to wire the corporate attorney:

"Forward original share certificates to Bank of Geneva, W1, London.
Respectfully, Susie Grass."

It worked, and when Winton and Susie arrived in the States for the damage control made inevitable by their father's careening psyche, they were minority shareholders with a big advantage: their mother, ungraciously shucked like a limp raincoat, brandished her claim to the remaining shares.

So there were torrid legal battles, with all the violence and ferocity that attends any struggle between parent and child. There was everything primal about it, although conducted by high-priced lawyers in hand-sewn suits. And like most ego contests in Hollywood or New York, the principals started it but the lawyers were paid to fuel the scorching flames.

"A skirmish over lifestyle," I shrugged, indifferent.

"It's more than that, Rider," Christian corrected me. "For people like us, lifestyle is survival."

7.

Bunker Dodge

In the weeks following Christian's party, I worked at Filmland mostly. It was a pleasant, stimulating life entailing about four hours of real work a day, six days a week. Our corporate offices were in the elegant old Hollywood Roosevelt building on Sunset Boulevard, where I hung around Irving's corner suite discussing deals, mega-deals. We had guys flying in from all over. Lightweights. Heavyweights. We were instant luminaries.

We didn't bother with loan applications, underwriting or anything like due diligence. We relied on our gut. "Yes" or "no" in ten minutes. Oh, sure there was a loan committee, genteel vice presidents who had come with the bank. And they asked polite and puzzled questions. But that was the end of it.

One morning in March I looked up an acquaintance of Alex who styled himself a guru to the rich. Bunker Dodge, that's what this duck called himself, and it wasn't any coincidence most people associate the surname with old wealth.

There were things you would have noticed about Dodge. Couldn't help but notice. And you'd ask yourself, as I did, first time I saw him flicking his dirty gray ponytail over the pink collar of his raw silk jacket, "Who the hell is that?"

Dodge was an older guy, late fifties, slightly paunchy, with a round sun-beaten face. His costume was slightly remarkable, silky pants, sock-less Gucci sandals and a common canvas bank pouch tossed beside his right hand like a tennis towel.

Everybody has a wallet, but the well-used pouch, stenciled with black letters spelling BANK OF AMERICA, held a literal bankroll of hundreds large enough to gag an Arabian horse.

In an interesting ballet, too well rehearsed to seem spontaneous, Dodge would raise the purse, toss back the flap with a flourish, peel off one or two of the outside layers and brandish them in the air to summon a check, the faint yellow hairs glistening along the backs of his febrile hands.

Six days a week he sat casually alert at his corner table in the patio of the Beverly Hills Hotel, attracting conversations with wealthy patrons, drawing them out with somnolent flattery.

As I waited in the Polo Lounge for Alex that morning, a prospect approached Dodge's table and I observed him working.

"Are you Mr. Dodge?" the prospect asked.

"Ye-es." Dodge drew back as if unsure whether to permit the intrusion.

"Bunker Dodge?"

"The Third," he said, flapped a hand gracefully at the empty deck chair facing him. "Take a seat. May I offer you something?"

The man—let's call him Mr. Jones—settled his bulky form in the chair. Dodge unfurled two fingers at the waiter, lifted a polite brow of inquiry to which his guest replied, "Chilled Absolut, please."

"Of course." Dodge smiled as if remembering an innocent time of selling chilled Absolut at a makeshift roadside stand, five cents a glass.

I watched, fascinated.

"Might we," Dodge paused, "—share some small refreshment—cashews—what have you?"

The waiter, Louie, bowed. Nearly bowed. An exercise in

small gestures, and Louie had been carefully coached.

"Of course, Mr. Dodge." Louie hustled off in his best imitation of respectful efficiency.

"Now," Dodge smiled a refined, obliging smile. "I'm afraid you have the advantage of me, sir, may I know who you are?"

He could almost have added, 'Mr. Jones.' And I wonder sometimes if he ever committed that error. For he vetted every prospect—despite the way it appeared, he knew every trout he lured to the shallows.

Dodge studied financial statements, 10K's, Dun and Bradstreet. But nothing proved quite as informative as the rumor mill. If a guy had money, or was about to come into some, he suddenly had a lot of acquaintances.

Dodge learned from simple conversations. A first class flight to New York, or the Savoy Bar in London. That dinner party in Rancho Santa Fe. Montecito. Or Montauk.

An ex-wife wouldn't remember what they talked about. The unusual man with impeccable manners—wasn't his name Dodge, like the family who'd made their money in copper? She'd mention her former husband's place in Nassau, Martinique, Careyes. They'd traveled so much when they were together. And she might let it slip, entre nous, "an income of $2 million is almost nothing these days." Wistfully offered, sympathetically agreed.

So this guy at Dodge's table, this Mr. Jones, who'd been introduced by another in his circle, was known to Dodge almost intimately, at least so far as his finances were concerned, despite a studied performance to the contrary.

"Forgive me if I—if we've—do we know each other, Mr. Jones?" he asked. Dodge had all the time in the world. When it's a sure thing, there's time to spare. He nursed his l'eau minerale and waited, his smile slightly puzzled.

Mr. Jones lowered his voice. "I hear you're the man to see for investment advice." Hopeful, eager.

Dodge trilled a deprecating laugh, "Me?" Swished the ponytail languidly, letting his fingers hover over the sterling bowl of cashews. "I simply manage my own—portfolio. Oh, there are things that excite me from time to time, of course." He set his full lips, frowned attractively. "Through friends, family. ."

"I see."

Louie placed the Absolut before the disheartened Jones. The man shifted forward, reached for his blazer pocket.

I watched Dodge's tanned, bejeweled hand float across to Jones' arm, "May I? I'm grateful for your—interest." Dodge spoke in the manner of someone pitching a gracious white lie. Jones needn't have worried. Dodge would reel him in eventually. First he must move from mere greed to gluttony, then he'd be offered the hook.

Alex arrived at my table, and we waited until Dodge was alone. Alex introduced me with an aside, "Bunker has impeccable contacts."

Thus it was that I engaged Dodge to market Filmland's partnership interests, a complex scheme which Dodge translated into simplicity. For $10,000 a unit, an investor purchased the right to participate in a package of ten films. Dodge presented it like an invitation to a private investment club.

I think that accounted for his success in selling the interests for Filmland. The first week he sold partnership units equal to $200,000. And it was a rare Brink's delivery from Bunker's "office" at the Polo Lounge that didn't match that sum. I instructed Wingdot, a vice president, to place the money in an investment account at Filmland, and put a man in charge who moved it daily among international currencies, until we could fund the partnerships.

Would I say Dodge's contacts were impeccable? I think now, it was his pigeons that enjoyed that reputation. His contacts, I could not be sure about.

Φ

Alex could walk to our offices from the Chateau Marmont, where he resided during renovations to Tower Hill, his Moorish villa above Lake Hollywood. He started dropping by to chat about films. We'd go to lunch. Consequently, I got little done after one o'clock.

My fruitful hours were eight to noon, before any serious dilettante would think of making a phone call. Alex used those hours to bathe, contemplate, study the writings of Machiavelli, or the philosophy of Wittgenstein. So it was with surprise one morning at ten o'clock that I greeted Alex in Filmland's lobby, where he bristled with bluff vitality.

"Rider, old man, let me offer you an incomparable opportunity." I took it he meant to talk business.

Filmland Credit occupied the top three floors of the Hollywood Roosevelt building, opulently restored. New elevators of brushed steel whisked us to the penthouse where Irving and I disported ourselves in offices like sultans' suites.

Our private lift opened onto a shimmering granite waterfall which licked delicately downward into a dark pool that lay behind a marble console of rare verde jade. The marble had traveled from Tangiers to Long Beach, then been conveyed by flatbed to Hollywood, where it was lifted, carved, polished and installed on site, to form a seamless, sensuous surface of polished rock.

There, illuminated by artful lighting, an exquisite redhead with an empty smile clipped out an automatic greeting in LA's phoniest accent.

I led Alex to the conference room where he assumed a chair at the head of our conference table, an imposing rectangle of Moroccan rosewood and beveled glass. A silver samovar of espresso was brought in, with a large bottle of Perrier on its own filigreed tray.

The receptionist poured two demitasses, offered lemon zest from a Wedgewood saucer. "No thanks," I said. I've always been a wimp when it comes to espresso. Much as I like the idea of that super-bitter macho brew, I must soften its acid with milk.

"I'm found a little short, Rider," Alex began, stroked his clean-shaven jaw, slightly reddened from the scented bracer he used. He was dressed this day in a blue oxford cloth shirt with burnt orange ascot tucked at his throat, his leather jacket, the color of his espresso, flowing open. "I must begin immediately,"

"Begin what?" I asked.

Alex spoke as though his words might bring about revolution. "To reshoot all principal scenes of Danse du Sang for American tastes."

Gina Paloma was pressing Alex to get her scenes out of the way, as she had several studio commitments in Rome.

"I could of course go to Ramòn Brulée," Alex said before I could reply.

I'd seen Brulée, a short, chisel-nosed Belgian whose toupée yelped like a terrier.

"I wouldn't be terribly pleased to have him involved," Alex went on. "Quite frankly, he has the morals of an Oriental Satrap. Frightfully rich, gets his way all along, not very simpàtico, not terribly attractive, hangs around with bad characters."

"I don't know him," I said, wondering how we had gotten diverted to said Brulée character.

"Don't know him?" Now it was Alex's turn to disapprove.

He raised one finger to summon a secretary going by the open door, elevated his brow and pointed to the samovar, "Could you? This has grown rather cooled."

He waited until she withdrew.

"I hear on very good counsel he schemes with the Arabs. A man who will make bad business with anyone. Brulée bought silver with the Hunts, engaged in highly questionable accounting behavior. Bunker tells me they're suing him. And he purchased the new house of Jean-Paul, Getty's son, for two million American dollars—had it bombarded immediately."

"You mean razed?"

"Destructed. Blown up. So he could build some other monstrosity. A man of frightfully poor taste."

"I understand," I said.

"Of course, eventually, my own money will come through. It's held up only in Liechtenstein." Alex assumed a sudden arrogance, "You know, Rider, my family's wealth is such I need never work in my lifetime, need never study, as you have done, how to make money off the backs of my fellow man."

This amused me. The dons of Yale Law School—my alma mater—would have been very surprised to learn Alex's opinion of its curriculum. Yale is not known for its practical approach to the professions. You could hardly find a law school more esoteric. Even our class in criminal procedure— which focused only on the proper time for a police officer to deliver the Miranda speech—was regarded as metaphysical by Yale's faculty.

"Alex," I said. "How much do you need?"

He tossed two fingers in a slight gesture like the Pope's parade salute, "Only, I should say, a couple million."

It wasn't that I needed Irving's approval. We operated independently at first, two profligates with a joint checking account. Rather, I perceived lending to a friend slightly tricky, as Alex himself might have said. Or perhaps I had my doubts. In any case, my intercom request brought my partner Irving charging from his suite.

Irving lived for the contest. Every phone call, every meeting served as an occasion for conflict. He blustered upon us, a cyclone of nerves and ego, glanced at his watch impatiently—a gambit meant to imply urgency.

"One word," Irving said, as he extended his large manicured hand. "Give me one word on the two principal characters, one line on the plot. I'll tell ya if it's commercial."

"My film is enormously valuable," Alex replied. " Gina Paloma is tremendously big now. Did you see Time magazine's little piece last month on the most beautiful women in Europe?"

"Yeah?" Irving said, "Star-driven? We could take a chance."

"I hired Gunnar Fischer, Bergman's cinematographer, the entire crew was hand-chosen by him."

Irving threw himself in the latest of ergonomic chairs. "Nobody gives a damn about Bergman," he said. "Bergman's not commercial, he's anti-commercial."

Alex drew up in protest. "Gunnar is the greatest cinematographer in the world."

"Yeah?" Irving's eyes quickened. "That's what interests me. The territories. Any deal we strike has gotta include foreign."

"My film has already proved itself in the foreign marketplace. There was enormous controversy in Italy."

"You already sold in Italy? What other territories are unavailable?" Irving gave me a dangerous look.

"Well, you know I really don't know." Alex said.

"What d'ya mean you don't know? You sold theatrical. Didya sell video too?"

"I can't say."

Irving slapped the smoky glass table with the flat of his palm, "Are you tied up with a foreign distributor?"

"I fired him," Alex proclaimed, darkly.

"What rights did he sell? France?"

Alex pulled in his chin like a pigeon put off his food.

"I don't think so."

"Spain? South America?"

Alex threw back his shoulders, thrust his chest forward. "You place the carriage in front of the horse," he said, with comical formality.

I admit to enjoying Alex's distress under Irving's persecution, even as I felt somewhat disloyal to my new friend. Perhaps that's why I intervened.

"Irving, Alex should give you some idea of the film," I said.

"What's it called?" Irving demanded.

"Danse du Sang."

"What's that mean?"

Alex clicked his tongue as if any educated person should know. "Dance of Blood."

"Gotta have a new title."

"An adulteration!" said Alex, "You must see the film. Then I will hear your surmises."

"I got to get the frigging foreign rights. That's what I gotta do," Irving said. "Are they available or aren't they?"

Alex flushed under his Gallic complexion, "I sold theatrical under another title."

Irving dropped his fist on the table. "Well, how d'ya imagine you could assign the territories then?"

Alex slumped back, Irving waited, curious onlooker to a drowning man.

Alex's reply, when it came, was nothing if not inventive: "We'll shoot to a new script—the new print will be so distinct, we can sell the foreign rights—again."

Irving stopped him wearily, "Okay. We'll take it under advisement. We've got vice presidents here," he flapped his hand vaguely toward the floors below, "others to answer to besides just me and Rider."

Alex stood up, raising his palms in a grand gesture, "We'll screen it immediately," he said, cheerful again. "You will decide the fate of Danse du Sang!"

A limousine was dispatched to the Marmont where Alex kept the film while Tower Hill suffered his renovations. We moved to Irving's corner suite, where a panel concealed a screening room in which the three of us, together with one of the more befuddled but discreet vice presidents from the floor below, prepared to view Danse du Sang.

I accepted Alex's belief in film as Art as much as I approved Irving's commitment to profit. I didn't see the two as incompatible—French romantic comedies were doing very well in New York.

I confess I didn't know, that morning, what to make of a film so artistically pure and so desperately European. The story had been adapted from an obscure French novelette. Practically all of Alex's highborn friends and relations were featured in the cast, including Christian Ruhl and Marina

Loge, and Christian so becharmed himself with his screen persona he'd decided then and there to pursue an American film career.

Irving barked out his question during the fifth reel, "The nude scene. Will Gina Paloma match the other print? Let's say she's still luscious, she's still gorgeous. Okay. But it's been three years. She ain't young. She ain't creamy."

I could feel Alex draw up in his chair. "She was my mistress," he said.

During the long beautiful shots of Italian village life, with youths glowering at a seductive Gina Paloma and comical cuts to leering priests vacuuming the steps of the Duomo in order to keep an eye on her, I found myself seduced. By the producer's credit Alex had offered Irving and me the opportunity of meeting Gina Paloma. But for me, it was mostly about the chance to enter Alex's world.

When the lights came on, Irving just looked at me and shrugged. "Your call," he said. "It's pretty, but it's art," before he lumbered out.

8.

The Linens in Greenwich

Everyone suspects himself of at least one secret virtue. Honesty. Sound judgment. For me, it's style. I have good taste.

I cannot see a regimental tie without remembering my first: real silk, circus red, with standing lions glittering fiercely glittering over a golden lance.

When I was six, my Parisian mother was employed as governess to a household in Greenwich, Connecticut. The Linen mansion was a square, forbidding dungeon with formal gardens, hedged by Teutonic gardeners into geometric shapes. Wesley Linen, called "Waffy" by his boisterous Newport friends, enjoyed a position as publisher in his family's media empire. Both sides came from money, and he and his wife "Babe," a crisp, athletic blonde in tailored shirts and Capri pants, were stuffy beyond their years.

Their manner to my mother and me was always correct, with a veneer of solicitude that felt patronizing. In the spirit of noblesse oblige, Babe passed on to me the wardrobe of her middle son—a sissified collection of sailor suits and short pants I detested. Under a rationale still obscure to me, the Linens embraced the sartorial dictates of Britain's royal family, scorning long pants for boys until age eight.

The summer of 1957 I journeyed to England for the first of many brief, unsatisfying visits to my father. I arrived at Heathrow a frail Fauntleroy of six years, in too-precious linen suit, matching cap, and tall, cabled socks.

Having been instructed in the taking of a cab, I waited

at the taxi queue, anxiously clutching my valise, until some Cockney-gargling native could ferry me to my father's estate. When we reached the curving drive, with its faded Jaguar parked in front, my father and stepbrother came out to greet me.

Rory was six months younger than I, a miniature of my father, down to jodhpurs and riding boots. My father surveyed my appearance with obvious distaste. "He'll have a trip to Harrods out of it anyway," he observed.

Rory nodded in schoolboy sympathy. "Maxwell must have long pants."

Next morning, I was dispatched to Harrods with my father's secretary Page, and a hasty list of components for my first blazer uniform.

Harrods affected a giant movie lot, its various departments like miniature sound stages. Boys' furnishings were in "Egypt," a dimly lit room of pyramids and friezes, with the sound of ceiling fans whirring overhead. Amphoras of cattails evoked the banks of the Nile, as Tutankhamun, the boy-king, surveyed all from his throne with dark, unseeing eyes.

I dashed about taking in everything while Page and a frock-coated clerk assembled the first items, a Navy blazer and regimental tie.

In an ante-room outfitted as a feudal hunting hall, thousands of blazer buttons and pocket crests reposed in shallow drawers of oak highboys. Scribbled hieroglyphs foretold the contents of each drawer. The clerk dubiously studied each, comparing it to a sample of my father's stationary. When at last he held a set of brass buttons bearing my father's coat of arms, a tailor was summoned and the buttons attached with alarming dexterity. Over the blazer's pocket he tacked the family crest. Back in Egypt, a shirt of cream-colored India cotton was produced, with the centerpiece of the ensemble—gray flannel trousers with shallow cuffs.

While I was in England, puzzling out the reasons for my father's detachment, the Linen family laid plans for a lavish late-summer reception for Babe's youngest sister, who had become engaged to a French talk-show host.

This French fiancé had a daughter, whose photo enchanted me. Nicole Legrande was seven, with wavy hair and haughty eyes. More than that, she had the glamour of an orphan: her mother having plunged into the Seine and been slivered smartly by the rescue boat.

The morning I returned to the Linen estate, day workers from the "village" (pretension of Babe's—Greenwich was a thriving town of sixty thousand, even in 1957) were at work installing tables on the south lawn. The east wing, which the Linen twins and I employed as a rainy-day playground, had undergone a transformation. Gilt sconces glittered along the gallery. Tables for six and eight filled the entry hall, set with porcelain and crystal stemware. Hallmarked silver trays, released from their anti-tarnish blankets, were set about on lowboys in readiness.

Too humorless to conceive a theme affair on their own, Babe and Waffy acceded to my mother's whimsical proposal of a "sur la mer" effect.

The sous-chef devoted the entire afternoon to carving sea creatures from blocks of ice. Tablecloths embroidered in coral and French-sailor blue featured schools of crustaceans swimming gaily around their hand-stitched hems. Real Koi fish filled the fountains. And kerosene lily pads floated in the pool, awaiting nightfall, when they would flame like fireflies on the water.

Babe conferred special permission for the occasion. I was to join the Linen children for dinner in the garden. Thanks to my mother, my French was fluent. Nicole Legrande would have a dashing younger man—an American—as consort.

I attended the preparations as if I were in charge, materializing at critical moments, hands plunged into pockets, to offer a diffident suggestion here and there—reminding the sous-chef for example, "Fishes don't have tails like that."

When the guests started to arrive, I raced upstairs. From the motor court, I could hear excited conversation. A small strident voice clattered over the scales of the French language with emphatic petulance. Even without seeing her, I could have choreographed Nicole's pouts, her lifted shoulders and sailing hands.

Anticipating glory, I buttoned up my shirt of India cotton, attached the red silk tie. Suffused in guilty grandiosity for the crime I was about to commit (an immature Raskolnikov lurking in his rooms) I drew the cuffed trousers from my suitcase, hitched them up with striped suspenders, and struggled into the blazer. I touched my father's crest for courage. And waited.

It was seven-fifteen by my Flash Gordon wristwatch when at last I heard my mother leave her room.

Furtively, I descended the back staircase into the Great Hall.

Acute as any Tom Sawyer for his Becky Thatcher, I sensed immediately the radiant presence of Nicole Legrande, and flashed a brilliant, foolish smile in her direction.

She was, if anything, more beautiful than her snapshot. A delicate weariness shrouded her features, which I imputed to the homicidal bungling of the Seine Harbor Patrol. Her lips were small and deftly drawn, a sulky sketch of charming temperament. Her hair in soft brown waves was restrained by pink poodle hair clips. As noted, haughty eyes. No suitor could ever be good enough—a potent aphrodisiac.

I fully intended then and there to marry Nicole Legrande after completing second grade.

"Très charmant!" Babe's younger sister cooed to her jaded husband to be.

She turned to Nicole. "Here is a nice young gentleman to meet you."

I searched the cool gaze of my intended. Did she admire me?

Lost in ardor, I didn't see or feel the gathering clouds behind me.

Abruptly, Babe's swing skirt eclipsed the sun. Eclipsed the moon too, and every light. In one miserable instant of fused impressions, I recognized the reason for Babe's antipathy to wearing skirts—her thick ankles seemed to throb with rage.

Babe's hands flew to her hips in a frightening parody of a fairytale witch. She spoke to my mother in a voice of great control.

"Elène? What is this?"

"It is only that his father—"

Babe cut her off, and turned to me. "Please change your attire before you presume to greet my guests."

My mother quickly scuttled me upstairs to my bedroom. My cheeks burned from shame and fury. She shut the door and said nothing, but extracted from my closet the second-hand tunic and short pants.

She struggled with my blazer first. I stiffened my body, locked my arms to my sides, hard as marble in my resistance. Exasperated, she simply threw the hand-me-down sailor suit on the bed, and left the room. I felt choked by humiliation. Tears burned through the wool of my trousers.

Lifted by the late summer breeze, laughter floated up through the window. I could hear joyful music, and the lilting voice of Babe's sister speaking French on the terrace. The kerosene lily pads shimmered on the pool. Ice creatures glimmered, fey ghosts in the moonlight. There were my cavorting lobsters and frolicking dolphins. And there was Nicole Legrande. She met my gaze, then turned away.

In every childhood, there's a time when one accepts magic. Events line up to confirm one's special locus in the universe. My first suit of trousers, delivered up by Harrods to my father's order, was such a magical event.

The next morning my mother scolded me so harshly I suspect my gesture had touched some tragic hope within her. When I was finally allowed to wear my father's gift, I had outgrown it.

9

Susie at Michel Richard's

"I feel so envious," Susie Grass said one crisp Thursday in April, after she'd greeted me from her table outside Michel Richard's on Robertson. You know—where West Hollywood passes itself off as Beverly Hills, and a patron can get gunned down over his croissant and coffee. "The girls in LA are so ordinary, it's very attractive."

I guess anyone can have self-esteem problems. But she looked like, if she had one, it was an entirely new experience. She was perfectly dressed in a Chanel-style jacket and pleated skirt. Her slender legs twined together in nylon stockings the color of fairy dust. The straps of her ivory pumps lay just so at her ankles, and her box handbag sat between us like a seriously refined maiden aunt.

"Wardrobe is protection too," she said, as if reading my thoughts.

I took a seat across from her. I'd brought with me The New York Times. She glanced at its headline, which seemed to interest her: "Carter Freezes Billions in Iranian Assets as Khomeini Regime Tries to Withdraw Them. "

"He knew it was coming," she said.

"Who are you referring to?"

"Ramòn Brulée, surely you know him?"

I shrugged. Alex had mentioned Brulée in passing. And it seemed the man's most important defect, in Alex's perception, lay in his bad taste.

The sun shone pleasantly in the galactic blue sky. The French roast coffee was good. The air was fragrant with scent from Richard's cakes—lemon, chocolate, Grande Marnier. But she hadn't called me for a contribution to Girls' League.

"Allow me to come to the point, Maxwell," she said. "Winton and I have run through quite a sum of private money pursuing our rights to the gold mine."

Susie toyed with her lemon cake, observing me slyly like a kitten prods a crippled lizard.

"Where do I come in?" I asked her.

"You own a bank."

She had it wrong, Irving owned the bank. But I didn't correct her, it was a distinction rarely appreciated then, even by bank directors.

She leaned back, studied the Tiffany charms on her bracelet as if she'd never seen them before. "Winton and I intend to overcome our current—challenge. We intend to bring the Inca Princess to profit. Winton is willing to accept your bank's investment in our enterprise. And, of course, anything Winton approves..." She fanned her hand, the bracelet jangled.

I leaned back in the chair. One thing we learned in the 1970s was rapport—how to mirror other people to get what we want. So I thought it'd be amusing to mirror her mirroring me. Of course, one can carry this game too far. Like the Irish—with their intimate speech, intense gaze. They lean into you, hush their words, lock you with troubled eyes. I've come away cross-eyed. This time she beat me to it, folded her hands across her lap.

"You want the bank to invest in your gold mine," I said.

"Well—yes."

"We're in the business of financing films, not gold mines," I said.

"You're in the business of making money."

"What kind of returns are you projecting?" I can't believe I asked this for I couldn't have cared less. I had no intention of risking Irving's faith and friendship by lending money on a gold mine—especially one whose ownership was in issue. But carnal excitement rang in my ears, and an answer— already formed—raced through my thoughts like a headline. If I do this for you, it's because you're a part of myself I have to know.

Something made me glance up, and I became aware of a Rolls Royce Corniche paused at the curb. Tinted windows obscured its occupant. I rose quickly as if to shield Susie, and stood looking down at her through dark glasses.

"Who's that?"

She gave a charming shrug. "Will you or won't you?" she said.

Suddenly, I wasn't thinking of Filmland anymore or the pallid prospects of a desert gold mine, but of this pristine doll before me, hard as crystal or rock candy.

10.

Mona and Lainie in Santa Monica

Manhattan has its brownstones, London, its row houses. And you don't have to troll the streets in Pacific Heights to identify San Francisco's gingerbread Victorians. There's an architecture ubiquitous to LA too. You haven't seen it in film clips, newsbytes, studio stills. One has to live there to know it. And after you've been there awhile, it sort of disappears.

It's LA's bungalows I mean—diminutive dwellings that sit like silent old folks in Hollywood, Los Feliz, Santa Monica. It's Santa Monica I'm thinking of. Those dark streets of cruel pines that dwarf the charmed cottages like a malevolent fairy forest.

That's where Mona Andrews lived with our child Lainie Rider. Mona and I had separated by the time I met Susie Grass. We gave our reasons, traded disappointments. But even now I don't know why she left me. I suspect, sometimes, she sensed my immaturity and fear of being a father. Fear that I wasn't up to it. That I would be a father like my own.

I visited Mona and Lainie every Saturday morning.

Mona's bungalow was one of four set long-ways on a deep lot, with a path down the center. She'd secured the rent-controlled apartment through bribery of its previous tenant, a stewardess who was lucky enough to have engaged the attentions of a Mercedes dealer who invited her to move to the canyons.

Each apartment enjoyed a front patch of tough, scrubby grass, with a faded beach chair confirming the single-hood of its occupant.

Inside, a tiny coved living room led through an archway into a dining room the size of a closet. The kitchen recalled pullman quarters on a train and you imagined a bed might fold down next to the toaster. Indeed, a doll-sized ironing board was released from a pantry near the stove, where Mona ironed Lainie's dresses my mother ordered from abroad.

Lainie slept in a den with the dimensions of a child's playhouse, and Mona's bedroom was not much grander. The decor was, by accident, minimalist—before the term had acceptance outside the art world. And I was never there when the place wasn't tidy and serene as a monk's temple.

"Tell me, Max," Mona said one Saturday morning after Filmland got going, "about Alex's film."

I shifted in the beige beanbag chair of Mona's living room while Lainie—Eléne Elizabeth Rider, after my mother— played at my feet. Lainie loved Mona's beanbag chair as much as I abhorred it, disparaged it as tacky and nouveau.

"When are you getting rid of this chair?" I asked, allowing Lainie to climb onto my legs and entertain me with phrases borrowed from Big Bird and his pals.

"Tell me about the film," Mona insisted.

From her bedroom, Mona encouraged the monologue of my success as she dressed for her job at a fitness club on Beverly Drive. There were few enough positions where a mother could bring along her three-year old, and Roby's 'Robics was such a job.

Mona had followed me from New York where she'd begun a modeling career. Too late. Not that she was past her bloom. Far from it. She was only 23, a serene midwest madonna whose wholesome beauty would never fade. Mona worked afternoons at Roby's. And though she called in, made the rounds as much as she could, it wasn't easy caring for a child and pursuing the vocation of an actress.

"Is there a part in it for me?" Mona asked.

From Mona's beanbag chair I pitched the plot of Danse du Sang while Lainie guided her miniature red Corvette, hand-me-down toy from her cousin Nils, along the matted shag carpet. Across my handsewn Gucci loafers it travelled, the inscrutable male passenger windblown in his flying white scarf. The car traced the diamond pattern of my cashmere sock, drifted into the tunnel of my cuffed trouser of English gabardine.

But this was no Sunday drive on Savile Row.

Lainie's goal, her real intention, was to summon my attention to her game, compelling me to touch my ankle as I spoke, and flick away the tickle of fragile fingers on my leg. My simple gesture, hand to cuff, flashing gold from Hermès studs, Cartier watch, delighted Lainie, broke her up, with joy that repetition never dulled.

I've never imparted so much pleasure since. And I failed to appreciate then how rare a gift it was. But I complied with Mona's request, and the scene in Alex's film that I described to Mona and Lainie that day remains vivid:

"A dazzling golden meadow. A nude nymph luxuriates in a footed tub of breaking eggs. Close-up, Gina Paloma. Brittle eggshells rive against her milky skin, shiny yolk seeps like liquid topaz along her shoulders. The girl cavorts sensuously in the tub, her breasts heavy, sumptuous with movement."

As Gina moved, the shells broke. And for some reason known only to its director Alex des Prairies, Gina reveled in the viscous stream of raw egg, slitting her eyes with false coquettishness. From the sidelines, lascivious priests and cardinals leered salaciously.

"Strong sub-text," I assured Mona. "Dichotomy of art

versus evil, fecundity versus death. Not to mention the obvious—corruption and hypocrisy of organized religion."

My remarks sounded academic even to myself, and the pause from Mona's bedroom began to concern me. What would she think of the movie? Finally, she spoke, her soft, flat vowels recognized anywhere as the natural speech of the American Midwest.

"Maxwell, I'm sorry, I missed the story for a moment— why is that girl in the field? Are those priests the Mafia or something?"

I laughed out loud, as much in delight at Mona's summing-up of Alex's film, as at Lainie's fingers driving the red Corvette up my trouser-leg.

Mona emerged from the bedroom in tights and leotard, uniform of Roby's `Robics, and swept around the room gathering our child's effects into a vinyl tote. In a kind of graceful choreography of modern motherhood, Mona bundled our child in one hand, saddled her on one hip, smiled at me the perfect smile of the natural American beauty she was.

Suddenly, a transient memory of my own estrangement from my father pained me like a bruise. And though I longed to change the pattern that day, choices I had made were insisting that I should repeat it.

11

Alex and Rider at the Inca Princess

At nine o'clock one morning in April, Alex liberated his midnight-colored Bentley from the joy-riding valet at Chateau Marmont, settled himself upon the sun-cracked leather, and proceeded along the Sunset strip to Filmland.

"Good morning, Rider old man," he greeted me when I joined him at the curb, having been summoned by the doorman. "I thought we'd take a ride out to Grass's gold mine."

He saw me looking with admiration at the car. The Bentley was, even then, a classic. Alex's family acquired it during his father's last post in London in the early nineteen-fifties and, until Alex coaxed it from his father—employing, I suppose, the argument that in Los Angeles, rental cars had a curious habit of "taking fire"— it had been used to deliver Alex' old man to and from events of state.

The car was a rich navy with biscuit interior, bright with chrome, and sleek enough to sport a partition window between front and back compartments. The fragrance of old leather drew me into the front passenger seat and, leaving word with the doorman, we started for Bakersfield and the Inca Princess mine.

The air was warm, the kind of day that passes for summer everywhere else. A sky the color of a Portofino postcard was crisply hatched by shiny, black power lines. Dried palm fronds shimmered against the billboards, and images of actresses and perfume merchants grinned down at us with maniacal sociability.

Alex was oblivious to the attention we drew. Right-hand drive automobiles were rare. But the profanity that trailed us was produced by Alex's motoring etiquette. Alex had learned to drive in Belgium and the British Isles. He resolved conflicts between the two systems democratically: half the time he drove on the right, half the time on the left, which worked for him, if not the other "road boars" of Sunset Boulevard.

As we drove, Alex began an account of his sudden interest in the Grass family gold mine.

"Winton's made me a very attractive offer. You know him? Double-breasted blazer, yachting trousers, sueded shoes?"

I nodded, thinking of his sister.

"Ten percent fee for arranging introduction to my friends in Europe. So long as they buy shares in the gold mine, of course."

I was not surprised to learn Winton and Susie were flogging interests in the Inca Princess for $10,000 a share. More curious that Alex should take an interest. It seems a school chum of Alex's was a dilettante geologist whose father had made a fortune in De Beers and Alex was impressed.

"Winton's eccentric," I said cautiously.

"A bit mad actually," Alex agreed. "Yet I find the twins attractive. Winton and Susie are romantics. They act from a sense of destiny."

I almost blurted laughter, for I thought it a strange synonym for desperation.

"It's a matter of class really," he continued. "The Grass twins belong to the American aristocracy. In Europe, the holdings of one's family over centuries confers nobility."

He unfurled two fingers in a gesture I came to associate with discussions of class. "Winton's family has owned these mining interests for three generations. In America that is the equivalent of barony."

"What good is barony if they're broke?" I asked casually.

Alex glanced at me sympathetically. "Your business—it's a little vulgar, isn't it? Moneylenders have always washed the bed sheets of the aristocracy."

I reeled from the unfairness of this remark, "They've asked me for a loan!"

Alex dismissed this with a wave of his hand. "The occasional advance is a necessary inconvenience. In no sense is that business between gentlemen."

I must have winced. Alex had never asked me about my family. I relied on my Ivy League education to purchase entrée. And something else assured my welcome, I never knew what. But in that moment I felt the stab of shame for my illegitimacy, as if he knew, and degraded me for it.

We rode for some moments in silence. Alex glanced at me sideways several times, but I held out against his penitent impulse. Finally, in a hearty tone which I took to be conciliatory, he announced that he'd finished the script on Danse du Sang.

Irving and I had approved Alex's credit line of $2 million. And Alex began drawing against it immediately. With the new script, we planned to include Danse du Sang in a package of ten films whose foreign rights we hoped to sell at Cannes in May. Although still annoyed with Alex's disdain for my profession, the prospect of recouping at least part of our investment cheered me.

"After we've toured the mine, I hope you'll lunch with me at Port's." Alex paused, "I have a bit of news you'll find extraordinary."

"Why wait?" I said impatiently.

"At its own time," he replied with an air of mystery.

I hadn't the faintest idea what this "bit of news" might be. But I was more annoyed than interested. For one thing, I didn't feel at all like whiling away the afternoon at Port's.

Alex's cheerfulness grew on him as we neared Bakersfield, a sprawling landscape of farms and oil fields at the south tip of the San Joaquin Valley. The sky was hooded with the ugly brown sludge of the petroleum industry, and a thick odor like underarm sweat assailed us.

"Part of the Grass baronial estate, no doubt," I observed. Alex barked indulgently.

From Bakersfield we sped east with the efficiency of an English motorcar exempt from smog controls. Ten minutes outside the city the land became a vast desert, the highway narrowed to a tumbleweed track. I pulled out a map Winton had drawn.

The roads which intersected ours grew less frequent, and we amused ourselves with their ironic appellations. "115th Street," for example, implied a bureaucratic fancy for Manhattan, though it suggested nothing so much as a tractor crossing.

We reached an unmarked road and passed through a wooden gate listing on one hinge. The road was furrowed with ruts. We proceeded along its diminishing lines toward the horizon, pitching and tossing for at least twenty minutes. This precluded all conversation.

Abruptly, we came upon a tiny shack rising from sagebrush, and lurched to a halt in front of a striped crossing bar that prohibited further passage.

"We were greeted at gunpoint," Alex recounted to Winton later that day. Indeed, a pair of bearded thugs regarded us with guns drawn. With an effort, I managed to restrain my incredulous laughter. It struck me how ridiculous we must appear, our Bentley romping to a halt among blankets of dust.

Alex stepped from the car and straightened himself. We were oddly dressed for a trip to the desert. I wore a Panama styled suit with yellow pocket handkerchief. Alex's houndstooth wool jacket and silk ascot seemed equally out of place.

"Get back in the car." The man who spoke was the larger of the two, baring incisors which appeared useful for grinding glass. He was at least six foot two and something about the way he held the pistol made his hands look enormous.

"We're here to tour the mine," Alex said.

"Our orders say no one gets in without permission."

Alex stalked around to the front of the Bentley and stood with his hands at his hips. "What is so top secret about this mining operation?" he demanded. "Anyone with a four-wheel vehicle can go around your alleg-ed checkpoint."

"Back in the car, mister." He snapped the gun at Alex's face. "When I pistol-whip your ass, you'll get the picture." He made a show of taking in Alex's outfit, "Percy."

I opened the door to step from the Bentley. "Just a minute," I said. "Whose orders are these? We have Winton Grass's authority to tour the mine." I reached for Winton's map.

Suddenly, a shot rang in my ears and the dirt leaped at my feet, a slug had passed into the sand not two inches from the Bentley's tire.

"That's irresponsible! You could have hit me."

Instinctively I appealed to the man who hadn't fired. "What's going on here?"

"We admit no one." The smaller man was dressed very casually in khakis and Weejuns. He spoke with an educated accent I couldn't place. "You had better go back." He nodded slyly at his companion. "Before an accident occurs."

Under different circumstances I might have persisted. Demanded to call Winton. After all, we had his consent. But we were alone in the desert two and a half hours from Los Angeles. And the only man who knew our whereabouts was the doorman at Filmland.

"American gangsters!" Alex expostulated as we retreated back down the washboard track we'd only recently negotiated. "Pistol-whip me," Alex sputtered. But he was secretly thrilled; the incident appealed to his sense of adventure and stirred a restive spirit of chivalry.

"They never put away their guns!" he said with his eyes fixed on the rear-view mirror. Then he shook his head sternly, "One should always pack a pistol in America, Rider."

Suddenly he stopped the car and peered through the dust behind us. "Get the guns I have in the boot, Max, we'll sneak back and ambush those molls."

It was characteristic that I should be in conflict whether to correct Alex's vocabulary or address his ill-advised plan to bushwhack our assailants.

"What guns?"

"Rifles. For thrush hunting, of course."

"Alex, in the first place, molls are the girlfriends of gangsters. In the second place..."

But Alex had already swung the car onto the shoulder.

"I'm going back," Alex said excitedly. He bolted from the Bentley and ran to the trunk from which he produced two twenty-two rifles and a box of ammunition. He began packing one of the rifles with birdshot.

Oh, great. It occurred to me there was an elementary physics lesson here somewhere.

"In the second place," I continued, "they were armed with

pistols, not birdshot!"

Alex paused and squinted toward the checkpoint with his hand shading his eyes. The men were quivering specks in the heat radiating upward from the sand. The land was barren, with fewer than thirty stunted shrubs between us.

"This isn't going to work," I said. "We can see them. They can see us."

"Oh." Alex's disappointment was great. "Yes. I see. Well," he brightened, "we'll come back when we're properly armed. Then we'll see whose ass gets pistol-whipped."

Resuming our positions in the elegant car, I thought I heard him mutter under his breath, "Always pack a pistol."

I had plenty to consider on the ride back. Alex had almost gotten us killed. My reaction troubled me. If tolerance can be a fault, my ambiguity about these events suggested a character flaw. I found the risk of danger exciting. And dismissed quickly thoughts of what might have happened. As for Winton Grass, Alex and I remained puzzled. He had promised to meet us there, and supplied a map. What had gone wrong?

Φ

It was almost two o'clock when Alex's Bentley glided along the curb in front of Port's. Three brown-eyed valets swarmed the car. "Park it there," Alex directed them.

Ruben, Ports' maitre d', led us to a back patio, pleasantly set with white linen in a casually tended garden.

We seated ourselves at a table set under an umbrella. Sun-warmed air encircled us and I removed my jacket. Port's employed a German chef at that time whose mussel soup Alex particularly admired. Among plump, green-tipped

New Zealand mussels floated parsley and thin wafers of mushroom. Served with a light, freshly baked Parmesan loaf and a bottle of Bordeaux, it was a meal to be reckoned with.

Of course, Alex was accustomed to a full meal at midday and went on to chops and vegetables, boiled potato, pear, créme frâiche and espresso. So we lingered at Port's for several hours.

I'd been there a couple times with Alex, observed the same woman seated at the same table. Her skull was finely formed, yellow hair skimmed back to a tidy knot wrapped with silvery cord. She could be thirty or fifty, one could not tell. Large, tortoise-framed sunglasses rested on soft powdered skin. And her lips were carefully lined in a cherry color, filled in with pale mauve.

With her, a white dog with black spots, large as a small tyrannosaurus. Whenever she rose, the dog rose too, and clicked along the black slate patio, slightly worried he'd get left behind, until she twiddled her fingers lightly on his fine brow.

"Come, Mister D, nothing bad happen," she said.

Today she sat writing in a lesson book. The cover was black and white like Mister D. She wore an olive suede glove on her right hand, the hand she used to smooth the page. This day she rose from her seat earlier than usual, swung past our table on her way to the door.

"Countess," Alex said.

She turned, flashed a sparkling smile in our direction. "Alex des Prairies, lovely," she said. "Is this your friend?"

Countess deftly removed her glove at our introduction, clasped my hand in a forthright way. A diamond the size of a briquette dazzled me with fragmented light. She restored her glove, this time slipping her left one on as well. "Alex, what do you do here?" she asked.

"Well, Countess, just now we are discussing the good surprise of my investing in a gold mine." His phrase disturbed me. If Alex intended to invest his own money in the Inca Princess, he'd chosen an oblique way of announcing it to me.

"Gold?" Countess said. "Lovely. " She regarded me with flattering curiosity. "Do you also invest in gold?"

"Films," I answered.

"The cinema" she said. She moved her head in a teasing way. "Isn't film the hard currency of this town?"

I felt tongue-tied, as she appraised us coolly.

"Alex, you know my friend Susie Grass. She owns a gold mine. Perhaps you are involved in that?"

"No, no. Pure coincidence. Probably not the same," Alex lied.

She shrugged. "Sadly, Mister D and I have to leave. Good luck with your gold, Mr. Rider," she said.

When we were alone, Alex resumed the topic of Winton Grass. I studied my estate Bordeaux to hide my uneasiness.

"He's offered me a seat on the Board of Directors."

I shrugged—easy to offer.

"Really. Winton expects to be appointed Chairman during the litigation. What he says goes."

"At this time," I said coldly.

"You know what I told him? The very first thing I will do as a member of the Board is to replace him as Chairman."

"How did he react to that?"

Alex balanced a slice of red pear on the blade of his knife. "He took it rather badly, actually."

I was forced to laugh, amused at Alex's impudence

"You're not really thinking of investing?"

Alex raised one brow. "Why not?"

"If your money's come through," I said carefully, "you could pay something on your account. The disbursements on Danse du Sang will shortly exceed your credit line. Irving is concerned."

There was more to it than that. Government scrutiny of banks had heated up and Irving feared attracting attention to the risks we undertook—in financing Alex's film and others. Irving put it succinctly, "I got something to worry about, Rider, I put up cash."

Alex dismissed our unease with a wave. "That's my good news, Rider, I have a buyer for Danse du Sang. Fellow from Buenos Aires, Costa Brava Films—loves the script. I've talked him into a nice profit after Filmland's kind advance is repaid."

"That's great, Alex," I said, relieved. "But if you have a few dollars in the meantime… "

Alex tapped a fresh cigarillo on the white cloth. We sat in silence a few moments. "You know Winton is suing his father to gain control of the mine?" I said.

"What? Sues his father?" Alex regarded me as if I'd revealed Winton Grass had a third ear issuing from one side of his head.

"That's a bad business," he said in a low voice. "Too bad."

I'd rarely seen Alex disappointed. He shook his head regretfully. "I can't make business with a man who sues his father."

"Old man Grass is still going strong at sixty," I said.

Alex pitched forward. "What! Sixty years old?" He snapped shut his cigarette case of fretted silver. "The man should be tending roses. Have a bimbo. Gather sea shells! What business has he to be involved in the mine?"

Alex glared at me as if Tom Grass' persistence were a

crime against nature which I condoned. " If the old man won't take to pasture, he must be pushed."

He adjusted his posture to summon the check. It was like him to reverse himself for his own whims. He quickly excused Winton's faux pas of suing his father, on the grounds the old man defied the natural order for retirement from the world's affairs.

"I've promised to stop over there after lunch," Alex said. "Grass' place in Hancock Park, do you want to come?"

Φ

Two weeks had passed since our meeting at Michel Richard, and Susie hadn't been out of my thoughts for one night.

"You have a classical profile," she said, in her soft articulate voice. We were alone in the living room of the Grass home in Hancock Park, a neighborhood of blue-bloods and displaced Euro-crats. I was grateful to Alex for trotting off with Winton to view a diorama of the gold mine in the library, while I offered to keep Susie company.

"Like the 'David,' in Firenze. First time one sees it—it's—terribly moving."

Susie could be very affected. Not every man would find that attractive. But I liked her as much for her artifice as I did her sensuality. I wondered if Susie's affectations concealed something else, like the vague sense of loss underlying my own.

"Your profile," she said, tracing a line along my cheekbone to the curling hair at my collar. I accepted this as encouragement and moved against her. Very pleasant. In high heels she seemed half an inch taller. Flawless posture, and a slender waist with a curve like an Austrian luge run. My hand was very comfortable there.

It was my nature to observe the setting, to assess the possibilities for moving things along. The room seemed little used. It was too large like a hotel lobby, and formally arranged around two fireplaces.

I don't mind neoclassical. There's something vulnerable about striving to revive the past. Thick Italian fabrics were swagged and tasseled into draperies at the windows. A pair of gilded torchieres idled in corners like haughty butlers. The chandelier made you think of Empress Eugenie. And a Persian rug scattered gold medallions under our feet.

Susie's outfit kept faith with the decor. Her gown of silk plissé was bound in empire fashion. Its aqua folds illuminated her eyes like lapis stones.

I was getting somewhere. In a nice way. And we couldn't tell whose breathing was whose—when the cleric strolled in.

I'd forgot some of the best stories about the Grass twins featured a short solemn duck in a cleric's collar, wearing a gigantic renaissance cross that flopped against his chest when he walked. I knew he was the third member of the Inca Princess board and 'special friend' to Mrs. Grass. But I didn't expect him to turn up here. Not in Susie Grass' living room while I plotted her seduction.

Susie turned coy, started a conversation midstream. "You know she married an Italian count. Quite the old Nazi." She pronounced it 'Nazzi,' gave the unnamed Italian Count a flick of her head.

"And they arrested this old Nazzi in Argentina. After her divorce, she married a Persian, a friend of the Shah's, who came to LA through Europe to avoid the freeze. Ramòn's helping him, of course. And she's agreed to keep up this phony marriage until his assets are safe."

Two weeks before, President Carter had impounded $13 billion in Iranian assets to force the release of hostages. I remember the date, because I met Susie at Michel Richard that morning. Although no one I knew was Persian, a lot of people claimed their wealth was tied up in the freeze, because it seemed fashionable to have interests in the Persian Gulf.

I regarded the whole thing as a tangle of political intrigue. It was obvious Carter was under siege from major financial interests. David Rockefeller, for his part, had manipulated the Shah's exile to the States. While the State Department applied pressure to deport him again, the Shah's friends among the CIA and other covert interests worked to keep him in New York. It was political farce of the highest order and I didn't doubt Ramòn Brulée played a part in the affair.

"Always—always," Susie resumed her obscure history, "she must be attracted to social exiles. Older men who are slightly—declassé."

She looked at me as if I'd aided and abetted this unnamed cohort, whoever she was. "Of course, there's something terribly attractive about degenerate men."

The cleric appeared unaware of us. He floated around the room, placing a bejeweled hand lightly on various surfaces, as if bestowing a benediction on the inanimate world. Finally, he sidled up to Susie. "Your mother serves tea, my darling," he said.

As we followed Father Rob into the library, I whispered, "Who are we discussing?"

Susie moved discreetly against me and took my arm. "I thought you knew. My friend Countess."

The library was a much smaller room with apricot walls and cream moldings. An austere fireplace of tobacco-colored marble formed a centerpiece. On either side were painted book shelves holding faded volumes of the classics.

A framed photograph showed two tow-haired children regarding the world with serious eyes and betrayed mouths. Both were in sailor suits—short pants, for the boy, pleated skirt for the girl—standing so close they seemed connected. The twins.

Alex and Winton breezed in behind us. Alex made the introductions and I found myself clasping the dry, frail hand of Mrs. Grass, a precious, twittery bird who spoke in an arch, affected rasp. She was soft and blushed as a peach. One whose downy skin is almost imperceptibly withered so if you get close, you're warned—it's all parched and pulpy inside. She wore a wispy caftan whose sleeves bared a crepey, spotted arm as she poured.

"You will have Earl Grey, won't you, Alex? It's the only tea we drank at Connaught's when we visited the twins at Oxford. You knew Winton and Susie studied abroad?"

Susie and Winton seated themselves next to each other, rigid and watchful. I glanced at the children in the framed photograph. And felt uneasy, without quite knowing why.

"We arrived at gunpoint." Alex began his account of our trip to the Inca Princess mine. And I attempted to quell my sexual tension with a tepid brew passed off as jasmine tea.

"For someone who allegedly owns the mine, Winton, you seem to have little control over things," Alex observed.

My sense of annoyance returned from earlier in the day. "Didn't you let the guards know we were coming?"

Winton stiffened. "They're excellent men. See how they follow my orders? To a fine point. And if they did not? They can be quite sure I'd kick their ass!"

I regarded Winton's speech as something out of a play.

And I found myself wondering whether Winton himself had access to the mine.

"Did you call them?" I pursued.

Winton stared into his teacup so long that Alex and I exchanged a glance of puzzlement. Finally, he lifted his head to meet his sister's eyes before he spoke, "Those are my father's men," he admitted. "He must have countermanded my instructions."

The sun was brilliant through crisply painted French doors, but every so often a shade passed over the room and the winter chill revealed itself. When the cleric wasn't hovering uselessly near the tea cart—apparently he served as general gofer—he shuffled the periphery repeating his mysterious benediction ritual. Despite Alex's dependable vitality, I felt like a guest at a séance for unappealing souls.

Then I learned Susie Grass had a lover. At least I supposed it was her lover.

"Susie's fiancé, Ramòn Brulée. Do you know him, Mr. Rider? Lovely man, owns a racetrack I believe."

Cut-throat asshole, I'd heard. 'Makes bad business with anyone,' Alex had declared. That explained his appearance at Michel Richard's the morning Susie and I met there.

Relief seized me. I'd briefly imagined Winton Grass challenging me to a duel of honor, transporting me to the high desert cuffed to the cleric, with two armed henchmen offering weapons, and serving as seconds. Now it seemed, my rival was a short racketeer with a bad hair piece.

"He's not really my fiancé, Mother," Susie Grass said calmly.

"Brulée's merely a suitor, I should say," Winton smiled patronizingly at his sister. "Among many, I should say."

Alex tossed me his quick glance of skepticism.

"He's very influential," Susie went on, speaking to me. "with interesting connections."

Winton nodded his head seriously.

"He's been so helpful to Winton and me with our little—"

"Difficulties," Winton said, winked at Alex. "Nuisances really."

Their mother's hand trembled on the handle of the Spode teapot, while the cleric clutched his cross, nervously fingering its glass stones.

I was wondering when the homage to Brulée would end, when Winton Grass said brightly. "Alex has subscribed to buy two hundred shares of the Inca Princess stock."

"What—when?" Evidently Alex's intention was accomplished fact. I spoke so sharply Father Rob moved to Alex's chair and raised his cross.

"Right," said Alex to no one in particular.

"My goodness!" tittered Mrs. Grass. "My little tea party must rise to the occasion of celebration. It's really quite mischievous of you not to have told me. " She simpered her face into a little girl's smile of small perfect teeth, her eyes too bright.

Alex offered his tea cup in a toast, avoiding my eyes. "Excellent tea. Superb, really. Thank you. Now, we must be off, I'm afraid. Max, are you coming?" Alex rose.

I stood, bowed slightly to Mrs. Grass, exchanged a disconcertingly sexual look with Susie, and followed Alex swiftly to his car. The only question on my mind at that time applied as much to Alex's line of credit as to Susie's seduction. When?

12.

The Grass Twins in San Marino

Alex was right about the Grass twins. They were the American equivalent of barony. There was enough wealth to sustain three generations, in a style that can only be called aristocratic. Their grandfather grew rich through a form of American genius we call ambition, while their father slogged through the pretense of preserving the legacy.

Susie, like Marina Loge, had been presented abroad, in a kind of traveling deb program. At seventeen, she danced with dukes. And princes. And would have married one of these eligible admirers but for Winton's possessiveness.

It wasn't Winton or Susie who confided these facts to me. They lacked the detachment of historians. Alex's cousin Christian Ruhl really knew the twins, from their years in England.

Christian knew the family before its rupture. Before Tom Grass' debauchery rent the paternal bond and shattered the twins' illusion of wealth. Susie regarded their struggles as epic. Winton too. The conflict, marking the time I knew them, resembled Greek tragedy. Like another good melodrama, it began with father and son.

Tom Grass, Susie's father, posed as working geologist. But unlike the patriarch, his ideas were trivial. There was the gold case he invented to carry one's favorite poker chip, inspired by his own indulgence in the betting life. Unfortunately, gold was priced at eight-hundred dollars an ounce at the time; there weren't many takers.

Failure in financial matters is one thing a man cannot

forgive himself. And it's the one thing a self-made man like Susie's grandfather could not forgive his only son. In 1955 the twins were born. Their grandfather was then eighty-five. The old man waned in health but not in spirit. Even as the son, Tom Junior, softened toward his parent, trying on the spirit of forgiveness that attends the certainty of a vast bequest, Grass Senior composed a secret trust to issue upon his death. A series of trusts actually, Chinese boxes calculated to hoard principal for the benefit of the twins, and with the intended consequence of denying their father authority over financial matters.

The terms of the trusts were strict. The purse was managed by the old man's cronies, hard-bitten conservatives like himself who'd ripened into heads of banks and trust firms. When he passed on, Tom Junior received an evergreen allowance. Discretion to invest, participate in business ventures, or to manage his living expenses—all were subject to a corp of needle-eyed trustees.

Even the family's sallow scrivener, senior partner in a downtown firm, raised a faint brow at the charity provision: Tom Grass had no discretion to make bequests.

There's more to charity among the rich than noblesse oblige. The power to endow is the power to attract friends. And the acquaintances most valued are the ones who can be bought: curators, directors and trustees of philanthropic organizations. Because then the wealthy know the terms on which friendship is based. Depriving Tom Grass of philanthropy was nothing short of cruel, for it cut him off from his peer group and the collection of toadies who'd have been his lifelong pals.

13.

Susie at Café Chapeau

For a while, I lost sight of Susie Grass. I accepted her alleged engagement to Brulée as convenient, if unsatisfying. I suspect other men feel the same—a kind of fastidious aversion to the complications of romance. And I still felt a connection to Mona. If Fate threw Susie and I together, well, I'd pursue it. If not—then.

Irving and I kept busy at Filmland. I applied myself to perfecting the presentation we would take to Europe in May. I sought appointments from international names I'd only read about, and studied their films so I'd be well versed when the time came.

My knowledge of French was valuable. I could phone abroad without a translator. If you know French, you can pick up Italian. And Spanish. At least enough to get by. So our trip was taking shape, thanks to my efforts.

And then, in a Pasadena garden where almost nothing but French was spoken, I found Susie again, entertaining the Belgian consul with amusing speculation upon the origin of "cold duck."

With its waxy magnolias and draping bougainvillea, the garden revived Susie's ethereal spirit and rekindled my imagination. After that evening, I served as Susie's casual escort when Brulée was out of town.

I felt flattered to go places with her. The powerful effect of her arrival in the company of Winton—for he was invariably chaperone No. 1—was compelling, her pale hair fastened in a French braid along her back, her penetrating eyes drilling you like blue ice.

At first it was erotic fascination that drew me to her. And then, it was something more.

I forgave Susie, in advance, her infidelities. Calculation is a quality one admires in a woman as her prerogative, a form of retribution for all the inequities that attach to being female. From the moment Susie signaled her intention to exploit my position at Filmland, I regarded her with approval as I would a child who is selfish at play.

I longed to know her. Though I enjoyed our time together, there was no physical satisfaction in it. Winton was always present. Or Father Rob. And Winton and Susie indulged an annoying habit of lapsing into whispers concerning the gold mine. According to Winton, their father was having them followed. I gathered there were covert trysts with agents employed by their father, and secret transactions of all kinds.

"My father's lawyers would have us killed sooner than relinquish his legacy," Winton announced at the Belgian consul's, his eyes wild and dark.

"Don't be ludicrous," I said impatiently. But this earned me a cool lifting of Susie's brow, so I listened politely to Winton's ravings.

I perceived a toughness in Susie's nature completely lacking in Winton. And the alluring danger of that landscape drew me to her.

Perhaps two weeks after our meeting at the Belgian consul's, Susie asked me to invest in the Inca Princess. "We need a loan of half a million dollars," she said with unblinking directness. I replied it was not something I could decide on my own. Irving must concur.

"I understand," she said thoughtfully. The next day she telephoned to schedule a presentation at Filmland. I couldn't talk then, and we agreed to meet at Café Chapeau for a coffee. I had a brief wait before she arrived, half-taking in the hopeful conversations of the writers and actresses who hang out there.

The gist of it was, the twins' father was trouncing them in the litigation. They had spent hundreds of thousands so far pursuing a lead in Venezuela that turned out to be a ruse, tracking a man rumored to be their father's partner. They demanded copies of records and their father's lawyers stonewalled, claiming the records were destroyed in a fire. So the twins had no records of the income of the mine and no idea of its expenses.

And they were quickly running low on trust capital from their mother's side. That's why, I suppose, Winton tapped Alex and some of their other acquaintances for money. And why Susie pressed me for Filmland's support.

Susie arrived at the café like a fairy princess, a very determined one, and swept over to my table in the farthest corner of the room. Winton followed and held her chair for her before seating himself.

"It's critical we have the money now," she said almost immediately. "We want to purchase father's interest in the mine."

"What's it worth?" I asked casually.

"That's the difficulty," Winton said.

"Most of father's accounts are international," Susie said. "From Libya, Syria, Iran, Iraq. Places where it's difficult for the rich to change their assets."

She lowered her voice. "They buy gold."

"They send cash by courier," Winton continued in an agitated way. "Cash—how can Susie and I trace it? How can we calculate how much the mine is really worth?"

I felt thick-headed. I didn't get it. "But what's the cash for?"

"To buy gold contracts," Susie replied. "They're not delivered—obviously. Gold is not allowed to leave the United States. The bullion is stored in vaults at the Inca Princess and used to buy property here." She silenced Winton with a gesture. "I've heard Khasoggi and his entourage own Park Avenue apartments purchased with our gold."

"Why don't these investors simply wire their cash into a bank?"

She swung her braid impatiently. "You know very well, Maxwell, cash deposits over $10,000 are reported to the Treasury Department. Most gold purchases start at $100,000."

I realized later she'd given me an idea how Filmland might finance their litigation. If we backed our partnership units with gold bullion contracts from the Inca Princess, we eliminated investor risk. And provided an immediate source of income to Susie and Winton by way of gold contracts and vault fees.

But something else concerned me. The stratagem Susie described sounded uncommonly sophisticated for a dilettante geologist like her father. "Who negotiates these contracts?"

"Ramòn, of course. He set it up for father. Ramòn has extraordinary contacts. People in high places. Governments you and I wouldn't even know exist." She took a breath, "That's why, of course, it's so terribly awkward for Ramòn to aid Winton and I. Technically, he's still in business with father."

It took a moment for this to sink in.

"Are you saying Brulée refuses to help you with the litigation?"

"It's very hard for Ramòn. Sometimes we quarrel."

Brulée again. She tossed her head in petulance, the luxuriant golden braid moving like a whisper between her shoulders.

Susie's vanity was an affectation that drew me to her. I allowed my hand to trace the curve of her spine beneath the v-backed sheath she wore.

Her eyes turned suddenly very green. "You know what I'd like to do?" She let her eyes sweep down to the long hem of the cloth. "If Winton weren't here."

The said Winton character scowled disapprovingly, but made no gesture of leaving.

"Do you think we could get away with it?" she spoke with schoolgirl excitement. I glanced at the tables of actors earnestly mining their conversations.

"Winton, get lost," I said.

"Here's my purse, darling—pay the check, will you?" Winton's eyes flickered disdain. He rose stiffly, like a suspect in a bad British movie, and stalked outside, leaving the purse on the table.

There was something in the gesture that made me know it was all a game they'd played before. But a skillful one. Her voice, and her demeanor, suggested every moment her words implied: I fantasized her sliding beneath our small table, crouching hidden by the cloth, lifting the interested party from its place among my trouser folds…

"Let's try it," I said.

I guided her to me and felt her skin hot beneath my hand. Her mouth was hot too. Moist, small kisses on my lips, teasing me. I let my hand rest in the small of her back. The satin fabric felt silky and crisp. She wore a common scent, Chanel No. 5. On her it turned warm like an over-heated blossom.

Abruptly an actor started reading lines aloud, and she

turned business-like again, reviving the subject of a loan. I felt the sharp catch of disappointment in my groin.

"May we have Filmland's promise?" She asked it seductively, almost sweetly.

Her timing was excruciating. But I didn't bother with evasion. If ever I was to get close to her, it wouldn't be through lying.

"It's not possible," I said, "we're leaving for Cannes in two weeks."

She shrugged my hand from her back. "I see." She drew her mouth into a spinster's purse and signaled Winton that she was leaving. "You can call me when you return, but I cannot promise I'll see you then."

I tried reaching her after that but my calls were not returned. I ran into Susie with Countess the week before Irving and I left for Europe. Countess smiled warmly. Even Mister D sniffed my legs with dubious interest. But Susie only nodded coolly with the faintest of smiles. When we parted, she swept her eyes down, murmured, "À bientôt." If you know French, you'll think it strange, but I took comfort from her phrase. After all, she hadn't said adieu.

14.

Costa Brava Productions

"Sub-scribed, Rider," Alex said impatiently on our way to meet Alex's alleged buyer of Danse du Sang. " I've merely subscribed for Grass's shares, I haven't paid for them."

I appreciated the difference. Yet I felt uncomfortable over Alex's promise to invest in the Inca Princess mine. When I aborted my career as junior partner at the New York firm of Muller, Fagan & Luft I left behind the gloomy pessimism of law and lawyerly thinking. But my education continued to intrude and, though Alex insisted his money was held up in Liechtenstein (just saying it over in my mind imparted an exotic aspect to Alex's affairs) I made it clear that when it came through I expected him to repay Filmland before meeting his obligation to the Grass twins.

"Of course," Alex assured me as I relaxed into the fragrant leather of his Bentley. "The film is proceeding fabulously."

I'd seen a rough cut of what he had, and the cinematography was stunning. But the film wasn't finished. I'd hoped to enter Alex's film in the festival at Cannes a few months away. Several scenes remained to be shot. Even Gina's close-ups hadn't wrapped. And it would need to be looped and edited. A final cut was unlikely, so I instructed Alex to prepare a trailer, artfully patched together from the original film and new cut.

"Who are these guys?" I inquired about this morning's prospect, Costa Brava Productions.

"Referred by Bunker Dodge. He has impeccable contacts."

Alex had said the same thing upon my introduction to

Dodge. While I admired Bunker's discreet marketing skills, I didn't find his judgment reliable.

Alex deftly avoided a Mercedes, restoring the Bentley to its own lane with a graceful swerve. The startled driver screwed his head backward to glower at us, but his epithets were lost in the rush of our passing. Alex continued without pause.

"Bunker thinks Trujillo, the chairman of Costa Brava, descends from the Parma family, one of the five grandee families of Spain."

"I thought he came from Argentina."

Alex conferred on this incongruity his serious attention, and the Bentley lurched abruptly to avoid running down a yarmulke'd ancient in a crosswalk.

"Alex!"

"Oh, sorry. As I say, he's well-connected. Could be from Argentina."

I confess to having limited patience that morning. With Irving and I leaving for Europe in May, my schedule was tight. Alex had ransomed my time with the promise it would take only an hour to work out a distribution package with his new contacts.

"Well, anyway, I've never heard of Costa Brava. Are you sure they're on the up and up? The top guy, Trujillo, will I meet him this morning?"

Alex brightened. "He wants to meet you, too. They've offered to produce my next film, based on the Raft of the Medusa."

"The 19th century painting?"

"Well done, Rider! Your good American education is almost equal to a bad European one."

"Your next film's a tragedy at sea?"

"The research for this film is immensely interesting. You

know, of course, it's a true incident. The officers abandoned the ship. The survivors on the raft practiced cannibalism before they were rescued. "His glance took a dangerous shift to the horizon. "I must depict that realistically."

This conversation wasn't doing much to illuminate the terms he'd discussed with Costa Brava. "So they're going to buy Danse du Sang and they're going to produce Raft of the Medusa. Ambitious. Where are they getting the money?"

"That's why Trujillo wants to meet you. He asked me how Filmland works it."

"Works what?"

"Oh, you know. The money end. Your syndications."

Now I understood. "It's all wrong," I said. "I'm not telling them anything of Filmland's business. Either they want distribution rights to Danse du Sang or they don't."

We both desired a negative pick-up deal with a major distributor who would agree to pick up the cost of distribution to all theaters, pay for the advertising, the cost of prints, and all promotion. It would also mean an immediate recovery of Alex's costs and Filmland's investment and, if we could pump it up a bit, a split of profits between ourselves.

"I've never heard of them," I went on. "What theaters are in their pocket?"

"No one has heard of them," Alex replied. "I discovered them!"

I sighed with exasperation. "Just finish the trailer so we can sell it at Cannes. If we still need your new protegés when I return from Europe, we'll talk then."

Alex protested. "You have to meet them now. Dodge tells me they're swimming in cash."

We pulled onto that sedate mysterious street called Beverly Place. A lane, really, just off La Brea above Melrose.

A place out of time, it has always worn an air of Bond Street elegance foreign to LA.

Behind Georgian doors and ornamental gates lay dimly lit antique shops—to the Trade mostly—and a few clandestine film companies with enigmatic names like White Dove Productions, Bluebird Films, and so on.

I wanted to impress upon Alex that no deal was to be struck unless Trujillo was prepared to supply references. But Alex leapt from the Bentley as soon as we parked, and squinted up the deserted street for the address.

The only activity issued from a limo with shaded windows pulling up to Le Restaurant, a secluded lunch spot for those few industry notables who preferred obscurity. We started walking and our shoes clicked on the sidewalk.

At 122 Beverly Place, we paused before an iron gate with its lock un-joined. The gate creaked as we passed inside and I felt a boyish dread, as if we were trespassers at a haunted house. A brass plate fixed to the door announced, curiously, A. Jamul.

"Are you sure this is it?"

Alex glanced at a business card, "Yes, yes," he said impatiently and pushed the bell. We stood there several minutes, an interval long enough to invoke the bell several more times, and were about to turn away when we heard a man's steps rushing for the door.

We were welcomed into the foyer by a trim man in a pale blue jumpsuit with loops and epaulets. His hair had been buzzed short and his shave was so close his Adam's apple practically shone. Military, I thought, shaking his hand.

The man introduced himself as Arthur Jamul, putting an end to my curiosity about the door plate. Yet there was nothing remotely Latin about his appearance, and his accent—Akron, if I had to speculate.

Jamul led us swiftly down a hall with offices on either side. I glanced into one of the offices and felt astonished by its air of vacancy. The room was barely furnished. I saw nothing to demonstrate any work was done there. Telephone, typewriter, sofa, desk, and chair. Strange I should remember this, but there were no pencil holders.

Jamul hustled us into the kitchen where two men were seated at a table of gray formica. After introductions, we seated ourselves around the table, while cokes were brought from the refrigerator. and Jamul initiated the conversation. "Tell us a little about your business, Max."

You might have noticed I'm not one who seizes the conversational pigskin and takes off charging downfield with it. I preferred to hear what Jamul had to say.

"Quite frankly," I said, "We've come today because you've offered to buy Danse du Sang. I'm here to further that process. My office is prepared to confirm a letter of agreement between Costa Brava and Mr. des Prairies, assuming you can assure Filmland, by way of an audited financial statement, that you have the resources to distribute the film."

Alex was aghast, and I saw anger cloud the face of our host in powder blue.

"Pro forma," he snapped, "plenty of time for the formalities. As I understand it from Mr. des Prairies, Danse du Sang isn't even finished."

"Then why are we here?"

"We're interested in a long-term relationship," Jamul said smoothly.

Alex broke in, "The Raft of the Medusa, they want to finance my next film."

"What about it?" I looked directly at the man in blue.

"We're interested in Filmland's capital resources."

"What do our capital resources have to do with anything?"

"According to Mr. des Prairies, you aspire to become a major player in this town, where will you get the money?"

I was beginning to get annoyed. I'd known my share of muscle-headed simpletons but this guy left the cake out in the rain. "We run a bank. Banks have depositors. It makes loans. It takes in interest and fees. What else do you need to know?"

My answer had the curious effect of arousing excitement among the troops. The three men looked at each other. Then, the younger one spoke up. He nearly stammered his question.

"Depositors. Yes. How does it work? Where does the money come from? If—if Filmland finances a film—Raft of the Medusa, for example—who would the investors be?"

I didn't see this was getting us anywhere. I started to rise. "Look, I'm on a very tight schedule. I'm leaving for France. No time to discuss projects that may materialize in the distant future. If you're ready to make a commitment on Danse du Sang, I'll see that appropriate agreements are drawn. Filmland will of course require that your funds repay our loan according to a schedule we approve." I didn't want them going behind my back and paying Alex for the film.

"Wait." At a signal from Jamul, one of the men drew from his shirt pocket a business check and threw it on my briefcase. "There! There's our commitment."

Alex and I stared at the draft. We'd come here for this, why should a voice of caution beat out a warning, Don't touch that check!

I picked it up and read it, printed with the name and address of Costa Brava Productions, made out to Filmland for $300,000—10% of the sale price—and signed with one signature, Trujillo. So where was the elusive Trujillo?

I turned to Alex, "What's the understanding?"

"They will repay our costs, and we split profits, one-third to us, two-thirds to Costa Brava."

I resumed my seat. I had to credit Alex with negotiating a very attractive package, assuming that's what the absent Trujillo had agreed to.

"I've never heard of Costa Brava," I said cautiously. "What theaters are you associated with?"

"We'll get the film into the theaters," Jamul said.

Alex and I exchanged a look. "What theaters?" I pressed.

"We can rent the theaters."

Too easy. They were setting us up for a four-wall deal. It wouldn't do. When a producer is forced to four-wall a picture, it means he can't get a straight distribution deal. He has to rent the theaters, which takes a lot of cash and time. Costa Brava appeared to have the cash, but they hadn't demonstrated the connections. And I couldn't see Alex or me flogging Danse du Sang to theater owners in our spare time.

I stood up again, Alex did too. "Feel free to call me when I return."

Jamul moved to detain me. "We want a relationship. We could start working on finding cash for your partnerships. We may have investors for you."

Who said anything about Filmland's investors or partnerships?

"I really don't have any more time. Keep in touch."

I collected my briefcase, replacing the check in front of Jamul with a deliberation I didn't feel. He stood up, grim with frustration, and I saw a question pass among the three men. I caught the quick snap of Jamul's head in a negative gesture.

For the second time, Alex and I took the brisk march

down the hall in the company of Jamul. This time all the doors were closed. In the foyer I turned to Jamul with sudden intuition.

"Vietnam?" I asked.

His eyes flickered and he frowned. "I wasn't called," he said. "What made you ask that?"

"Your watch and ring," I said casually. "Military." Something made me glance at his shoes as the door closed behind us. I knew he was lying.

15.

Lainie's Chair

One Friday evening at Yale, five years before I met Alex, Christian or the Grass twins, a classmate drew me along to fill a foursome at Mrs. Palsgraf's. I was twenty-two. The girl I disappointed was petite and vibrant, a Jewess from Jersey, as different from Susie Grass as lager from champagne.

"I knew a guy once," she said, tilted her head and slit her flashing eyes. "Nostalgic—like you."

I set my faux-German stein between us. "Nostalgic?"

"Only thing is," she continued, philosophically, "you're nostalgic for things that don't exist."

The girl, Shelley, was not the sort of girl I could have more than a laconic interest in, though she was beautiful enough. But she lacked grace, and a quality I guess you'd call refinement. For some reason I can't explain, her remark affected me. And for several years after that evening, every time I thought of her I got depressed.

Φ

After Filmland got going, I wrote a check once a month, and made regular visits to 1342 Euclid in Santa Monica. Thirteenth street below Montana Avenue for the cognoscenti, is now an upscale area of sitcom writers and actors with a series. Then, it was the bungalows.

Regular visits. I can console myself with that. Cruising to Santa Monica from Beverly Hills in my red XKE, bought off a Persian prince at Dan Tana's when the valet key-nicked a small chrome piece on its door, I often arrived aloof and defensive.

"Dad! Daddy!"

Sensing my arrival with stubborn acuity, Lainie would stumble down the path to my car in alarming defiance of the natural laws of equilibrium. Behind her, Mona smiling, yoga smile.

Sensuous woman, beautiful child. Their gentle regard transformed me against my will. For several lost hours once a week on Saturdays, I became part of nature's scheme in a role larger than myself.

Lainie turned four the Saturday before I left for Europe. I had an inspiration for a birthday surprise. Alex had pirated the family heirlooms on his last trip to Brussels, in anticipation of a move to Tower Hill. He couldn't use everything, and it passed to me to store some of the best pieces at Mona's bungalow.

As the hired truck pulled up to Mona's with two of Filmland's office crew, I jogged up the path to make room for Alex's things.

The first item I hauled out of the ant-farm that was their home was Lainie's beanbag chair, which I set, forlorn and beige, next to the aluminum lawn chair. While the boys from Filmland trotted in Alex's antiques, Lainie watched with troubled eyes.

Alex's heirlooms, from his family's twelve-bedroom chateau, formed a collection of carved mahogany on a scale intended for the courts of kings. Each was carved to resemble various animal parts. Every table ended in a lion's paw, the love seat rested on some prancing reindeer's forelegs and twin griffins stared backward from its arm rests. A pair of chairs—there were two of everything it seemed, were supported by massive limbs.

In half an hour Mona's small living room was crowded with animalia of polished mahogany, overstuffed down pillows, a Renaissance tapestry where the Monet poster used to be and a giant Chinese bowl on a footed rosewood stand.

I puttered around adjusting things, while Lainie tiptoed after me. Her small figure mirrored my gestures, then studied me for approval.

"Don't touch, Lainie," I cautioned. "Visual appreciation only."

But she watched intently, miming my movements.

Mona's reception of these new things was subdued, as if I had delivered a kennel of yapping poodles. But she didn't protest. Instead she graciously offered my helpers Red Zinger sun tea.

"Je prefére café au lait, s'il vous plait," I said.

Since Lainie's first words, I'd imposed on Mona my desire for our daughter's fluency in French as well as English. Mona gamely tried to cooperate. But language lab at Santa Monica City College modified only slightly her soft midwestern accent.

When Alex's furniture was unpacked and settled in the cottage, Mona asked me haltingly in French, "Does this mean you'll be a real father to Lainie?"

This surprised me, for we had broken off even before I moved West—before Lainie was born. I did not know then, or suspect, the issue was my fear of failure. Mona's question forced me to consider what it meant to fail as a husband, a father. And, pushing the feelings away, I assumed a manner that, I think now, must have resembled my own father's.

"I'm not ready," I answered her in French, "I have another life."

"You act as if we're a family. You choose our furniture,

you pay our rent, you dictate the language we speak. Are we your family, Max?" Her blue eyes regarded me as truthfully as Lainie's.

"I did not choose this," I said with unforgivable presumption, "You did."

"Choose us now Maxwell."

I can't forget her look of pain when I resisted, "Look, I've got to go. This has to wait until I return. Don't try to change things."

"Things change whether we want them to or not," she answered in English. "Lainie changes every day and you're not here to see it."

I didn't reply. Instead, I moved toward the open door. Lainie followed, as if to leave too. It was then she saw the movers pick up the last of Mona's things, the beanbag chair.

Blonde, sturdy (she looked just like me, except for Mona's golden hair), Lainie rushed outside. She threw herself on the torn plastic chair and screamed with infant rage. And fear.

"No! Beam-bag chair, beam-bag chair." She looked wildly at her mother, accusingly at me.

"No, no! Beam-bag chair!" She made a chant of it, moving her head side to side like a German doll.

The other single mothers in the complex came out, observed us with the grateful detachment of parents whose screaming kid it wasn't, for a change.

Mona raised a sympathetic brow as if to say, "We better keep the chair." But I knew it wouldn't fit. And it would have spoiled the effect of Alex's things.

"Wait, Lainie, we'll take pictures." I raced to the Jaguar, collected an old Polaroid from the trunk.

"We'll keep a picture of the chair," I said, "until it comes back."

I snapped one then, an angry, tear-streaked toddler almost swallowed by the formless cushion.

Twenty minutes passed before Lainie left the chair. Twenty minutes of Mona's coaxing: "Daddy's things are from Europe, a far-away place. Like the Land of Oz."

It's the small acts of selfishness one regrets. The stubborn resistance to grace and generosity that seems to come from nowhere to spoil things. It disappears as quickly as it comes, leaving you to wonder, why couldn't I have just—

When at last Lainie climbed down she moved slowly, weary and resigned. Mona led her to the sideyard where a faded swing diverted her until the movers bore the chair away.

Among the snapshots from that day is a portrait of Lainie and me, Santa Monica, 1979. An eerie shot, those enormous pines casting long shadows on the grass. My younger self holding a little girl smiling radiantly through her tears. So clear now what I missed then. Lainie used her grief to unit us, however briefly. All she wanted was me and Mona—a family, and a chair.

16

Rider at Heatherton

Once I learned to write and speak on the telephone, I sought my father out. I forced myself on him at a time when he was content to place me second to his crystal decanter collection. To the extent my school routine and finances allowed, I wrote him every week, telephoned at Christmas and Easter, and anticipated my custody visits with the avid attention of a beagle at an open door. My father, for his part, tolerated me like the local constable, a necessary but not particularly welcome part of the scenery.

With my stepbrother Rory absent at public school, my father enjoyed the life he'd been born for: riding, sports, dabbling in local politics, in short, the sterile, if satisfying, routines of an English country gentleman. His only real pursuit involved stretching his finances, a dwindling sum which he used sparingly to support his pleasures. Concealed from Rory and me was the secret selling of antiques to Americans, secret because it was bad form to admit to financial need, even to one's own children.

As a concession to my mother, I was allowed a yearly visit to Heatherton, my father's estate outside London. June through August, my father faced the uncomfortable prospect of a visit from his American son—bright and curious, good at squash and tennis—emotionally over-refined—slightly, failingly, idealistic.

After the summer I returned to prep school where I found myself among the poorest of my schoolmates. Academic scholarship covered my tuition. And my father's support, always modest, was reluctantly advanced.

The spring I turned thirteen, I received a shock. I wasn't going abroad. My father wrote my mother in May—estate expenditures prevented his paying my fare. I saw treachery in this—an opportunity for my father to sever the idea of my existence. And I panicked. I began to put away savings toward my summer at Heatherton.

By the next week I had a job at the village soda fountain, scooping Sealtest ice cream into cones for co-eds from the University. $1.65 an hour, plus tips, and I quickly learned to offer myself for deliveries, to housewives nearly always grateful to be spared a trip to the village for dessert.

By finals I had enough to secure my ticket to Heathrow. It wasn't all my own money. My mother slipped fifty dollars of her savings in the envelope with my birthday letter. Convinced that Fate could jinx me, I carried my ticket in my book-satchel until the day I left for England.

I arrived on a weekend when guests were gathered, many were my father's friends from school. Rory wasn't home yet, as he often stayed in town with schoolmates. I arrived late, and took my place at the table just as dinner was being served.

Page served the meal, with the help of an Irish girl who lived in the village. It had been a year since I'd dined in this manner, among adults at a dinner party—a custom much more common in Europe than in America. I was engaged in the clumsy conveyance of veal chop from platter to plate when my father chose that moment to introduce me.

"My son," he announced drily. "I do wish he'd come a little later—a few decades perhaps."

I felt stunned by his meaning but the guests tittered appreciatively—a generous drinks hour preceded dinner— and the sly smile of my stepmother Carol may have encouraged my father to be cruel.

"His mother's an actress," Father lied. "French. "He pursed his mouth into a tight, silly smile. "What can one do? She turned me down—I had to force myself on an English girl." An exchange of glances with my stepmother was trotted out to illustrate this company fiction—the flighty, romantic French actress turning down the English Lord, and legitimacy for her son.

That wasn't how it was. The end of my mother's acting career coincided neatly with my fetal development; she was a passionate, serious woman with a strong sense of duty, who loved my father and expected to marry him.

"Mixed blood tells," Carol offered sympathetically. "You know the French intermarried over centuries with the Spanish. It's well known the southern cultures are too passionate for their own good."

"You might introduce a bill into Parliament, Henry," my father addressed his neighbor, the district M.P., who flushed at the attention, "Let's do something for the blighted French. We don't have enough social problems in England. We ought to rally 'round the French!"

My father seemed to think he'd been amusing and surveyed the table for approval. "I'm sure the cause would be a welcome diversion from local issues."

"Quite," replied Sir Henry Thompson. But his face reddened, even as my own grew warm to feel everyone's eyes upon me.

I suffered through the rest of dinner in a silent rage. How dare he insult my mother? I'd show him. My anger attached itself to my stepmother. She had stolen my mother's life and title. She'd taken what should have ours.

The larger irony eluded me. My father's dalliance had

produced an illegitimate son whom he was too cowardly to claim. It was he who'd acted basely, transforming filial responsibility into condescension.

The next morning, I descended the stairs to the dining room at seven o'clock. Always the first in the household to breakfast, I usually ate alone. But that morning my father joined me, his mood subdued from the evening before.

I'd made up my mind to return that day to New York. I didn't know how to accomplish this, my return ticket was set. Yet I could not remain where my mother was dismissed as a silly Parisian actress. It had been a miscalculation to force myself on my father when he'd made up his mind that I should be erased. I felt incredibly sad, yet strong in my resolute plan.

I returned his good morning soberly, turning the page of my Black Tower comic book which I'd brought with me from the States.

Instead of taking his seat at the head of the table, he set his plate across from me, and regarded me over kippers and eggs.

"You're sprouting, I see," he said, referring to the smallest and palest of hairs on my upper lip. He surprised me by brushing my cheek with his hand, tracing his index finger under my nose. I could feel the slight resistance of pale growth I'd noted myself.

Tears sprang to my eyes from his gesture. I wanted very much at that moment for my father to apologize to my mother, and to accept me.

He blinked his eyes rapidly over the Mason teacup. "I've asked Page to set out your grandfather's shaving things, including his Georgian straight razor—it's hallmarked, and monogrammed. A wry smile flickered briefly, "Never had much of a beard. But yours may well come in thick and blonde like my father's."

My father began stirring sugar into his tea with a relentlessness that could have served as Chinese water torture. "Can't demonstrate the damn implements, I'm afraid. A talent beyond me. Likely to slit my throat if I tried."

He claimed his London Times then, opened it in front of his face and commenced an exercise of folding it into a precise rectangle beside his place setting. I too folded something—my feelings, folded them into a tight rectangle of my own, and pressed them neatly behind my sternum for another day.

Φ

Rory and I enjoyed a good relationship. I've seen what passes for regard between siblings, and I think we had something different. Formal. And yet, sympathetic.

He was taller than I, brown hair where I was light, freckled in place of the pale bronze of my mother's family. And he wore an endearing expression of polite concern that there should be no conflict.

My stepbrother was scrupulously courteous, he planned his schedule to include me when he was present at home. And besides all that—we had fun. Although slight, I enjoyed a cheerful disregard for physical safety. I introduced Rory to the pleasure of leaping off the portico fifteen feet onto a trampoline, which I urged him to acquire from a neighbor when they installed a permanent one in their playroom. This extravagant talent made me extremely popular among Rory's friends, and enhanced my reputation as a reckless American.

My father showed his preference for Rory in curiously

patent ways. My stepbrother had his own mount and hand-made saddle, while I was consigned to ride Snowball, an equine shrub-aholic who could not pass a birch branch without pausing for a snack.

Coaxing Snowball was like driving a cockroach, with as much potential for success. On the first morning that my father wore his new orange breeches, his mount Diablo lowered himself to roll in the mud on the lane. Nothing my father did could prevent it. Rory and I were greatly amused. And though Snowball made the most of the occasion, snuffling up leaves along the path like a starving gourmand, the whole party was detained while my father released himself from his stirrups, and stood swearing at Diablo, his flame-colored jodhpurs brown with muck.

My father's severity was most pronounced on hunt weekends. Generally, I had returned to New England by autumn. But that year, I was present for the hunt.

"You don't have the proper attire," my father insisted, though Rory had offered to lend his old ensemble. "It wouldn't fit," Father replied. "And I can't afford to buy you a new one."

I wouldn't deny myself the excitement of the occasion, and stood stubbornly in the drive until they rode off, Rory turning back with a curt embarrassed wave. The jubilance of hunt stories upon their return gave a second blow to my unhappiness. I found it hard then, as later, to be the outsider.

My father's wife, Carol, was all right. An excellent sportswoman and strong competitor, she hadn't time for Rory or me. Having claimed my father and secured him to England by producing his heir, her job was done. She then settled herself into club life. And never gave another thought to her son. It was even more remote that she should acknowledge me.

I needed a friend in that household. Especially during the weeks when Rory stayed in London. Margaret, the Irish girl, came in four days a week. She wasn't destined to be a servant, having been accepted at Trinity to study the classics in the Fall. Slender, with glossy auburn hair and night blue eyes, her skin shone with impeccable whiteness. Margaret spoke little, but when she did her crisp, soft speech nourished me like an April rain.

"Young Master American," she referred to me drily when my father wasn't present, to distinguish me from Rory, whom she dubbed "Young Master London."

Margaret spent her mornings in the large, tiled kitchen at the back of the house. It was sunny there, and the deep windows looked over unruly gardens of foxglove and red squirrels. I started drifting in about eleven. "It's a cup of tea ye're after, is it?" she asked. While she polished the silver, wiped the glassware, revived the floral arrangements, I spoke to her about America.

Margaret said little but listened to my accounts with an air of fascinated interest. "Really?" she whispered softly as if the truth of it were a secret between ourselves.

My father's chiding about our friendship puzzled me. "Your friends should reflect your background," he told me. It seemed to me he missed the irony in his words. Apparently even I, his unwelcome son, must not blur distinctions between staff and gentry.

During the last weeks at Heatherton, my thoughts were conflicted. I could have admitted she was my friend. But my father's resentment had a way of disorienting me, I lacked the navigational skills to make it back to the shores of my own soul.

When Margaret left at the end of the summer, I could only manage to shake her hand. She returned a tender smile.

"Good-by, Young Master American," she said in front of my father.

What was the outcome of this connection to my father which I scrupulously tended and from which he withdrew? I used to say I came to know him, and not to like him very well. And yet there was one more curious affect to it after all. For decades after I was grown, I still longed for him to admire me.

17.

Irving and Rider in Florence

There came a pause in my association with Alex's affairs. Late April to June, I didn't see Alex or yield to his energetic charm over the telephone. Mostly I was in Milan, Athens, Paris, Madrid, trotting around with Irving, trying to ingratiate ourselves among the barons of Europe's film industry.

"Why would individuals invest?" Roger Vadim, the French producer, asked me in Paris. "Films are risky."

"Glamour," I replied. "Wouldn't you rather invest in films than in bonds?"

Vadim raised a brow and placed his fingers at his lips. He was a swashbuckling figure in French film, with a gift like Roger Corman for commercializing cheap product. Since his early success with "And God Created Woman," whereby Bardot created her director, his films followed the Vadim formula: cartoon set, campy script, stunning starlet. "Barbarella" was a case in point, made in 1968 with Jane Fonda, whose sarongs of torn leopardskin captured box office while better French efforts languished in art houses.

"What does Filmland get out of it?"

I explained the profit participation split, using "Barbarella" as a guide. "Twenty-five percent of gross revenues on the front end. Fees for packaging, commissions on sales."

"No strings," I assured him regarding creative control.

"Percentage of gross—you take the profit away!"

As we parried profit participations in the Ritz lobby bar, Vadim engaged in eye-flirtation with a mademoiselle seated between her proper, aging parents.

"She's attractive—yes?"

I shrugged my reply, slightly annoyed. Irving and I had flown almost six thousand miles over the Artic circle. Couldn't I expect his attention?

"I will let you know."

Vadim had the good manners to stand and let me make it to the lobby before sidling over to the girl's table.

Ф

From press coverage of the film festival in Cannes, you might infer it's merely a publicity stunt for starlets, or a screening venue for subtitled films. But for most who attend, it serves as an international marketplace where films are bought and sold, and real money is exchanged.

Of our ten films, only one was completed, Malibu Shear, a low-budget tribute to Psycho, in which a deranged cowboy attacks his girlfriend with her sewing scissors to a weird driving musical score that resembled Hitchcok's original. Malibu Shear was popular, especially among the Spanish-language producers, who planned to dub a popular actor's baritone for the wimpy lead.

Irving and I held out for distribution of the whole package. And it paid off. That put us about $1 million to the plus side by the end of the week when we departed Cannes for Madrid.

Before leaving the States I'd made a bold plan of calling on every major filmmaker who exhibited in the U.S. in the past decade. Thanks to my planning, we came close to achieving it. But my journal entries from the time will give you a better idea of whose fortunes touched Filmland's in those heady days.

April 15. Arrive Heathrow. Brown's Hotel. 5:00, tea, Antonioni [Blow Up, Zabriski Point]

April 17. Arrive Dublin. The Sherbourne, car to Huston's estate. [Discuss distribution for The Man Who Would Be King.]

April 19—April 26. Dublin to Paris. Ritz Hotel. Truffaut re: Day for Night; Malle re: Le Combe Lucien, dinner.

April 20. Vadim, cocktails, discuss Don Juan. *Arthur Hiller may be in Paris at the same time. Discuss American distribution for The Man in the Glass Booth.

April 22. Godard (assistant insists we call on arrival).

May 2—May 9. Cannes Film Market.

May 16—May 21. Eurail, Nice to Madrid. Fly to Athens. Theo Angelopoulos – new project?

May 22—May 31. Rome. Fellini, call to confirm invitation. (discuss U.S. distribution Amarcord).

Φ

With some effort, I strove to cut a provocative figure in leather bomber's jacket, chinos, and English mocs. I borrowed flair from Alex with a silk ascot, and brushed my hair straight back with a gel I picked up at Boots. The effect was—quite possibly—interesting.

During the six weeks Irving and I peddled our Wild West Show, I kept in contact with Alex about the progress of Danse du Sang. I was disappointed we couldn't show it at Cannes, and still hoped miraculously to receive a rough cut. It was a shock to find that Alex had prevailed upon Wingdot, Filmland's disbursements officer, for further advances. Panic set in when Wingdot wired me to say that two dacron-shirted auditors had showed up from the Federal Bank Board.

"Christ, Rider, we gotta go back," Irving said.

I thought of going back too, but it seemed to me Wingdot might be overstating things. He tended to look at his shoes when he walked, and that affords a dismal perspective. Besides, there was every possibility the audit would be extended if Filmland's co-chairmen arrived.

Instead, I crafted two very explicit telexes, one to Wingdot prohibiting any further outlays to Danse du Sang until a principal payment had been made on the account, the second to Alex at the Chateau Marmont:

Alex—trouble with bank regulators. Wire $2 million principal reduction to Filmland immediately. Call Wingdot re: wiring instructions. Rider.

I thought I'd hear something after the telexes. But Wingdot was difficult to reach. He seemed to have his hands full trotting back and forth to the auditors delivering files.

When a week passed with no reply I decided to follow up with Alex.

"Max! What a good surprise. How's Madrid? I forgot to mention you must look up a good friend of mine when you get to Rome. Terribly good fellow. Tied up somehow with Fellini. Fabulous connection."

"Thanks, Alex. Thanks very much. Did you receive my telex last week?"

"Oh? Yes?" Alex sounded dubious. "Yes I did. Round here somewhere. And I meant to reply. Quite slipped my mind. But here's the thing. I'll arrange immediately for the wiring. I'll call Wingdot. Good chap, slightly obtuse, he'll arrange it. It will be done today. Don't worry, I'll take care of it. But say, call Rocco Gigli in Naples. Here's the number. He'll be delighted to talk to you, have dinner any time, give him my best."

We rang off, I turned to Irving. "We can relax," I said. But I continued to feel unsettled and that evening I arranged for an early return after Florence.

I called Rocco Gigli before we left Spain but the number Alex gave me had been associated, for centuries it seemed, with the Curci family, who as far as I could elicit, had no knowledge of Signoré Gigli. Fellini's studios were in Rome, not Naples, and there was no Rocco Gigli in the phone listings.

We found Fellini without Alex's help. An outgoing man, and generous, he invited us to lunch at his polo estate outside Rome, an austere-looking convent set upon beautiful grounds. His photographer was there, Gianni de Venanzo, whose work on 8½ I'd admired enough to watch three times in one weekend.

It seemed Fellini was something of a polo player. And although there was no polo that day, he welcomed us in jodhpurs, boots, and riding crop.

Following a long Italian lunch of many courses, served upon his loggia in the sunshine, it struck me how like his films the setting was.

Children chased each other under the trees, dashing in

and out of sunlight like dappled spirits. Count and Countess something-or-other rode up on horseback. And I realized the life Fellini filmed was the life he led.

As we lingered in the waning afternoon, I found myself thinking of Susie and wishing she were there. European sensibilities are often attracted to the scions of American wealth. Fellini would have found the Grass twins fascinating, if only for their superficiality. I even imagined he might portray them in a film.

The talk grew less emphatic. The air became dense with mist, softening the landscape. Quite suddenly I felt intensely interested in hearing Susie's voice.

"Of course," Fellini replied when I asked to use his phone. He gestured toward the club room off the stables.

I excused myself and made my way across the grass to the stone paddock, which, in its earlier incarnation as a convent, had served as dormitories for the novitiates. A separate door led to a high-walled office filled with polished woods and leather seating. The scents of harness and hide soap almost knocked me back with their bracing familiarity, and I paused willingly in the cool masculine rooms.

I reached Susie in New York, recalling that she and Winton were meeting lawyers there. It was ten am New York time. She'd received my Botticelli postcards—goddesses in profile that recalled her bland intensity to me—and cryptic messages on hotel note paper. My thoughts expressed themselves more intimately in writing than in person.

"I realize I've let you down—declining to lend you the money from Filmland, but I don't want finance, or money, or anything, between us. I haven't forgotten. But first—you and me."

Not the most romantic jargon. And I left a lot unsaid.

Though I hoped she could read my intention.

I felt buoyant when I heard her voice—glad she was in New York, that she'd been the one to answer instead of Winton. Glad of her existence. And my own.

"Susie," I said in a warm rush of emotion as if it were necessary to catch her before she vanished. "I'm calling from Rome. It's Max—Maxwell Rider," I added foolishly, in case she should still despise me.

"Maxwell?" Her voice floated dreamily through the tunnel of the Italian telephone system. "What are you doing there now? It must be four o'clock this afternoon. You're calling from the future!"

I described for her Fellini, his estate, and his guests. The Count and Countess Something-or-Other, which I knew would please her. The children. And their ponies. The dense, expectant air. The falling afternoon.

"Susie. I needed to hear your voice. I—well, we have to make this trip together next time."

There was a pause in the voice tunnel, when I could only hear the echo of my own phrases. And I thought I'd lost her. Then her voice came, excited, happy. "You must bring me something exquisite. Something terribly unique. From Florence, please make it be from Florence. Don't forget, Maxwell, will you?"

Her words were just the superficial chatter that passes for conversation for girls like Susie, who have been sequestered at private schools. But it made no difference to me. Her voice was lush with all the possibilities that could exist between us. With her teasing words, she had deliberately shifted our relations. And I knew then that I loved her.

I returned to the party just as it was breaking up. Fellini embraced us warmly. The shifting light brought a romantic fade-out, complete with ambiguous European ending. We left with the impression Fellini might call us for financing on Casanova.

Φ

We rented a car the next day and drove north to Florence where we would catch our flight back to California. I called a girl there, a friend of Susie's, and she agreed to join Irving and I for our last night in Italy. Gabra was a slender Argentine with naked arms and swaying hips. Irving was attracted to her. Any man would have been. But Gabra preferred aging playboys, autocratic figures who sat smoking indolently at cafés, expounding on their aristocratic backgrounds.

When we met her, Gabra was between father figures, the last one had broken her heart.

"The jealousy I can forgive. He is passionate. But to borrow my money, when he knows I am an artist," she turned her large and lovely hazel eyes on me. "It is—" she groped for the English word, "immoral. Terribly, terribly corrupt."

I agreed with her, although I realized my carnal interest in her was no less corrupt than her last fiancé's.

"Max, Irving, tiens, I must show you the quaintest Etruscan ruins. Come with me."

She led us through the streets of Florence to the train station, where we caught a bus for the hills above the city.

On the clean, modern bus we gripped the leather straps and braced ourselves, careful not to pitch into the laps of the polite and private citizens of Florence. The view behind us unfolded, a lazy panning shot in technicolor. At Fiesole, we jumped off, the spectacular beauty of Florence spreading out below us like shards of ancient pottery. Through short pines and whitewashed villas, we viewed the sky, a vibrant teal, and perfect scalloped clouds.

We strolled a few steps to a small hotel where a terrace bar jutted from the hillside. We ordered Campari and soda. What else? Gabra related, again, with charming intensity, the tale of her disaffected lover. We ordered more Campari and denounced him emphatically. Around five o'clock, the sun turned mauve and I started to question my resolution of celibacy.

"There is one thing I cannot stand," Gabra was saying. She swung her hair in disapproval. "It is a man who bares his chest at table, it is the rudest thing."

I glanced around at three Italians drinking Ouzo nearby. One of them the others called Guido, dark, bold, with the peculiar affectation of wearing his watch strapped to his shirt cuff, initiated smoldering eye passion with Gabra, even as he unloosened his shirt nearly to his navel, exposing his chest.

Gabra lowered her lashes in rebuke. Guido pouted his lips audaciously.

After a half hour of this, Guido swaggered over to our table.

"I could not help listening," he said in beautifully accented English. "You are in the film business." He spoke suggestively, without once removing his glance from Gabra.

"I am an artist," she said.

"Really?" Guido raised a dark brow as if this were of great significance. "I am looking for paintings for my villa. Will you help me choose them?"

I found this entré tastefully brief but I couldn't ignore its subtext. And soon, despite my reserve, we were joined by Guido and his friends.

The Italians revealed themselves as great American film

buffs, expressing admiration for Irving and me as some kind of celebrities. We began to expand under the influence of the liqueurs—

"Actually, we own a bank," Irving said. "A bank for filmmakers." He leaned back expansively. "We got problems. In the States, sources are drying up. No dough. My partner and I, we came up with a plan."

"We intend to attract all film financing to the States," I added. "From Milan, Rome, Paris, Madrid. Every major film will be financed through our bank."

"Packaging. Advance sales—we'll make the market in video—full service to the film business." By this time Irving had slipped into his native Bronx syntax.

"Bah," Guido offered a rare interjection. "What is so original about that?"

"Listen pal," Irving said, "Nobody's ever done this before. We're talking syndication. Nobody ever used a bank to draw investors to films. Tax advantages are gone—okay? Kaput. But we got something better—glamour and security— security and glamour. You're gonna' frickin' fall on your frickin' hands and knees to buy shares in our film syndicate."

"What do we have, Irving," I asked casually, "a billion in assets?" A billion dollars. Irving and I looked at each other. We hadn't stopped to appreciate our wealth. Filmland had more resources than any studio.

"Yeah," Irving said, "a billion dollars. If we don't finance it, it ain't going to get made."

"We'll have our own international currency," I improvised, "set the rate of exchange. Convert all film revenues into dollars, whether they're earned in Florence or," I smiled toward Gabra, "Buenos Aires."

Irving shrugged grandly, "We'll be recognized by all

foreign governments."

"And," I thought of Susie and her gold mine, "shares will be backed by gold bullion."

"Yeah, yeah. Revive the gold standard," Irving said emphatically.

"We'll issue our own coins, and call them Chaplins," I said, with a burst of inspiration.

At some point we forgot Gabra, Guido and the others. We snatched a stack of bar napkins, uncapped our pens, and began to plan feverishly. Charts and graphs, darts and arrows—sketches as obscure as the art of the Etruscans. Dollars in, dollars out. And profits. Points to Filmland for financing. Fees to Bronx Arts for packaging. Producer credits to Irving and me. Our own studio.

And so it went. Through the night. Through the Campari, wine and Ouzo.

Transformed by an exotic place, exquisite setting, and the seductive presence of a beautiful woman, we spun our brilliant schemes, honing and polishing our future like rushing water over slate.

We didn't even notice, until the day-man brought a carafe of thick espresso nègro, that Gabra had slipped away with the Italian sometime in the middle of Irving's and my destiny.

At dawn, we parted from our new friends into the awakening street. Shook hands all around. Something momentous had happened. The smiles, the warmth of our companions documented it. And though we never visited the museum of Etruscan artifacts, I found a clay figurine lying on the path, a replica of an ancient canine, unfurling a small bronze scroll in its teeth—so delicate, so refined I thought immediately of Susie. Its message, in Latin script, took me by surprise: "Expect the Unexpected."

We may have overlooked some things, that splendid night in Fiesole. The beauty of the place can blind you. Tiny fault lines beneath the stones should have warned us—terremota.

18

Irving and Rider in Beverly Hills

The week of our return, Irving and I were scheduled to panel an industry breakfast in the Bengal Room of the Beverly Hills Hotel.

With its painted murals of jungle scenes the room wore a spooky charm. Some local psychotic, a modern Rousseau, had been given a free hand. Sinister chimps and malevolent tigers lurked behind rubber tree fronds as large as a man's torso. Neurotic tree ferns writhed upward along either side of the podium, with a pair of demonic parrots glinting furiously. I found the whole effect unsettling despite the Hotel's party pink linens and daisy centerpieces.

From Europe we'd engaged a publicist, Sunny Garbo, who arranged the event. Our fellow panelists were two Hollywood legends: Tristan Mills, the showbiz lawyer who perfected conflict of interest. And William Morris, Jr., grand old man of talent agents. Good company, you might say.

It was their presence, not ours, that commanded a packed house. Robert Altman, Robert Evans, Billy Wilder. John Huston was there. Roger Corman. Stanley Kubrick. Coppola. They showed up the first Friday in June to hear our thoughts on the subject of Film Financing for the '80s.

Our publicist, Sunny, wasn't. Sunny, that is. A daughter of old Hollywood, though not related to the film star of the same name, Sunny was ambitious. She refused to skulk the periphery of the business like other Hollywood orphans. Rather, she flogged shamelessly her alleged connection to "the" Garbo and traded on the star's celebrity.

Sunny's access to the legendary and powerful didn't come cheaply. We were willing to pay. We had glimpsed what it might mean to see our dreams achieved, that night in Fiesole. And to Irving and I, failure to gain admission to Hollywood's inner circle was an outcome so repellent neither of us could mention it, even between ourselves.

Outsider. The word exudes a powerful repugnance. To live in LA beyond the charmed circle of the film business is to live aggrieved, like anxious puppies snuffling at the glass. I would not wish that on anyone. And I certainly did not accept it for myself.

Irving wore a red tie, which he tucked inside the snug vest of his navy pinstripe from Barney's New York. My Italian costume—leather jacket, oxford shirt, ascot—seemed pretentious for LA, and I settled on an olive suit of Milano wool, which drew the dubious envy of the Hotel's truculent waiters.

We arrived early to assay the crowd, mingling among faces we knew from Cannes. And Ma Maison. As the hour drew near, Irving's St. Tropez tan turned damp with sweat and my stomach dipped like a flock of swallows eluding a Gulf storm.

"What's it all about?" A short man with a cigar came up to me. Before I could reply, another man I recognized as a crony of Irving's answered.

"Currency. These guys from Filmland—bank on Sunset— they created a new currency just for the film business. They package films into syndicates, backed by a gold standard. You wanna make a film? Anywhere—foreign, domestic. Everything in U.S. dollars. They set the rate of exchange. Right here in LA." He poked the air with his cigar.

"Where do you get this new currency?" the first man asked.

"Right here. In Hollywood. It's like Vegas for gambling."

"Oh, yeah? Who are these guys?"

"Irving Fain? You don't know Irving? He produced Hot Dawg."

"Oh yeah?"

"Listen, I know the inside on this thing. They own a bank, for Christ's sake. So they got money. It's going to be like having a major studio in your pocket. Green light for every project. No more scrounging for two years for pocket change."

"California gold rush."

"Damn right."

Irving's crony exaggerated. About green-lighting every project, for example. As for a new currency, however, we had brought with us gold tokens to hand out at the conclusion of our remarks. The coins were beautifully made, Chaplin on one side, the Hollywoodland sign on the other. They glittered before us, a tangible talisman of our plan.

Five minutes before the presentation was scheduled to begin we took our places at a microphoned table on the dais. From there I observed a sea of Hollywood insiders lounging skeptically at tables of eight.

The last man to arrive compelled the most attention. David Lean swept in, the British director, his air of cheery affectation enhanced by a tweed hunting jacket which sailed from his shoulders as if attached by cup-hooks.

Sir David Lean had long been my private hero. I turned eight the year he won the Academy Award for The Bridge on the River Kwai, a plucky tale of English glory, with a jaunty score that could still ignite an anglophile's patriotism. Five years later Lawrence of Arabia galloped across my imagination, a modern knight who lived his dreams. Before our eyes could meet, the program began.

Pacing was swift. The Mayor of Beverly Hills had been importuned to slick up the introductions. Garrulous blowhard, he fit the task. His fawning welcome of Morris and Mills was classic Hollywood sycophancy. Irving and I didn't mind. When our turn came, we bowed our heads modestly as Sunny's script exalted our slender achievements.

"As we sit here today," I began forcefully, "there are no major sources of film financing. Private investment is finished, due to recent changes in the tax code. Yet the allure of financing a blockbuster film is stronger than ever. Our firm, Filmland Credit, has the potential to dominate this market, not just in the United States but globally. With our banking and investment structure, we can attract billions of dollars in film revenues to Hollywood from foreign capitals, and to Filmland in particular."

Irving stalked the narrow dais behind me like Julius Caesar, punctuating my remarks with charts set upon an easel at one end.

Still jetlagged but high, we pressed our ideas. The rapid pace infused the program with energy. We undoubtedly seemed brash or arrogant—but a cautious nodding of heads confirmed that our audience was with us. After early challenges from our co-panelists, the celebrity-lawyer Mills was reduced to sputtering, while the super-agent retained his dignity through silence. The haughtiest maitre d' in Beverly Hills stood dumb as we scattered our Chaplin coins for an exultant climax.

Applause was generous. An air of exuberance prevailed. I could almost hear that schmaltzy tune There's No Business Like Show Business and visualize a stage of swooning actors. But we weren't selling nostalgia. Our game was money—in a time and place where almost nothing else mattered. For that brief moment we were heroes.

The crowd pressed forward.

"Great presentation."

"Got a card?"

Each man (there were few women studio heads then) picked up a golden coin.

I descended a few steps to shake hands and found myself meeting the friendly gaze of Sir David Lean. "Well done," he said.

I was the first to notice the suits at the back of the room. Six cloddish figures in black wingtips had surreptitiously entered. In a sudden annoyance of sound and movement, the men splintered into teams of three, rushing the aisles for the platform. A hulking Baby Huey in forty-six extra-long boomed out a terrifying baritone.

"Don't move, you're under arrest. Maxwell Rider, Irving Fain. You have the right to remain silent, you have the right to an attorney. Anything you say can, and will be used against you in a court of law…"

Irving and I were spun rudely, wrestled into handcuffs and pushed swiftly from the Bengal Room of the Beverly Hills Hotel, leaving a stunned, electrified crowd of film executives.

Outside, photographers from the trades and gossip sheets were already there. It's not unknown for law enforcement to use a few tipsters among the press. Irving raised his coat to shield his face and drilled me a look I'll never forget. It was his gesture, rather than my own humiliation, that stung tears to my eyes.

19

Irving and Rider at the Federal Courthouse

I'd been fingerprinted before, twice, once for admission to the New York Bar, once for California's. But Irving hadn't. It's a coercive process. More so, under the twist of a cop's grip.

LA's federal courthouse is very clean. The large vinyl floor tiles are buffed shiny. The walls, cream-painted enamel, are free of smoke or smudge. Something about the place inhibits the city's graffiti artists and litterers, though they might well be represented along its corridors of lounging criminal defendants.

Perhaps it's the architecture, 1930s Federalism. Or modern chrome metal detectors, manned by female officers in neat pressed uniforms. Or maybe, it's their guns.

I had plenty of time to think about the events which had just occurred. Federal agents rushed us through the courtyard side of the building, then took their time with the debasing procedures we've seen depicted on television cop shows. We were booked, four counts each of banking violations. Then we slumped on a bench, hangdog, until Tom Latham—our $400 an hour consigliere limo'd downtown to apply for bail. While we waited, I took stock.

I tried to tell myself the scene at the Hotel was a sham performance by the Feds to warn off copycat banking. The high-profile drama of our arrest was meant to splash the trades, call attention to the risks of expansive thinking. That was how I rallied to the cause at first—but after the effects of adrenaline had worn off my spirits turned bleak.

Somehow I'd managed to betray, not just myself, but Irving too. "Just keep us on the straight and narrow," he'd said at Le Dôme. And I'd failed. I wasn't the first lawyer to choose adventure over law, and feel stunned at the consequences.

"Irving," I said. "This is bogus. What's the deal? It's not like we streaked the Courthouse."

"Scumbag technocrats," Irving replied, "Friggin' government scumbaggery."

"Exactly," I said, inspecting the creases on the sleeves of my jacket where my arms had been twisted behind me. "Look at these guys. They're clerks." The team from the FBI's banking division still lumbered through the corridors like Hannibal's horde.

"Frocking scumbags."

That kind of talk is reassuring. Irving started to feel better, he spoke with his old pugnacity. And I started feeling better too.

"Face it, they work for the Government. They've never seen guys like us. Filmland's unique. We're talking global syndication of the movie business. These notepad-lawyers and pea-brained cops, they can't comprehend it."

"Balls," Irving agreed.

"Precisely. They resent our success. That's the problem. Tom will explain it to them. Where the hell is he?"

Beneath my bravado, Maxwell Rider, Yale law graduate, entertained a more conservative view. The Government could make a case. We had failed to register our partnerships with the Securities and Exchange Commission, relying on an exclusion called "private placement," which assumed that Bunker Dodge's investors were all personally known to him. I'd chosen not to examine Bunker's investor lists, and that could prove embarrassing.

Just then, Tom Latham arrived. Tom was the best WASP lawyer in town for white collar crime. His firm of thirty smug partners from Pasadena had been taken over by an even larger Washington firm, lured to LA for its Hollywood connections

Tom resembled Dr. Kildare's father, if he had one— powdery white hair, crisp blue eyes, buffed nails. He had an annoying habit of flicking his Rolex. But Nancy Vaughn, the assistant U.S Attorney assigned to our case, didn't seem to notice.

Our interview took place in a spartan room painted the color of canned peas. A beige metal table pinched against my thighs, though the padded chairs were surprisingly comfortable.

Ms. Vaughn displayed little enthusiasm for the finer points of our case.

"Securities fraud," she said immediately.

Tom smiled. A little patronizingly, I thought. "Let's discuss this."

"Wait a minute," I said. "I'm an attorney, I'd like to speak on our behalf."

She registered my remark with an efficient toss of her waist-length tawny hair.

"Yes, counselor?"

"If I remember correctly, fraud is an intentional tort."

"You don't think a lawyer has reason to know SEC regulations?"

"I suppose that will be the government's position," I said lamely.

She aggressively opened the file.

"Let's get to it. In or about March, 1979, defendant Maxwell Rider hired one Bunker Dodge III to sell Filmland's partnership interests." She tilted her head smugly, "Mr.

Dodge's license to sell securities was suspended last year pursuant to a felony plea bargain."

I swallowed hard. "That can't be true."

She didn't bother to reply. "The government anticipated your 'private placement' defense. You might be interested to know Dodge's primary source for luring investors is a list containing the names of thousands of individuals—all current or past members of Lloyds of London insurance trusts."

She glanced up with a sour smile. "Section 10(b)(5) of the Securities Act of 1933 provides—" She didn't need to read it but she did, just to drive it home.

"'It is unlawful to sell, or attempt to procure the sale of, securities by one who has not been registered under the Act as a licensed securities dealer.'"

Vaughn's green eyes held the interest a night owl confers on a litter of rats. "So why am I thinking fraud?"

Tom cleared his throat, "These gentlemen are legitimate businessmen. They had no knowledge this fellow Dodge was unlicensed—apparently the man conducts his business affairs from the Polo Lounge."

Irving met my eyes, things were starting to look up for our side.

"You can have no proof that either of my clients knew Dodge was marketing those interests so broadly. Indeed, the purchasers may be personally known to this fellow Dodge."

Highly unlikely, I thought. But I kept quiet.

"These young men—" Tom swept his arm toward Irving and I—"have developed a very sophisticated business plan for Filmland Bank. If some aspects need refining, it's understandable."

"Exactly," I agreed.

Tom raised his palm to silence me.

"Irving Fain runs a successful film production company called Bronx Arts. Mr. Rider is a businessman with imposing credentials. A graduate of Columbia, and Yale Law School. Top five per cent of his class. I'm sure you can appreciate that accomplishment, counselor," he nodded to Ms. Vaughn with his signature smile of insincerity, "having been selected yourself to write for Law Review at the University of Southern California."

That's why you pay four hundred dollars an hour. Tom had studied Vaughn's profile on his way downtown. She shifted impatiently and scowled. But Tom blustered on in a verbose offensive calculated to wear her down.

"Mr. Rider apprenticed at Muller, Fagen & Luft, a reputable entertainment firm in New York. He enjoys the confidence of some of the wealthiest multinationals in LA." He lowered his voice to a tone of intimate sincerity. "I think the Justice Department would be making a mistake to pursue these gentlemen for a few minor oversights, due—very obviously—to mere inattention."

We waited, respectful as schoolboys. Vaughn allowed silence to speak her disdain. "Let's get something straight. Your clients have been operating Filmland like a family business. They seem to have forgotten it's a bank—with deposits insured by the Federal government."

She clicked off a list of violations. "Inadequate documentation for loans to filmmakers. No financial statements. No credit reports. No written evaluations of the films. Your clients failed to develop written lending policies. Any policies. They violated security laws—as previously mentioned. And there's the little matter of $10 million advanced without proper security."

Irving and I exchanged a glance. The audit. We hadn't had time to check the balance on Alex's line of credit. But the report she tossed to Tom, and then to me, confirmed her charge. In our absence, he'd drawn on the account as if tapping a private trust fund.

"These 'minor oversights' as you call them, are violations of federal law. We can seize Filmland. We can send your clients to Lompoc. You look good in prison denim, Mr. Rider?"

I felt Irving stiffen. I didn't feel too well myself. The government's seizure of Filmland would wipe out Irving's cash investment of $2 million. As for my demand note, which I'd signed so casually that evening at Le Dôme, the Feds would call it due immediately. One million dollars. I could hardly hope to pay it from a cell.

Ms. Vaughn leaned across the table to me. The stiff white front of her blouse puffed toward me in full sail. But I suddenly had little interest in noting the outline of her breasts. "In case you didn't know, counselor, the unsecured loan to Mr. des Prairies should not have exceeded $2 million. You've busted through your loan ceiling."

I strove to mute the natural arrogance of a lawyer with his back to the wall. "The film is security for the loan."

"An unfinished film." She dared me to continue. "What's it worth?"

"Any film is difficult to evaluate until it's finished. We have an offer to buy it," I said, hoping Alex's friend Trujillo and Costa Brava were still in the picture.

"Don't insult me." Vaughn was pretty in an American way. But not when she scowled.

"We're amenable to working something out," Tom interposed with bland understatement. "My clients will consent to a reasonable plea bargain.

"These gentlemen are not criminals," he added. "It's in the Government's best interest to rely on Mr. Rider's relationships."

Really? Maybe Tom had a point there. I thought of Alex—he could get us out of this.

"Your proposal?" she asked.

We sat silent as Tom drew her out on the terms of a deal she'd already plotted. "Capital infusion of $10 million in ninety days," she said, "or reduce the balance on Alex des Prairies' credit line to zero. Got it?"

And if we failed to comply with the terms of the plea bargain? Ms. Vaughn leaned back and read from the federal statute. "The Court shall impose financial sanctions in an amount not less than $1 million per violation, together with imprisonment in a federal penitentiary for a period not less than one year."

20

Bunker Dodge at the Polo Lounge

The next morning at eleven o'clock, I went immediately to the Beverly Hills Hotel to have it out with Dodge. He was open for business at his corner table, long legs splayed out at the heels, the soft pink bulge of his incipient paunch insinuated beneath a flaring silk shirt. A tumbler of grapefruit juice sat before him. The canvas bank pouch lay alluringly close, fat with hundreds.

I wasn't formal with my greeting. "You never said your securities license was revoked," I said darkly.

Dodge didn't seem at all surprised to see me, he flapped a hand toward a chair. "Suspended, ducky. Anyway, it's a private matter."

"Not private enough. Irving and I were arrested yesterday. Apparently, the Government takes issue with your qualifications."

"Too bad. But I don't need a securities license for what I do. Dear boy, don't you know the way my business works?"

"I know we were put through the thresher for it. What does the Justice Department have against you?"

Dodge surveyed the room casually to assure himself the bar was empty.

"Let me speak frankly—just entre nous. Select financial institutions—let's use Kidder, Peabody par example—reward me handsomely for suggesting a specific stock. One which, shall we say, no longer justifies their confidence?"

"A dog," I said.

"Bow-wow." He lifted his glass in toast to my remark. "I pump it up briefly through my contacts—the stock goes up and whoosh! Kidder sells, taking a tidy profit for its A-list clients, the only ones who count. I can't be blamed if my suggestions don't always pan out—anyway, I never let them lose too much—whoosh! Out of Mr. Bow-wow and into something else."

"Manipulating the market."

"Tut," he chastened me with a lanky finger, "all brokerage houses need pawn accounts like mine. And occasionally, they let me in on a runner. We book a tidy sum and whoosh! My star rises." He flapped a hand, "Trés simple."

I felt my spirit slump like one of Dodge's mongrel stocks. I'd hired a market shill to represent Filmland.

"What does Kidder pay you—for these recommendations of yours?"

"That—dear boy—is confidential."

"What about your clients? Mister Jones, for instance, does he make any money?"

"Ah, that's where my marketing talent comes in. Overall, just entre nous, he would be better off buying Treasuries. But remember, dear boy, there's more to financial planning than yield. I offer cachet."

He surveyed our surroundings. "Polo Lounge, Beverly Hills. And—" his eyes glittered with private irony, "access to one of the oldest and wealthiest families in the States."

I suppressed my reply, Dodge was no more connected to the old-line clan than I was. But he read my thoughts. "Poseur? I know what they say."

I shrugged. Isn't it true?

"No more than your friends," he said. "What's authentic about deriving one's identity from the past? Flogging hapless others with the inference of some alleged lineage from feudal times."

He twitched his mane like a snappish mare. "At least I've

managed to employ myself at something practical. I've put my gifts of style and invention to good purpose. And my efforts are lucrative. I'm well rewarded for picking the bones of those with capital, the few who haven't plundered their wealth—inherited wealth—on a fraudulent lifestyle."

Dodge's vehemence stunned me. He was wrong of course. Lifestyle could be proof of lineage, I wanted to say. And lineage derives from lifestyle. An elegant chair, exquisite urn can be purchased by anyone, but to have lived among rare things on impressive estates, that's exclusive. I thought of my father. Illegitimate or not, wasn't I better than this paunchy old schemer before me? What could he know about class?

I gestured impatiently. "The American view."

"Ho-ho! Is it titles you're so fond of? I broker those too. Anyone can buy a title dear boy."

"Or a surname?" I knew it was cruel, I almost thought I glimpsed his wounded eyes through the pastel lenses he wore.

"It wasn't me, you know, who turned you in. Beware your friends, Rider. Beware of style. It's your weakness."

I shook my head at my own stupidity. There were plenty of legitimate brokers I could have retained to sell Filmland's interests. Instead I chose Alex's acquaintance because of his claim to old money.

"Look, Bunker," I said, standing to leave him, "consider yourself fired. We'll pay the commissions you've earned. I suggest you work on getting your license restored."

I waited for him to say something. But he'd withdrawn to his lists—he only swished his ponytail as if to dismiss me.

I left him there, scanning the room for his ration of suckers. And I had to wonder, what flaw in myself had put me among them?

21

Christian at the Bel-Air Bay Club

After our arrest, a natural order for business suggested itself: see Alex, talk to Susie. Yet, several weeks passed with no progress on either front. Alex declined to return my calls to the Chateau Marmont. Susie and Winton were in New York deposing their father. And I didn't feel like revealing myself as a potential jailbird over the telephone.

One day in the locker room of the Bel-Air Bay Club, I ran into Christian Ruhl, under what I considered strange circumstances. Christian was Alex's second cousin, and it was he who filled me in on the subject of money.

Christian was twenty-four, graceful, athletic—boyish despite a certain Teutonic formality. Women were charmed, of course, for he was not long in the U.S. from his family's castle at Salzburg, and his greeting, to any member of the more interesting sex, included a subtle snap of his heels, and the brush of his lips across her hand. Pretty effective as an opening gambit. Democratic, too, though I could detect his preference for young girls.

Absorbed in inner dialogue with Alex—cursing him soundly, exhorting him to pay up—I was unaware of the other figure at the urinal until I caught his familiar movement in the mirror.

"Christian!" I hadn't seen him since our return from Europe. I was taken aback by his peculiar get-up—chauffeur's cap and driver's uniform. I found that extraordinary. How could Christian be reduced to driving for someone—an individual who'd been chauffeured most of his childhood?

I quickly assumed a mask of polite interest, "How are you, old man? Time for a coffee?"

"Just a lark, really, this," he said, touching his cap. "No need to mention it to anyone."

Christian was picking up his client in half an hour. "Maybe just an espresso," he agreed.

The Bel-Air Bay Club, one of three private beach clubs in Santa Monica, was a bastion of Eastern Republicans who lounged poolside on the phone, transmitting buy-sell orders over a chopped salad. They didn't serve espresso at the Bay Club. Too exotic. I ended up buying him a beer, we strolled outside.

The patio at weekday lunch bore an eerie tranquility. Only the remote echo of a tennis ball disturbed the hush of the surf.

We took a table apart, furthest out, where the deck dropped off abruptly into naked beach. Our conversation turned to Alex, and I complained of my inability to reach him and the urgency of my circumstances.

"Two things have plunged our friendship onto rocks," Christian replied sadly.

Christian had visited Alex at Chateau Marmont one morning.

"He's still there?" I asked. "I thought he must have moved into Tower Hill. It must be extremely expensive keeping two places."

"Four," Christian said. "He also maintains a villa on the Italian Riviera, an apartment in Paris, and stays often in New York at a private club."

Christian shrugged.

"He's too lazy to move, really. It's comfortable at the Marmont. He would have to employ servants, get a driver.

Terrible nuisance."

The morning referred to, Christian had walked in on Alex haranguing his father on the phone.

"Terrible, Rider," Christian continued, "Alex was, what is the English word, choleric. I have never seen him in a state like this. His father, you must understand, is a Count. By birth—not courtesy. And respected for his diplomatic service during the war. A true patriarch, no one would dare to speak to him in the way Alex did."

I found this curiously unlike Alex, as I knew his distaste for anything vulgar. Only months before he'd denounced Winton Grass for suing his father. "What was it all about?" I asked.

Christian lowered his voice. "Money. They keep him on a short chain you know. He demanded his legacy. And you must remember his father's ailing."

Christian slit his eyes toward the surf where two young girls were building a sand structure.

"I'd like to spank her," he confided suddenly to me, regarding the elder one, a slender nymphet. He lifted his chin and crowed exultantly like Red Riding Hood's fraudulent grandmother.

But my mind was occupied with something other than sex at that moment. Only thirty minutes before, I'd been ready to denounce Alex, his casualness with money, and his failure to attend to business.

But on this occasion I found myself championing him. The money was his inheritance, after all. His birth-right. What use had his father for it now? I thought bitterly of my own father and stepmother, that horsey English rose with a thin, determined mouth. Yet, even as I sided with Alex, a question had begun to shape itself, and I brushed it impatiently away—are we entitled to anything at our birth, besides our mother's love? Or is there only grace which we are expected to earn?

As if I had spoken my thoughts, Christian turned back to regard me earnestly. "Can you imagine how desperate one can become?" he asked. "In childhood each of us assumes a life philosophy. The more rigid his philosophy the more desperate he becomes when it is challenged. Alex, you may have noticed, never carries money in his pockets. He never leaves a tip, except for a few coins. He has only to sign his name, or leave a voucher on the strength of his crest. In that, we are the same. Our family's worth is our guaranty.

"In the culture in which we were raised we were forbidden to mention money. If it must not be mentioned, one cannot ask for it. And one certainly cannot earn it. That's the role of others."

"Alex doesn't need to work," I said, recalling his words to me at Filmland. 'I need never study, as you have done, how to make money off the backs of my fellow man.'

"Yes. Well…" Christian lifted his mouth in a curious smile. "You know, Rider, Alex had $20 million from his grandmother's estate?"

I had forgotten Christian mentioned it. "When was this?"

Christian reflected, "Three years ago?"

For the first time, it grew on me that inherited wealth could run out, run down, dissipate or, as Irving would observe, be pissed away. The part of me that is American was incredulous.

"How? How does one go through that kind of money in three years?"

Christian moved his head impatiently. Suddenly he seemed decades older. "If you maintain four homes—Rider be realistic. Servants, trips back and forth to Europe on the Concorde, every wine a private reserve, private clubs, polo fees, hunting jaunts. Add a crazy investment ploy here and there. How can I explain? I didn't have quite that much. Still," he indicated the cheap gray wool of his jacket, cut like a boy's public school uniform.

"But, well, for Alex, it's temporary, isn't it Christian?"

"Temporary—of course." It was only later I appreciated the hollow tone of his assurance.

"He'll get the money from Europe?"

"The family's in banking, blue chips. They won't let him starve."

Christian glanced at his Baume-Mercier watch, an exquisite antique. "I should wait by the limo," he said with a wry smile.

The girls playing on the beach were no more than twelve years old, soft as a Renoir in the hazy light. We strolled over to see their work, they started giggling. The sand castle formed the top of a huge penis.

"I guess all little girls reproduce penises these days," Christian remarked almost sadly. "It doesn't look much like the real thing though."

We paused by a gray limo stretch at the Bay Club entrance.

"I'll finish my scenes in Danse du Sang," Christian said, referring to his role in Alex's film. "Of course I am honorable. But I can't see Alex until he resolves this desperation over money. It is too distressing. "

His expression grew boyishly earnest, "You'll see some things in this town Rider, when the money runs out. Have you ever been on the luge run when the sled starts to roll?"

For the second time that day, a shadow darkened my thoughts. Christian had stirred my concerns about Alex. He claimed to be a gentleman. And gentlemen pay their debts.

Didn't they?

A dark, stocky man approached, inscrutable behind pink aviator's lenses. He charged steadily toward us with the hirsute virility of a record company executive. I recognized Ramòn Brulée. Too late I realized, I hadn't learned the other incident Christian had promised to relate. As I turned to avoid a confrontation with Brulée, Christian smiled at me once more in a peculiar and terrifying way.

I've not forgotten his clipped, exultant cry, "Let the games begin!"

Rider and Alex at Ma Maison

"You can always tell who belongs and who doesn't by the purse she carries," the owner of Ma Maison commented to Alex and me. "It tells so much about a woman, doesn't it?"

Neither Alex nor I had an answer to that. For all Alex's monologues on civilization and breeding, he'd never once mentioned handbags. And I can't say I gave it much thought either.

Susie Grass and Marina Loge were lunching at Ma Maison. The café's owner, P. Terrail, obviously approved. Two handbags, a black lizard from Hèrmes and Susie's gold Chanel obelisk, rested demurely on their table edge like pristine children in party dress. I thought of my former wife Mona and her vinyl satchel, in which she transported all our child might require over a two-hour period. I felt ashamed at the meanness of Terrail's remark, my acceptance of it, and the pride I felt in observing Susie's expensive purse.

Marina's black hair was pulled severely into a small knot at her nape in the style of mezzo sopranos who sing Carmen. Which was fitting. Because her pale beauty derived from early land grant Spanish on her mother's side. Susie's light hair was plaited into a French braid.

The two small heads ducked and whispered, darted and flicked over salade niçoise. Their jeweled hands fluttered incessantly like Latin conductors leading some wild, triumphant symphony. I could see they had things in common. Handbags, hairstyles, lost wealth.

I resisted an impulse to rush over and announce myself

to Susie. I had other things on my mind. Three weeks had passed since Irving's and my arrest. I hadn't seen Alex since our return from Cannes, although I'd tried to get him on the phone. After my chance meeting with Christian at the Bel-Air Bay Club, I'd focused my thoughts on securing Alex's immediate pay-down on his line of credit. Our chance encounter at Ma Maison was not as accidental as it seemed, I suspected he lunched there nearly every day.

"Life has taken a strange turn, old man," I said, trying on an English public school tone. "Banks in the States, they're insured. A group called FDIC. And they—well—they want to have a say in running things."

"Anything else would be fatuous," Alex said pleasantly.

He studied the wine list. "Fabulous. A '66 Lafite. Shall we? You knew old Toddy Rothschild. Marvelous character. I once toured his uncle's cellars." Alex waved the waiter away. "The day I was there, a butler followed Toddy and I around with a corkpull, and a tray of Lalique goblets that had been in his family since 1885."

Alex tapped Ma Maison's goblet with his fork tines, as if to demonstrate its lack of quality. "Toddy started pulling down wines outrageously, 'See this? Petrus '55. Nearly the entire vintage went to Rainier's family that year in Monaco. Quite frankly, not our best showing.'

"Toddy selected a 1945 Margaux, the valet poured us each a swallow. Amazing wine. You could taste the Allies' victory in it. 'This one's a little better,' Roddy said. 'Must be drunk this year or next.' When the valet offered the bottle again, Toddy waved it away—'pour it in the geraniums,' he said.

"Think of it, Max, these were the most astonishing wines in Europe at that time. We must have ruined twenty of his uncle's reserves. Toddy behaved outrageously, unspeakably extravagant. And, of course, we got a little drunk."

One of Ma Maison's pony-tailed servers pulled up to our table. Alex put up his hand to restrain the man from speaking. "Never really kept in touch poor fellow—I heard he suffered a stroke and died during menage à trois. Bad luck."

Alex at last turned his attention to our waiter, not a tolerant member of Europe's serving class but an aspiring actor whose pantomime of restless vexation surpassed anything de Niro could have achieved.

My interest wandered to our surroundings as Alex dictated the details of his meal. Perfectly suited to its location near Hollywood's back lots, Ma Maison could be described in a one-line pitch: 'Striped tent, in an LA parking lot of Rolls Royces, passes itself off as chic brasserie on the French Riviera.'

I would have chosen to draw Alex out over several courses, as I had during our earlier dining adventures—for Alex, indeed all of Alex's circle, were natural raconteurs. Yet on this occasion, hounded by the unyielding Ms. Vaughn, I coarsened my soul to the pleasure of his stories. As the waiter moved off, I resumed my tedious summary of banking regulations.

"The thing is Alex, federal agencies get obnoxious at times. Try to muscle in on how Filmland conducts its business— that kind of thing."

"Quite right," said Alex. He swirled the Lafite once around the bowl of his glass, shot it into his mouth with obvious relish. "Can you imagine, Max? If they did not. If, for example, they left the running of things entirely to you and Irving?"

He issued a short delighted bark. "Commerce in the States would be ruined. Financial markets in chaos and the government pulling its pockets out. All of Europe would lose complete confidence to watch your currency plunge into catastrophe."

I wasn't in a mood to appreciate his humor. The waiter set our first course before us. Alex dubiously regarded the avocado-leek soup, as I tacked into the wind.

"I'm not sure it would be quite as dramatic as all that," I said. "Here's the thing. The government's asked Irving to increase our capital base a notch or so. It's because of your overrun on Danse du Sang."

Alex tested the soup with a crust of sourdough. I shifted forward to compel his attention.

"This is not easy to say, Alex. You've let us down. Your line of credit was to have been paid down regularly to maintain a balance of no more than $2 million. While we were in Europe, you detonated the game-ball. It's hard to justify a $4 million outlay for re-shooting an already completed film."

"Quite good, actually," Alex said, splashed a drop of burgundy into his soup.

"Damn the soup!"

Alex straightened his shoulders and leaned forward, a spark of acknowledgment glittering in his eyes. I thought I had his attention at last and leaned forward too. Abruptly, Alex stood then, gestured with grand conviviality across the tented room of green astroturf. Before I could protest, he had summoned with a wave Marina Loge and Susie Grass.

Susie and Marina floated toward us through an atmosphere of glances, and posed at our table like two mannequins.

"What a good surprise!" Alex graced each woman with three kisses on alternating cheeks.

"Alex. You really must redeem yourself," Susie said, speaking only to Alex. "You promised to arrange a showing in Brussels for my watercolors."

"Quite right," Alex replied. "My brother-in-law owns a gallery near the Sablon. Très Chère, you know it?"

Alex glanced at his watch. "Too late to call him today—I'll call him tomorrow, you must remind me, Max."

Alex and I remained standing and I found myself struggling with conflicting impulses. I couldn't explain my arrest in front of Marina. Though I would have preferred to be alone with Susie, I was restrained by the need to bully Alex. Feeling dumb with frustration, I resigned myself to the awkwardness of the moment—there was nothing to do but wait out the pleasantries.

"I didn't know you paint, Susie," I said woodenly.

She let her pale unblinking gaze rest on me.

"I could meet you at Chiquita Lowe's gallery after lunch," she said. "My paintings are exhibited there."

"I'd like that," I said. I meant it. And I regretted I couldn't follow her at once. But the subject of Filmland charged my mind. I had to save Irving's investment.

When she saw my indecision, the air changed between us with the swiftness of a Malibu breeze. She raised her hand to acknowledge an effeminate-looking boy in chauffeur's cap who appeared at the entrance to Ma Maison. Hesitating briefly, he returned a small stub-nailed wave.

"My driver," Susie said. "Au revoir, Alex, à bientôt, Maxwell."

Alex looked at me curiously when they'd left our table. "Doesn't it bother you to think Susie's driver is a lesbian?"

"I wouldn't take any bets either way," I said.

The waiter set a plate of tartare in front of Alex, club sandwich for me. Alex eyed the tartare critically.

The chef at Ma Maison claimed credit for creating

California cuisine. And he affected disdain for the traditional dishes of Europe. The best tartare, as anyone knows, includes raw egg and cognac, judiciously combined. Vigorous kneading will toughen the veal. A too-casual effort by Terrail's under-chef had left ribbons of viscosity running through Alex's favorite starter.

Alex, frowning, raised two fingers to engage the waiter's attention. I maintained a stoic silence, determined to choose the right moment for resuming my campaign. The waiter removed the offending dish and we sat unspeaking until he returned with another.

"Look Alex," I said when he'd signaled his approbation. "I don't know any other way to put this. We need your money. Pronto. You have to repay the debt immediately."

I got it out. And waited, relieved, for his reply.

Alex commandeered a pepper mill from a penurious waiter, cranked it lustily over his steak. "Max, old man, don't you know?" He paused, "I'm down to my last two Rodins my aunt gave me. Stony bottom, as they say."

"What?" Apprehension made my voice drop. Sweat dampened the Egyptian cotton of my shirt. "What?" I said again, unbelieving, "What about your account in Liechtenstein?"

"Art was selling like crackers until recently," Alex mused, as if commenting on the weather, "the Rodins as if from the oven."

The actor-waiter hovered with a sauce boat. The wine steward—probably a Melrose comic—drew up with a second bottle of the Lafite. The cork had hardly been pulled—tendered to Alex in a ritual I suddenly found repugnant, when I waved them both away.

"Your money," I said hoarsely. "Liechtenstein."

"Impossible." He raised the claret to his glass, I shot my hand over its rim.

"Your trust fund," I insisted.

My hand trembled over the goblet. I felt the desire to crush it in my hand.

Alex lifted an amused brow, gently moved my hand away. "Americans—compulsively direct. It's embarrassing, actually. I don't know quite how to put it. I'm busted, flat, pockets out."

"You could pledge the Rodins."

"Impossible, Max. I don't have control. My family has put me on an allowance. Pay all my expenses. But—" He raised a graceful palm skyward, "—I'm on a short dog-leash."

Alex turned back to his meal, slightly reproving, "In Europe the topic of money is considered a poor excuse for dining conversation."

He pulled out the soft part of the baguette, scooped the tartare onto a crust. "Delicious!" he announced.

It probably was. But the recycled tartare compelled my disgust. All I saw, when I glanced at the gold-rimmed china plate, with its heap of minced sirloin, was raw flesh.

The waiter approached when I pushed the club sandwich away, uneaten. "I'm leaving," I said. I charged from Ma Maison without waiting for the bill. I wouldn't have taken the check that day if they had hanged me for it.

23

Days in Greenwich

Greenwich was a fashionable town, a faintly rural enclave of stately homes and feigned civility. The Linen residence—with its long gloomy drive and cold vacant windows—was a contrast to the town's village shops and smart galleries. For me, the pomp that attended the arrival of Babe and Waffy's guests by train from the city was a welcome diversion.

I remember the weekend the Choates came to visit. We had seen other celebrities on our trips to town: Dave Garroway, Pinky Lee, Paul Newman. And we knew John Cameron Swayze from his Timex commercial: it takes a licking and keeps on ticking. Of the Choate brothers, I knew only they were rich, and Waffy Linen had invited them to discuss his political aspirations.

Except for the occasional rift lasting half an hour, Lindsay, Harlan and I were inseparable. Wesley, Jr., a persistent toddler, rarely left the house without his nanny. I was eight and small for my age, with the skinny shoulders and slight build of a child too active to store calories from Cook's peanut butter sandwiches, eaten on the run in the kitchen, with one leg swinging restlessly.

It was the end of September. Indian summer, a season of transition between the humidity of August and October's early frost. And it was the last summer I was to spend at the Linen estate. Although I did not know it then.

Babe Linen herself drove the station wagon to Greenwich station, our pleas to tag along having been denied with firmness. We began a game of skipping slate in a vacant field, pretending to ignore Babe's parting admonition to avoid her garden of prize hyacinths dying in the waning sun.

Cray and Bif Choate were young men on the brink of their thirties. Their brother Edward was nineteen. They were stocky and coarse with hair like beach grass and piercing eyes the color of sky.

On Babe's return, they appeared on the threshold of the side porch, dressed in khaki Bermudas and cotton golf shirts, exuding a rough exuberance that seemed so provocative that I lobbed a cherry tomato at them.

"Ho!" the eldest of them shouted, as if he'd been waiting all along for just this introduction to the enemy. We dodged behind a crumbling stone wall, and waited to see what would happen next.

What happened next was a shock. The Choates mobbed the gravel path, whooping like Azande warriors. They trampled the fragile netting of the root-vegetable garden tended by Hans the chauffeur for the cook. Plucking up turnips and rutabagas, they hurled them violently in our direction.

The low wall was no protection from their expert shelling. Scraping our knees and elbows, we kept up a defensive effort, lobbing cherry tomatoes as fast as we could fumble them from the plants.

Edward Choate, the youngest, slipped along the wall to ambush us from the side. We jumped up and fled in the opposite direction, heads lowered and shoulders hunched. Bif and Cray moved in, pelting us with whatever the Linen garden offered. A sharp pain stung me in the shallow cleft of my shoulders—a giant turnip hit the ground behind me.

The worst was to come. Our rivals rushed our position until they reached Babe's hyacinths. Using the plants as their armory, they snapped off the blooms and pummeled us with them. The husks smashed into our bare arms like needles, spraying pollen into our eyes. Too late I saw we were trapped—our only path of retreat lay toward the open field.

This surreal contest seemed to go on forever. When the gardens lay in ruin, with all Babe's flowers tattered on the ground or limp and smashed against the wall, the Choates went inside, leaving echoes of cruel jeers and victory taunts in their Boston twang. We hid out until nightfall, as terrified to face Babe as we were to meet her guests.

That evening I was summoned to the great room by Babe Linen. Harlan and Lindsay stood like soldiers about to be shot. Babe began to speak in an angry controlled voice, when the eldest of the Choates strolled in, relaxed and casual in white trousers and crew neck sweater. He threw himself into one of the wing chairs, observing our disgrace with amusement.

Babe's pose of fairness included Harlan and Lindsay in this scene, but I was the target of her sting of punishment.

"No Walt Disney Hour on Sunday nights for three weeks. No cartoons Saturday morning. And no playing with Maxwell during the same period. I will not tolerate vandalism or lack of respect for property. My flowers are ruined. And you boys are responsible." She locked me with her eyes. "It's obvious you're a bad influence on each other."

Cray Choate never spoke up nor interceded. I thought with disgust what I'd tell him if I got the chance. But on Sunday evening as Hans held the door of the Rolls Royce for the Choate brothers' return to the station, Bif turned and waved. "Good arm, sluggah," he called to me. And smiled.

My anger slipped away. I knew, in that lesson, the prerogative of wealth. That fall I went away to private school. I never saw the Linen house again.

24

Rider at Elysée

After that fateful lunch with Alex, I took up jogging. Pretty tepid I guess. Another man might have trounced him. Pummeled him. Denounced him as a blackguard. At least scuffed his shoes. But I was plunged into a kind of shock.

While there was still a chance that Alex would repay the funds, I had denied the gravity of our situation. Irving and I both approached the government's charges that way: an accounting problem. But after —well—I was beginning to appreciate the full impact of where we stood.

"Does he know you?" Tristan Mills' secretary bluntly asked me, when I tried to renew contact in the weeks after the indictment. Our calls went unreturned. The best tables were "taken." Deals we thought were solid, fell through. And all the heavy players who rushed to shake our hands that June morning at the Beverly Hills Hotel were "unavailable" a week later.

As Filmland's credibility went on life support,I could think of nothing that would bring it around. Except cash.

Jarred awake each morning at four a.m. in dread and sweat, I jogged the charmed streets of Westwood Village, an urban hamlet just beyond the gates of UCLA. I'd rented a guest house there, on a hillside opposite the campus. It was a neighborhood then, where one could stroll to shops and linger in cafés.

As a late September mist lay on the spires of the Fox Cinema, I jogged until I hurt. Panic grew into an obese creature who blocked the narrow door of my emotions. I ran from it. This action, running for my life, expressed my fear that nothing had changed, would ever change, I was the same undeserving child my father had appraised and found unworthy.

I rarely varied my routine. Six miles, six days a week. In October the oven blast that was the Santa Ana winds sucked my breath, hollowed my limbs into dry husks like corpses in the desert. Then suddenly, November. Daylight Savings Time eclipsed the sun. And a hostile chill made me mourn the heat.

North of Sunset Boulevard lies Bel Air, one of the most exclusive enclaves in the world. Through its East Gate lay lavish estates as close as LA could come to the manor homes in Europe. Wooded. Silent. A strange secluded glen, straight from the Brothers Grimm. You could prick your finger there. Or eat a poison apple. And no one would know. Or care.

Occasionally I glimpsed a pink cabaña. Or trellised court. I heard the whip crack of a tennis ball. And voices, faint and broken like early transmissions from the moon. Through the smoky panes of lumbering Bentleys, I glimpsed the area's inhabitants—rich dwarfs and trophy wives, who secluded themselves from wrathful Rumplestiltskins like me.

I stood defiantly in the private drives of strangers, staring into a distrustful lens and jogging in place, until I heard the rapid clicking on the bricks of Dobermans, who scanned the air to know me with their exquisite sensory equipment. Only then did I move away, my Nikes on the road tapping out the faint pulse of my existence.

One morning in late November, two weeks before Irving and I were scheduled to present ourselves to Ms. Vaughn with $10 million or our toothbrushes, an incident occurred which offered inspiration.

After my run, I stopped in Westwood Village for coffee. Running in place, I ordered an espresso, waited while the red-haired Frenchman cheerfully bagged my brioche.

A café diva swept in. Black and stunning, an inch of fleece for hair, gauzy garments swirled at her ankles. She possessed a presence so keen, I instinctively improved my posture which is, I forgot to mention, along with my smashed nose, a source of secret vanity.

This ravishing Diana indulged the company of a lesser mortal, a fat girlfriend with lumpen smile, whom she addressed like Catherine the Great instructing her generals.

"Ask for what you want—whatever it is—stupid honkey bullshit—ask for it girl. That's the only way you gonna know for sure you ain't gonna get it."

Her words had the force of command. On a bus bench under the emerging sun I gulped my croissant and coffee with sweat pooling on my face. And I knew what I would do. Then I jogged home, having spoken to no one, like some robotic athlete.

By eight that morning I drew up to Filmland's offices to begin my quest for capital. I placed my calls to New York and Europe. Reached out in delicate inquiry to the contacts Irving and I had made. I had to be tactful. The vaguest reminder of our financial need could send our reputation tumbling like a card house.

When the black goddess imprinted her fierce philosophy on me, I'd felt renewed. Ask for what you want, she'd said. At nine o'clock, I telephoned Ms. Vaughn.

"We need another sixty days," I said, after she'd dismissed the usual courtesies.

"No way, cowboy."

Her finality stunned me. I almost stuttered.

"Why not?"

"Sixty days, that was the deal." I could hear the dry percussion of pages being scanned.

"Danse du Sang has a buyer, it's just a matter of time."

"That's perfection then, isn't it? Short fuse."

"But the film's not finished yet. The buyer won't lock in without a completed American version."

"That's why I'm putting you in charge, Mr. Rider. As executive producer you're responsible. Finish it yourself if you have to. Or force the buyer to take it as is. We don't care how you solve your problems."

I tried silence, but she continued, "The plea bargain was a fair chance for you and your partner Irving Fain to avoid losing the bank and going to jail. If you're not up to it, you're obviously unqualified to run Filmland."

I braced myself, "We need more time."

The sound of slitting envelopes were shots from a firing squad. "You've got two weeks. We're happy to replace you with someone who can do the job—legally."

Whew. It was my morning for powerful women. They had the force to ignite. Or defuse. I slumped discouraged after the call. That's the only way you gonna know you ain't gonna get it. So I knew. And I knew Ms. Vaughn was right about Danse du Sang. I might get the money from Costa Brava or I might not, but I had to stay involved with Alex's film. And that meant reconciliation with Alex.

Φ

That afternoon I received a note on thick ecru stationary, with engraved lettering at the top: Comtessa Francesca Bianchi de Santanelli. A graceful sketch of Countess'

152

doberman, Mister D, distinguished the lower right corner of the page.

Dear Mr. Rider,

May I ask that you forgive my presumption in what I am about to suggest? I have heard of your temporary business misfortune. An acquaintance of mine is known for his broad financial interests. Could I assist you by arranging an introduction to my friend, with the idea of securing his investment in Filmland?

My warmest regards,
Countess

I phoned Susie immediately.

"I received Countess' letter," I began, "I know you put her up to this, I barely know the woman. Are you suggesting I approach your fiancé for a hand-out?"

"You heard from Countess?"

"Don't get ethereal, just answer my question. Is this what you expect me to do?"

"Maxwell, darling," Her procrastination drove me crazy. "As I understand things from Winton unless you raise $10 million, we cannot rely on you to finance our campaign against father. God knows Ramòn has more money than he needs and is always looking for an investment opportunity…"

"If he's so bloody charmed by investment opportunities why doesn't he simply throw his money at the Inca Princess?"

"Oh, he's much too scrupulous for that. He would never mix finance and love."

"Apparently I lack Brulée's integrity since you asked me to back your fight for the mine."

"But that's what banks do, darling," Susie replied. "And you and I—we have something."

"I'm glad you brought that up. What do we have?"

With a clarity of vision that comes with desperation, I began to see my part in this, some ambivalence that had kept our affair as superficial as the plastic bride and groom on a wedding cake.

"Darling. Maxwell. Sweetie. Your passion is so flattering. But don't let it suffocate you. Alex des Prairies has arranged an exhibit of my paintings in Brussels at the end of the year. I'm leaving on January 1st. If your problems are cleared up by then—we might travel to Cannes together, spend the spring at Countess' villa in Florence."

I tried to prolong my pique. "What about Brulée?"

"Ramòn knows about you, darling. I've kept no secrets. I've already mentioned you might approach him with a business proposal. He's interested. And he's been quite civilized about it."

"What does that mean?"

"He's offered to invite you, through Countess, of course, to weekend at his ranch in Montecito."

"What's Countess got to do with me?"

"Sweetie, don't you know? It's an accommodation to your pride. Ramòn's terribly sensitive to things like that, the insecurities that can arise between gentlemen and all that."

"It's all too damn civilized for me."

"Calm, calm. It's a lovely drive to his ranch. Serene. Relaxing. Go there. Speak with him. Spend a country weekend. Trap shooting, riding, Ramòn has some lovely ponies. But please, darling, don't best him at polo. I've seen him glower over losing a chukker."

"Sure." The idea of socializing with Susie's lover was giving me a headache. "I'll think about it, that's all. I can't make a commitment to speak to Brulée. I have my own sources."

"Don't wait too long, Max, darling. Winton and I need to proceed with our plan for the Inca Princess. And I desperately want to share Europe with you in the spring."

We spoke a bit more after that, mostly x-rated. If Daisy Buchanan had a voice like money, Susie Grass' combined money with erotica. And she could propose the most alluring activities in a voice as arch and cultivated, you might say completely phoney, as a Noel Coward society girl.

"Countess is going to call you. Please be gracious."

"We'll see," I said.

The Ramòn Brulée connection was one of those proposals that sound plausible until you start to act on it. Then it reveals itself as completely foolhardy, incapable of artful execution.

I'd avoided meeting Brulée on the grounds of his unsavory character. A pit bull in business, I didn't doubt it. But when you include someone in your social circle, as I had Susie, you must be prepared to accept their associates as well.

The source of his wealth was mysterious. Variously, he was described as dabbling in "imports," owning a racetrack. And according to Susie, he channeled the plunder of third-world despots through the Inca Princess.

I had to admit, though, my desperation was such I might have called on Brulée but for Susie Grass. The idea of importuning a man whose mistress I coveted was repellent to me. As a result, I felt annoyed with myself for entertaining the idea. I avoided Countess and pursued my own plan for saving Irving and myself. I'd told Susie I had "other sources." In truth I could think of only one.

25

Invitation to Tower Hill

Bunker Dodge was a source for money among the Europeans when they found themselves short. They considered Dodge a posturer whose exploits held a mild provocation, for the sake of gossip. He was their court fool. But his favors didn't come cheaply. I'd submit to the guile of a two-bit faker before I'd petition Brulée for help.

As I left Filmland's offices that morning to find Dodge, I was detained in the lobby by a swaggering German. I recognized the man as the haughty chef from Port's, hired by Alex to oversee the kitchen at Tower Hill.

The German bowed, stiff with resentment for his messenger role, "Mr. des Prairies asked me to deliver this personally."

He handed me a lettered card announcing an affair at Tower Hill, a grand fête on New Year's Eve celebrating the completion of Danse du Sang, and honoring its star Gina Paloma.

He bowed a second time, "Count des Prairies would be honored for you to attend and announce the unveiling of the marketing campaign for Danse du Sang."

"Thank you," I said. I was too stunned to accept. And too ambivalent to refuse. It appeared Alex and I were to resume our friendship. Although he'd let me down—this act of grace, performed with style, drew me back again. And that was not an entirely comfortable feeling.

Φ

Of course Bunker Dodge moved on when the dough ran out like his other Concorde flapping pals. And when he could have been helpful, he was elusive as string. But on that November afternoon, when I sought him out on the subject of money for Filmland, he still reposed at his post at the Beverly Hills Hotel, solemn and punctual at his business of scoring suckers as a Wall Street lawyer brokering time.

I hesitated before approaching him. We'd parted on bad terms. He didn't regard me as a welsher, for I'd agreed to honor his commissions. He knew if Filmland went forward, there was a solid chance he would be paid.

For several minutes, I watched Dodge unobserved, his head bent over his lists, and his bleach-gray hair languishing along the back of a rumpled silk blazer. The albino pink of his long toes protruded like shiny embryos from the Gucci sandals. The bank pouch lay bloated beside his right hand.

I tried to see him through Alex's eyes. Fool. Poseur. But Dodge's words had changed that for me. `At least I am authentic.'

An authentic bounder of the old school, Dodge was my last resort—unless I could see myself limping back to Brulée, quivering in attendance like a dowager's lap dog—which I couldn't. I had the week to raise the money and I hoped Dodge would loan it to me, secured by Filmland's stock.

"A loan, dear boy? Never. I would never tie up my clients' funds like that. You know the way my business works."

I knew. The favors he earned as a market shill were far more generous than the broker's fee I could offer. "If you won't loan the $10 million, I don't see how you can help me," I said.

"Dear boy, the focus at this table is what you can do for me." He glanced at a well-dressed older man who had just drifted into the Lounge, taken a seat at the bar.

"Chairman of American Express," he said absently. He nodded to Louie the waiter, then glanced shrewdly at me.

"You're invited to Alex des Prairies's for the preview of Danse du Sang?"

"Of course." I put my hand to the invitation in my pocket.

"Alex's guest list could be a very lucrative source of business development for me. If you can take me along as your guest, I'll place $10 million of my clients' funds with Filmland for sixty days."

I leaned forward, astonished at his offer.

"But you already know Alex, I've seen you with him. Aren't you included?"

"I would never be included, as you put it. Oh, it's all right to claim a hefty fee for dropping the name of a wealthy chum, but stand an invitation? Never."

"Alex has referred clients to you for a fee?"

An expression of detached interest hovered at his lips.

"You're surprised? Trust fund pimps. I need them. They share the dirt on an old school tie, give him a push my way and I take it from there. I pay several hundred thousand in fees every year. I don't file 1099s if you see what I mean. But an invitation? Ungrateful snobs—or should I say nobs?" He snorted mirthlessly at his own joke.

"I've only a week, Bunker," I said.

"Let me see that invitation." He floated his hand across, spirited the thick ecru card from my coat pocket. It was engraved in dark blue with Alex's crest and lettering. The smaller reply card was also engraved, and its envelope addressed by hand to Alex at Tower Hill.

Dodge uncapped a maroon and gold Montblanc pen, handed it to me. "That's my offer. All interest on the funds

159

will be paid to me and not a word to anyone."

He twitched his lips in a smile. "Principle? Or principal?"

I hesitated. Sixty-day deposits were not as good as a loan. Too temporary. Dodge could withdraw the funds by paying the penalty. But it might get us by until Danse du Sang was sold. I thought about the Brulée-option. And Susie. Then I filled in the small card: Messrs. Maxwell Rider and Bunker Dodge will attend.

I slipped it into the stamped envelope, slid it toward him.

"A realist," Dodge said. "We Americans are, aren't we?"

A realist. I found his compliment distasteful. Although, if I wasn't one then, I became one.

I stood up, reached for my wallet. But Dodge was ahead of me. With a gesture calculated to draw the attention of the Chairman of American Express, he tossed open the pouch, drew out the wad of bills. "Allow me," he said.

Φ

My telephone conversation with Ms. Vaughn was short but sweet. She tried to muscle me, but her heart wasn't in it. It seemed she had bigger fish to fry.

"The government's deal called for a principal pay-down by Count des Prairies or a capital infusion by you and Mr. Fain. Why should we accept short-term deposits instead? Too much risk if the money can pull out."

It was secure, I argued. No release before the end of the year. By that time Danse du Sang would be sold, Alex's obligation paid off. Irving and I could resume our plans for Filmland, without government pressure.

Ms. Vaughn responded with unfeminine coarseness. I visualized her delicate ear with its crescent earring pressed against the handset.

"You bought yourself two months. But if the bank's deficit is not cured by January 1st ..."

I was about to end the call, but she couldn't resist cautioning me about Bunker Dodge, reciting an excerpt from the government's hodgepodge of repetitive, incoherent regulations, a short paragraph titled The Offering of Bribes to Secure Deposits, which began,

"The giving or accepting of money or any tangible gift, reward, or thing of value, to secure deposits or other benefit is expressly prohibited... "

But I didn't think I'd violated the spirit of the law. The way I saw it, an invitation to Tower Hill had tangible value only to Dodge.

26

Irving and Rider at Filmland

The period between my meeting with Dodge and Alex's party was invigorating with press of business. If I lacked a keen eye for detail, Irving's vision was glaucomic— I'd satisfied Ms. Vaughn. That's all that mattered.

He started glad-handing again. At Le Dôme, on the telephone, setting up investors for Filmland's partnerships. A typical call:

"Maury, how goes it?" Listening. "No big deal, we're back in the saddle. Whaddya mean? At least they heard of us now—"

Irving and I never spoke about how difficult it was during the weeks of our eclipse from Hollywood. We both suffered the humiliation of grown men whose phone calls are not returned. I made a private pledge that when we were on top again— if we were—I'd employ someone just to return the calls of poor outlaws like us, temporarily banished from the tribe.

While Irving revived our contacts, I put finishing touches to the prospectus required by Ms. Vaughn's plea agreement, on the remote chance we could still fund Filmland's film partnerships.

The days grew dark at five o'clock. That's when we drew the blinds in Irving's suite and screened films for inclusion in the financing pools. The first film we included was officially titled Phantom Love. But I called it Swirling Cameras.

Niko Krakas, its producer, had written the screenplay himself. It showed. He cast a stunning blonde, a simpering stud and billowing drapes. In place of plot, there were nightmares. Instead of suspense—vertigo.

Niko's hand-held camera lurched through a contemporary Malibu mansion like the deck of a ship in a storm. Awkward sex between the gorgeous girl and the sapless lead crippled Niko's already incoherent story line. And the soundtrack of moans was largely unconvincing.

I said pass, but not too forcefully. Irving was still crowing over the results of his bulldog negotiations, having strong-armed the feisty Greek into giving up ten percent of gross for another million to complete the film.

By the time Irving and Niko finished congratulating each other, there was nothing to be done but break out the Taitinger and chilled crystal. Vladimir Horowitz pounded his pure tones from the concealed state-of-the-art sound system in Irving's office as we toasted Filmland Partners.

There were, of course, better films than those which found their way to Filmland's opulent rooms. Phantom Love was poor cousin to the films we bragged about that magic night in Fiesole. But then, things had changed.

Major studios had the lock on blockbusters in that decade. Big-budget scripts with box-office stars. Partnering with a studio wasn't possible after our arrest. The government had placed a limit on the financial commitments we could make. Films produced by independents, and budgeted modestly, offered our only chance to share gross revenues with controlled risk. Far easier to recoup two million than eighteen, which was rapidly becoming the average film budget.

Despite the return to business at Filmland, I still awoke in panic over Danse du Sang. Alex kept up his assurances about Costa Brava, and its chairman Trujillo, whom I was to meet at Alex's party. Still I was concerned. Dodge had only pledged his deposits for sixty days. I began to show the film around myself.

Danse du Sang was exquisitely shot in the Tuscany countryside. Gina Paloma exuded a radiant presence. A luminous Venetian with dove-pillows for breasts and slender, milky hands and feet, she played a virginal woman denounced as a prostitute by Roman Catholic priests, and rejected by her fiancé as a whore. She avenged this betrayal by castrating a priest, and died heroically, immolated by angry Catholics in Siena's ancient square.

Our early decision to loan $2 million for its domestic release presented little risk—Gina had become an international siren since the film's success in Rome. But after Alex's excesses attracted the attention of Ms. Vaughan and her henchmen— well—I was anxious to close the deal with Trujillo.

I insisted Alex stop reworking the script and screen the new cut. Sensuous, surreal in its images, the new scenes felt ambiguous and obscure. Certainly nothing the American public, whose literary model was O. Henry, not Kafka, could understand.

"Alex, this can only go to the art film market. What deal have you struck with Costa Brava?"

"Oh, $10 million easy, and another ten, for Raft of the Medusa," he said.

I pressed him almost daily and urged another meeting with Costa Brava to confirm a letter of intent. "We have a gentleman's agreement," Alex insisted, "I won't trouble him with that."

Late November brought the dog days of distribution deals. After Milan. After Venice. I felt grateful we had the shadow of at least one buyer. I continued to show the film, and endure the sham promises of every slick hipster I could trick into a rented screening room.

Luckily, Alex still maintained offices at Samuel Goldwyn Studios a few miles from Filmland—he'd been forced to prepay the rent. So I was able to put on a credible show. For the screenings, I wore my best suit, European in taste, with a conservative tie. I introduced Danse du Sang to prospects as "unique, with special commercial appeal." And tried to avoid the epithet "art film."

In silk ascot, with collar elegantly threadbare, Alex lent his irrepressible presence to these affairs. But in fact, the outcome varied only by the degree of tact, or lack of it, possessed by the moguls for whom we screened the rough cut.

The scene which Alex called "the absolute key, Rider, I refuse to cut even one frame of it!" drew a dramatic response each time it played: "What is this baloney?" Or words to that effect.

Of course we didn't have a completed film to show. The final scene was scheduled for re-shooting the first week of January.

We argued over the scene, Alex's new script called for an ending less than Hollywood-happy: A stag's antler hurtles from an apocryphal sky, plunges into the staring eye of the mysterious drifter played by Christian Ruhl, whose pierced retina exudes a swollen tear of blood along his cheek. As credits roll.

The transition from the new scenes to the old ending were rough to say the least. But nothing like the afternoon Alex's projectionist switched the reels.

Over several weeks I'd cosseted a friendship with the chairman of United Artists, whose son I'd known back east. When he finally sent his "man from New York," a weasel named Coyne, he brought a call girl.

They arrived in a limo, uncommon at that time. As Coyne stepped out of it, paunchy and grotesque, he asked the running time of the film. The girl he was with, not more than eighteen, draped herself over him like a fringe coat.

Most people want to sit in the back. Coyne strode to the front, flashed a weird smile, "I want to get the full effect," he said.

Another potential buyer was also present that afternoon, two executives from New World, and we sat in the last rows. At first I didn't notice the projectionist's mistake, it was so beautifully photographed. When I did I wasn't sure what to do.

Embarrassed, I glanced around, the two executives from New World watched absorbed. Sheepishly, I strode back to the projectionist. He made the correction, but it was too late.

They stuck it out for nine reels, old and new shots, mixed up like hash.

"Too linear," New World's first lieutenant said as the lights went on.

The UA man didn't surface until we were leaving the screening room. He said nothing about the film. Just smiled, a weird dreamy smile, departed in the limo, with the tart pasted to his suit.

Alex took the reel mix up as further demonstration of class differences. "One works intensely at artistic perfection. For years, months, producing one's unique vision. Then, some lowly technician—tired, bored, inattentive—in one brief important showing, switches the reels." He lifted his shoulders disdainfully, "All ruined by the machine operator!"

Φ

The days were not all spent watching films. While I struggled with arcane banking rules, Susie and Winton Grass swept in weekly to press for a partnership with the Inca Princess.

The idea was to secure Filmland's investment units with bricks of gold bullion vaulted at the Inca Princess. If the plan came about, large fees would be paid to the mine. It was this aspect that made it imperative for Susie and Winton to buy their father out.

You might think my friendship with Susie Grass deepened during this period. But strangely, Susie remained as elusive as ever. And Winton's brotherly bond seemed more Siamese than fraternal. Still, something had changed between us when I was in Europe. And I felt, when the business distractions were clear, our affair could begin for real.

One afternoon, I walked Susie to their Lincoln Towncar parked in Filmland's garage. Susie's driver, that feeble androgyne who hovered relentlessly in her vicinity, had stepped away. And Winton was detained unwillingly by Irving's bombastic plan to feature the Inca Princess vault—under armed guard—in our solicitation brochure.

When we reached the car, I pressed Susie inside, onto the plush pale leather of the back seats.

"Darling, Maxwell, Winton's only upstairs …"

I could give a damn about Winton Grass. His yachting-party uniform. Pale sprouts of hair reaching for the sky. Brulée too. To hell with him. To hell with both of them.

She unzipped my trousers, which was a good start. I pulled her face to mine, unfastened her blouse, and gathered her silky skirt around her waist.

"Let's try something," I murmured, pretty sure of the physics of what I had in mind.

Suddenly, rudely, Susie's driver popped up from the front seat, stared at us myopically with round, mocking eyes. He—or she—wore a faint moustache like a sprinkling of white pepper on a boiled potato.

Susie feigned irritation but she was amused, "I believe you're perverted, Damon."

"Get out," I said, and slammed shut the privacy screen, glaring at Damon until he left the car.

"When can we be alone?" I demanded. Susie didn't answer but removed a compact from her handbag, pursed her lips into the haughty expression of a runway model.

"What about Cannes?" I pressed.

"I dream about it," she said evasively.

"Where does Brulée fit in?"

"He has no soul," she said. "I'm convinced of it."

"What do you mean?"

"Hush," she curved her hand around my mouth, "Top secret—really must go no further—we've gotten the money to purchase father's interest. And Ramòn has nothing to do with it."

I tried to draw her out, to elicit a clearer picture of the status of the Inca Princess. Filmland's prospectus required my Opinion of Counsel that the gold was secure. I needed assurance that Tom Grass, Susie's litigious patriarch, had toddled off for good—to tend roses, gather seashells or have a bimbo as Alex once declared he should.

But Susie and Winton were fellow travelers in some vague hemisphere of cryptic expression. So I was left to my own deduction that Brulée, having failed to finance their contest, was stripped of the mantle of Prince Charming.

"Where did you get the money?"

"Top secret," she smiled.

"Not from Alex?"

"Not exactly," she said.

I became aware of Winton hovering like a Nazi outside the limo, too self-consciously fastidious to open the door.

"Christ!" I closed the first buttons of her blouse. Her breasts were small but perfect beneath the gauzy silk.

"I want to see you alone," I said.

"You're going to Alex's party at Tower Hill, aren't you?" she asked. She tipped her head and licked her child's lips, and I knew nothing would keep me away.

27

Rider at Beverly Place

Ironically, my efforts to save Filmland led to the end of the Grass lawsuit—and a lot of other events from that like dominoes falling.

One day Winton recounted his recent conversation with the old man. "Father, let us place our cards on the table. I'm calling to proffer our invitation, Susie's and mine, to settle this dispute like gentlemen. We will meet at my club—your old club, father. We will shake hands over a glass of claret, and patch this thing over, like gentlemen."

I found Winton's approach laughable. In a contest like that you don't just telephone your adversary, that vicious embittered bully who has dedicated the last two years to burying you alive in ink—28 lines per sheet, 25% rag bond, watermark by Stuart F. Cooper, Engravers to the Bar. You don't just do that. Because, as well-intentioned as you might be, your rival—the guy who's squandered a million dollars in legal fees already, and pledged another $100K to attach all your bank accounts before trial—is not going to receive your overture with the grace of a sorority sister at homecoming.

It doesn't happen that way. Surprisingly, the one who appreciated that fact was Father Rob. Though he wore a black suit and cleric's collar, and a giant jeweled cross that flapped at his shirt front when he walked, I'm not completely sure Father Rob was ordained by any church. He claimed he'd been employed as a private investigator in San Bernardino. And he claimed to still be licensed.

"Rider," Winton Grass continued on the phone, in the

furtive voice of a character in a 1940s spy plot.

"We're coming over. Father Rob has learned something that—well, quite frankly, I need a second opinion about. You're a lawyer. This must be in confidence. Attorney-client privilege and all that."

"The privilege doesn't apply, Winton," I said. "I'm not your attorney."

"I'm retaining you," he said immediately.

Which illustrates the kind of thinking I was up against. Winton and Susie were desperately in arrears in payments due their attorneys. Accordingly, among their acquaintances with legal training, they were inclined to promote the idea of pro bono representation.

From his urgency I expected Winton within twenty minutes, driving time between Hancock Park and Filmland's offices on Sunset. Two hours later he rushed in, with Father Rob sauntering at his heels. I led them into the conference room.

Winton waved away my offer of refreshment, surveying the room skittishly.

"Father Rob's performed some diligence work on his own to help us with our—ahem—project." He glanced at the chandelier, and lowered his voice to a murmur.

I lacked patience with Grass' furtiveness. Evasions I thought charming in his sister grew intolerable in a business colleague. I swung a chair around, leaped up on it, and examined the chandelier. I dragged the chair over to each sconce, and peered inside. Inspected the telephone, speaker-com, tray and coffee service. Finally, I dropped down on hands and knees to study the underside of the marble conference table of rare palisander wood.

"The room's clean," I said in my best impression of

Philip Marlowe. His brow cleared with relief. He'd never have thought of checking for himself.

"Here, see this." Winton slid several documents toward me from a stack of micro-fiched checks going back five years. Each one was paid to Tom Grass for twenty thousand dollars a month, signed by Ramòn Brulée.

"Consulting fee?" I said, reading aloud the notation on each check. "For what?"

Winton's eyes changed to dark currants of approval, undoubtedly the first time he'd admired anything about me.

"Exactly."

I studied each page. Brulée's payments to Grass began in 1974, several years before he met Susie. That explained Brulée's refusal to finance the twins' litigation against their father. But what services did Tom Grass perform for Brulée? And why was he paid so well?

"Where did you get these?" I asked.

Grass searched the room for Father Rob, who was blessing the coffee service and intercom. "Father Rob and mother were sorting papers to establish a basis for support in the, ah-hem, dissolution proceeding."

"Your parents' divorce," I said.

"Yes. And they turned up a curious ledger sheet in father's handwriting. Just a single page attached through static to papers concerning the mine. Obviously some sort of record of Ramòn's payments to father. And Father Rob—" Grass waved a hand toward the beaming cleric—"ingratiated himself with a young man at Ramòn's bank, a former Jesuit as it turns out, who produced these checks."

"But how did you know where Brulée banks?"

Winton allowed a sly smile. "Susie's proved herself quite the Matahari in this episode." He drifted into a private trance.

173

"Quite the Matahari."

"Yes. Okay. But what are you going to do?"

He stood up excitedly. "That's why we're here, Rider."

I was flattered to be consulted. A tone of formality asserted itself in my response, vestige of the lawyer I might have been. "It's unlikely your father has reported this revenue—either to the IRS or on his income schedule in the divorce proceeding—"

Grass seized my suggestion before I'd offered it, "That's brilliant! We'll threaten to expose father on this unless he agrees to sell us the Inca Princess."

Father Rob gave a benevolent smile.

"Well, yes. That's the idea," I said, flat-footed by their reaction. "Of course, he may very well have owned up to it. In that case—"

I'd never heard the cleric say much. At Hancock Park, he'd only summoned us to tea and murmured a few benedictions. He had a low rumbling voice like a boulder shifting. It started slow but picked up speed.

"In that case, we will confront Mr. Brulée," Father Rob rumbled, "—and persuade him to withdraw his support of Mr. Grass."

I wasn't convinced. Ramon was no business ingénue.

Father Rob spoke again, "Mr. Brulée has several accounts. This one is called Rapunzel Project." He mused, "Will he want attention called to his accounts?"

Winton leaped up. Father Rob smiled beatifically.

"Well done!" Winton said. "We'll get the mine. We'll have what's ours. Thanks to you Rider. Good chap, you're a gentleman."

Father Rob fingered the samovar lovingly on their way out.

It was only after this meeting, after I'd been useful to Winton Grass, that Susie agreed to meet me alone.

Φ

The day after Winton Grass' revelation, I received another, in different terms and through unexpected adventure.

There remained a week until Alex's party for Danse du Sang. I'd grown impatient with his stalling as to Costa Brava, and determined to track down for myself this alleged white knight.

We placed a conference call from Irving's office. Irving knew the way the game works as intimately as anyone I've ever known. Few men, for example, could best Irving at scoring a good table in a power restaurant. For that, he relied on shameless schmoozing of the trades, speaking weekly to editors at The Hollywood Reporter and Daily Variety, and relaying some gossip or half-truth as a pretext for self-promotion.

His characteristic sign-off—"I'm on my way to Le Dôme (or Dominick's or The Palm)" —was calculated to grab a line in the upcoming issue:

"Irving Fain called en route to The Palm this morning to confirm… "

That's just an example of Irving's natural savvy. So I didn't fear his knowing the score when it came to Costa Brava.

Irving scowled at his desk phone, and the oscillating sound of an unanswered line. "Answer the friggin' phone!"

Periodically, Irving pledged to give up the other 'F' word and, like some nicotine addict hoarding five smokes a day, he reserved his ration of `F' words for special occasions.

"F'cockin' scumballs!" he said after twenty rings, and

ended the pulse from the speaker box with a jab of his finger.

I checked the Producer's Guild for a new number, and confirmed with the phone company that the old, unresponsive one was disconnected. Then I acknowledged to myself that Costa Brava's disappearance didn't surprise me. Somehow, I'd been expecting it. I felt gravely disappointed, nonetheless. And Irving's assessment—"Friggin' flakes—" seemed to sum up the situation nicely.

Φ

That morning, Alex's sound editor had scheduled the looping of several scenes at a studio near Beverly Place. `Looping' is the dubbing of sound effects to go with the action on the screen. I decided to drop by the studio, and take in Costa Brava's offices on the way.

This time, I parked in front. The iron gate was locked, the door plate removed, and two small holes remained where the brass screws had been.

Few experiences are as eerie as walking a deserted city street at midday, seeing no one, and hearing nothing. The windows of antique shops on Beverly Place were tinted to repel the sun's glare. Glimpses within produced only shadowy movements, as the proprietors floated about their rooms in the company of an occasional designer.

An alley ran behind the shops, where delivery vans pull in. I strolled up to the end of the street, turned the corner and headed down the alley. There was a truck parked about half way down, outside the back entrance of Costa Brava's offices.

Any noontime in LA, you'll find scores of trucks abandoned in alleys. It's my experience the average working man is prompt in taking his lunch, and thinks nothing of abandoning his vehicle and striding off to the nearest Jack-in-the-Box.

There was a takeout place on Melrose, but it wasn't around the corner. I could anticipate the van's driver would be absent at least twenty minutes.

There was an outer door of scrolled iron, and they'd left it ajar. The inner door was closed but it pushed inward to my touch. Too easy, I thought. And with the strange silence of the street, and my own apprehension, I almost retreated.

Instead, I entered a narrow hallway which dropped off to the right almost immediately into the kitchen where we had met Arthur Jamul months before. Styrofoam cartons and a soiled coffee cup greeted me. I moved down the corridor to an empty office where desks and chairs had been. I dodged inside and listened. It was as quiet as the street. There were covered boxes, like those used for moving office files, and I crouched down to go through them. The first file was titled "Confidential Communiques." I thought it a good title for a film of political intrigue, screenplay by Graham Greene. I was completely unprepared for what I found.

A document on FBI letterhead, in memorandum form, was addressed to the Drug Enforcement Agency. The content of the memo suggested the DEA had expanded its powers beyond sniffing bags at airports.

"The Agency agrees to commit $50,000 a month for an indefinite period to participate in your Operation Star Search to identify illegal sources of film financing in Hollywood. The Agency agrees to share, equally..."

It continued, but I tucked it into my coat to read later. Initials in ink beside the name of the FBI's bureau chief, Los Angeles, confirmed its author.

I heard the voices of men entering the kitchen, with the rustling of take-out wrappings and scraping of chairs. The movers were back.

Quickly, I tore the lids off the other boxes and scribbled notes on the files they contained. The word "Filmland" caught my eye, and one other, "Rapunzel Project." I concealed those files under my coat and stole toward the front door. When I got there, I hesitated, torn between retracing my steps to the exit on the alley, under observation of the movers in the kitchen, or slipping out the front to possible defeat at the wrought iron gate. Either way, I risked losing possession of my prize.

A third idea presented itself. In the office I'd just left there was a faux fireplace, with a shallow draft for the gas flames popular in the thirties. I rolled the two files together in a tube, securing it with one of my socks. The other sock I placed in my pocket.

When I was sure the files were tucked firmly in the fireplace shaft, I walked calmly out the back door, past the men. "Guess they left already," I said, offering a wave.

One of them frowned, and I heard him rush down the hall to make sure nothing was disturbed. But to his eye, nothing was.

I sat in my car for several minutes reviewing the memo. Quick-witted or paranoid, I can't say, but I pieced together a pattern that sounded very much like Irving and I had stumbled into a sting of Hollywood, carried out by the joint efforts of two agencies of the Justice Department—the Drug Enforcement Agency and the FBI.

For the second time in twenty-four hours, the phrase Rapunzel Project branded itself onto my curiosity. What was Brulée's part in this?

Φ

Tom Latham's view of the LA Country Club from the sixteenth floor of Latham & Frye—the law firm that had rushed to defend us from the relentless Ms. Vaughn—was a lush contrast to the concrete grid of Century City below. I drove there immediately after leaving Beverly Place.

The firm's decor suggested the private club of a devoted Anglophile. The walls were Regency-striped above mahogany wainscoting. Ship prints and hunting scenes lined the hallways, and a glass curio case displayed the firm's collection of antique drinking vessels.

Tom flicked his Rolex under his cuff as I drew to a close my breathless recitation. "Unfortunately, your theories concerning an inter-agency sting don't change anything." He squinted at the stick figures teeing off below.

"It's bogus," I protested. "Filmland was set up. It's a government conspiracy."

"The federal banking charges you and Irving are facing are legitimate."

"It's completely phony."

I stood up and began pacing in front of the window.

"A spurious movie company run by the government? They represented to us they were going to buy the movie rights to Alex's film! All perfectly legal, by the way. It was just a fictitious ploy for looking into our business practices."

Tom spread his hands, "What do you want me to do?"

Do? I assumed he'd call Ms. Vaughn, read her the riot act. I thought he'd be as outraged as I was at the deception. But I had to confess I hadn't thought it through. I didn't know exactly where to go with my new intelligence.

"Entrapment," I said.

Tom frowned, considering. He caught his reflection in the tinted window pane and smoothed a silvery strand of moussed hair.

I gave it another try. "Abuse of process. The DEA comes to Hollywood looking for drug kingpins serving the film industry. They're running out of cash, and fail to make a case. Someone suggests links to film financing—Bunker Dodge or someone—on the basis of which these yokels approach the FBI. The FBI agrees to jointly fund the operation. Et voila! But now they've got to come through with a prosecution. So they go after Filmland, send in the audit team, tally up the infractions. Do you realize the FDIC expects to take over our company?

Tom steepled his hands in front of his lips.

"And why?" I was beginning to get worked up again.

"Greed," Tom said. "You may have something there. I'm beginning to see your point. There's something repugnant in this setup—the U.S. government pursuing prosecution for profit."

"Maybe I should go back and get the files," I said quickly, as if I were James Bond on a new assignment.

Tom held up a hand. "Well now, that would be—theft." He paused. "Of course, you didn't actually remove the files from Costa Brava's offices. And it's questionable whether you entered the premises wrongfully. Let's say you return later—lawfully—when the location is occupied by another tenant, whereupon you 'find' those files and remove them for safekeeping."

I nodded. "What about Costa Brava's chairman Trujillo? He must be connected to this thing somehow."

The voice of Tom's secretary crackled through the speaker box on his desk. "Paramount is on the line Mr. Latham. They want to bring suit against that comic who's obsessed with `The Godfather.'"

"Thirty seconds," Tom replied. His manner grew brusque. "Meet with Trujillo. Draw him out. Take a mini-recorder. Try to get him to suggest a criminal enterprise, 'You want me to do what?' That kind of thing. Follow your instincts. And—" Tom frowned at my bare ankles as I paused at the door, "—buy some socks."

28

Susie Grass at Chiquita Lowe's

My moments with Susie Grass still play in my mind like silent-movie clips. In the week between Christmas and New Year's Eve she telephoned, although I hadn't expected to hear from her before Alex's party.

"Will you attend?" she asked me, before I'd even said hello. "Will you come to my show at Chiquita Lowe's?"

I'm not sure when it started—my fascination for selfishness in women. Nicole Legrand, age six, might have been the first. In Susie, I found charm in her vanity. She assumed I could read her mind, and she regarded strict attendance to her thoughts as nothing less than a command performance.

"When?" I asked.

"She's mounting my sketches today. The guests are arriving at four o'clock."

"Then I'll meet you there at three," I said. "Alone." I had no wish to stand before Brulée making small talk, or submit to Winton's whispered tales of intrigue at the mine. To my surprise, she assented.

"Lovely. You will have the choice of them. Even before Ramòn."

I parked on Melrose just west of PDC, the shiny blue hangar that serves as toyland to the design trade. Chiquita Lowe's gallery was new, part of a diffident row of napkin white spaces beneath finely lettered awnings along the street. Behind dark windows lay cool white walls and rich tiles, stark lava canvases and howling bronze figures.

I arrived first, nodded to the limpid young woman with

dark bangs and red lips, writing cards at a reception desk of brushed steel. A wall-sized acrylic the texture of bubbling tar dominated the wall behind her.

Chiquita Lowe was in her office, standing behind her desk, surveying two canvases taped to the floor. "Maxwell Rider," she said. She had the manicured look of a Pasadena social club president and the wide aggressive stance of a jock in high heels. Her ash blonde hair was convenience-cut in a blunt bob, she wore a citrus colored gabardine suit. Not my cup of tea but a power-figure in the West Hollywood art circuit.

"I'm meeting Susie Grass," I said.

Chiquita scowled. "There's a lot of interest in her gouaches and watercolors. What troubles me," she said, a look of corporate concern on her brow, "—is Susie's commitment. She has to decide which direction she's going, as a serious artist or," she gave a disagreeable sniff, "decorative."

"I understand she may show in Brussels," I said, just to give the conversation international dazzle. But Chiquita was not to be diverted.

"She appeals to the wrong people for the wrong reasons," she pronounced.

"What do you mean?"

"She sold works to put in people's homes."

"Isn't that what private collecting is all about?" I asked. "Aren't collectors like the Annandales the angels of contemporary art?"

Chiquita's eyes flicked boredom at my logic. "No gallery owner will touch her if she places her art as decoration."

"Susie's talented?" I said.

"Oh yes. There's no question. But she's social. I've got to know where her head is at before investing my time and reputation in her."

A patron timidly coughed to signal her presence—probably only spent half a million in the gallery over the past year. Chiquita dismissed me, and I moved into the cool rooms.

The street floor, a deep space, was divided into three galleries like chambers in a tomb. The lighting had been turned off and natural daylight from glass skylights imparted a dusky effect.

The first gallery contained huge canvases boldly slashed with pigment in primary colors. A closely clipped young man in overalls touched up one of the paintings from a tackle box of acrylic paint tubes.

The next gallery I entered was a strange murky space devoted to sensory stimulation. Television monitors on battery-operated chairs were randomly propelled around the room, creating pulsing shadows to an ominous soundtrack of wailing monks.

The third gallery, at the back, was as cramped as a coat closet. An installation à la Kienholz was recreated—a modern prairie scene of cast figures titled Virgin with Child. In a modern expression of that classic theme, a mechanical infant beat a lump of dirt with a spoon, while a hologram mother-image pinned laundry to a line with a wooden pin.

After I'd assayed the possibilities downstairs, I mounted the stairs to a sunny loft hung with watercolors. With tall windows on the street, the space contained a classically framed exhibition of Susie's paintings. If art is the expression of the soul, Susie's soul—like her art—was vapid and childlike.

The subject matter did not include nature, as I'd supposed. Rather, the paintings formed a collection of social glimpses; slender, slack-chinned people posed against backdrops of Monaco and Cannes.

The watercolors were clever and attractive. But I could now understand Chiquita's reservation, for I perceived them as airy little washes, with delicately lettered prices that seemed absurd. Trivial tributes to the society Susie and Winton had known abroad.

The space was silent. I could hear my watch ticking. Three-fifteen. She was late. Impatiently, I descended the stairs swiftly and made the rounds. I strode the long, cool concrete rooms looking for Susie. Stalking Susie.

On my second turn around, I saw her. She stood close to the artist in the first gallery. He'd finished his work, closed his paint box. He asked how she liked the exhibit.

"C'etais trés bonne," she said, "accessible but mysterious."

He grinned, "I am the artist!"

Quelle surprise. I had little interest in the artist or his work. Suddenly impatient, I rushed Susie, forced my mouth immediately on hers. I put my hands on her waist, moved her against me into the dark gallery of roving monitors and wailing monks.

My desire took us both by surprise. An erection strained against my trousers.

She wore a pale crèpe de chine dress draped in a vee at the front. I eased her breasts from the loose silk and pressed myself against her. I'd been dreaming of her a long time. I pulled her skirt up to her waist and put my face in her bikini'd buns, revolving her slowly until she could feel my hot breath. Then I moved up against her.

Until this moment she'd been passive, amused. "Really? " she said then.

I led her to the darkest shadows of the room, away from the skylights.

Her nylons were a dusky taupe, held up with black garters.

Black lace shimmered against the sandy blush of her skin, and soft blond hairs on her thighs waved like sea grass from the electricity of our clothes. I pulled her softly to the floor, where a harsh, nubby carpet muffled the whirring sounds of the pivoting chairs. I placed her head on my jacket, entered her and came immediately. She closed her eyes, turned her head toward the wall.

"Just wait," I said earnestly.

We didn't even speak. Just waited in the weird shadows with our chests heaving and the monks wailing. The second time I made things right.

We left the gallery holding hands. As we passed the gallery owner's office, Chiquita looked up. "I hope you're as avid in collecting art as you are at pursuing artists, Rider." She arched a pale eyebrow to indicate the security monitor on one corner of her wall. I glanced at it quickly to make sure—no tape.

That doesn't mean we started dating. Susie was still seeing Brulée. The whole time I had a thing for her, she was "engaged" to Ramòn.

29

Alex at Tower Hill

Squinting up from Sunset, you can still see the exotic minarets marking Tower Hill. Stark and dignified as an Arab prince, Alex's castle snaked elusively along the crest, shrouded in fog from Lake Hollywood. On New Year's Eve it stopped raining, and Alex had his party there.

After a year of renovations, Alex had found the courage to move from the Chateau Marmont, hiring a German couple as chef and housekeeper. I'd only seen Tower Hill under construction: But knowing Alex's affinity for style, I awaited the finished project with a sense of excitement.

At seven thirty, I cruised the valet entrance to the Beverly Hills Hotel to pick up Bunker Dodge, then jogged north to Mulholland Highway, that craggy rim from LA's dusty past that shields Bel Air from the dreaded Valley.

After negotiating a sleek ribbon of crooks and turns, we took a quick dive onto a dark and gated private road going nowhere. Ten minutes later, we spun onto a lighted disk of blacktop, chaotic with floodlights and parking rustlers.

I jumped out, leaving the Jaguar to a swarm of valets and swung around to face a ghostly turret, part of a mobster's castle built in 1929 that was stepped into the hillside like the tiers of a wedding cake.

A plank door shone at its center, painted blue, with iron letters announcing: Tower Hill.

The door creaked in and shut solidly behind us. Alone in a kind of ante-chamber, we faced another door which wouldn't budge. Our only hope for advancement appeared in the form of an intercom by which we attempted to announce ourselves.

As soon as I started to speak, an unknown male voice boomed forth, like a garbled Orson Welles reading "War of the Worlds. " I spoke again more quickly this time, but the voice did too. Third time, I rushed our names. Maxwell Rider, Bunker Dodge. The box crackled, then issued its final irritable command. The door clicked sharply and we entered a small blazing lift like a cage. We creaked skyward eight floors to the main living quarters.

I had known the stingy frugality of old-money parties in the East; nouveau-riche flamboyance too. Tiresome people. Dull populations. Listless posing among vast collections of new Lalique. Or The Hollywood Party, white rooms and garish paintings, daubed by business school graduates posing as artists. Sequined women, men in fur coats, jaded with their own celebrity—and still hungry for the celebrity of others. This was the world I expected. I was entirely unprepared for the impression Tower Hill made upon me that night.

Φ

The crash of voices drew Bunker and I toward a grand hall dazzling with light. There were mammoth chairs and davenports, starkly white, Spanish chests and carved figures from another age. A massive hearth of pink flames glowed before me like some remembered womb. A silk carpet of red and gold pentacles lapped the distant edges of dark polished floors. And rare tapestries, large as a wall in the Louvre, hung suspended from iron staffs.

A terrace along the front stretched over the sparkling velvet of Hollywood Boulevard below, its limestone balustrades and urns of dwarf lime trees standing guard like sentries.

At the back, matching sets of French doors opened onto a garden that glowed with light from dozens of fat candles on bronze candelabra.

Alex had chosen the evening for its full moon. Like a disc of ripe fontina, it shone its surreal light full upon the rear lawn where dozens of armchairs were arranged before a movie screen large as a billboard.

"Seventy-five sweating Mexicans," Alex replied when I asked how the screen had been installed. Indeed, they had carried off a dramatic feat—Tower Hill's eight levels rose like steppes into the hillside.

A score of tables offered all manner of refreshment. Ice swans, their bodies hollowed in the afternoon by tedious sculpting with hairdryers, held champagne punch, melon balls, and mixed cocktails. Bittersweet truffles were piled high on filigreed trays. Silver bowls like the shells of giant pearls contained crops of fresh strawberries for dipping in fondue pots of darkest Belgian chocolate.

I stood transfixed. Pale light had filtered time and I hovered, a quivering child from 1959. There are many parties, many nights in one's life. As I stood entranced at Tower Hill, observing an exotic sea of guests, I felt transported back in time to Greenwich, the Linen mansion, and the elusive expectations of a dreaming child.

Dodge lost no time in divorcing himself from me and I drifted slowly into the great room, not ready to catch anyone's eye, enjoying the intimacy of eavesdropped conversations.

"I've heard he cries to get his way."

"You're joking."

"No, it's true. He wanted to buy back his house from a sheik—you know it used to belong to Dietrich when she lived in Los Angeles—and he sobbed inconsolably for weeks. He'd sold it to the Arabs—can you imagine—well, of course he got it back. With half a Million Dollar profit to the sheik."

I couldn't avoid Marina Loge and I asked her how the Madame Europe photo layout went.

"They put in a lot of nonsense that was not true about my mother's family and they made my remarks seem facile and superficial."

I couldn't imagine how they would do that. Marina carried a copy of the article, removed it from her handbag and showed it to me. LA's Most Eligible Women Under Thirty. Marina looked fantastic. There was so much gauze on the lens she looked as plump and innocent as the Gerber baby with a chignon; I'd have bet a set of Steuben goblets not one of those girls had seen thirty for some time.

Marina's escort, a haughty Spaniard in the get-up of a toreador, affected the intellectual. "It was the Aztecs invented the zero."

"Really?" Marina asked. "Was that a significant invention?"

"I've found it useful," I said. That discovery belonged to the Arabs. But I didn't correct Marina's Spaniard, the Aztec civilization was reduced to zero anyway by the conquistadors.

We were casually absorbed into a group of elegant strangers all talking at once.

"Camilla is so simple, so unaffected in her lifestyle."

"You think so? If one's as broke as she is, one must travel all the time to conceal the limitations of her wardrobe."

"Speaking of travel, I just returned from Peru, blighted country! I was bitten by the Cambia fly who got under my scalp and laid its eggs. My fiancé put bacon on it and the worms wriggled into the bacon. But it was so obnoxious, I couldn't wash my hair. It was stiff and rose up from my head like whipped meringue. I had to meet her parents at the country club. So, I went to the clinic to have it excised. But the idiot—a priest— didn't use any bleeping anesthetic. I was out of my mind with pain. Unfortunately, I insulted the medic in front of my fiancée's parents—devout Catholics, you can be sure. I'm not engaged anymore but at least I don't have those blanking worms in my head."

Abruptly, someone shoved me, jerking his cigarette downward to flick an ash. I was thrust up against an exquisite brunette with a heart-shaped face. She wore a European pout and a Bob Mackie gown, which exposed one breast through thin black netting.

She regarded her dress front, pressed against my arm, with desultory interest. "My breasts—they are my beauty," she said. I had to agree. Plump, fine as travertine, her firm brown nipple pressed against my sleeve. I withdrew my arm.

"Do I intimidate you? Don't you want to touch me?" asked Gina Paloma, the star of Danse du Sang.

Impossible question.

"You're more alluring in person than on screen," I said.

"Of course I am. It is my gift." The actress fanned her lashes in the direction of her co-star in Alex's film, a knighted Shakespearean actor Alex had charmed into playing the male lead.

"Can you imagine how disgusting it was for me, humping that old crow?"

I winced. The aforesaid old crow had raised his hand theatrically in greeting and was starting over to us.

I moved against her with the swell of the room. Crowded parties hold the enticing probability we will be drawn into another's gravity—and not rejected. Gina slid her satin hand between us, tracing an outline of my anatomy with her fingertips.

"Lose something?" I responded to the moment, then moved her hand away. I had another seduction planned for the evening.

"Max," Alex strode up and planted himself before us with bluff grandiosity. He was charmingly got up in his glad-expatriate style. The frayed collar of his shirt lent an air of insouciance to an ascot of paisley silk. And his dark hair, still wet from the shower and combed back, resembled an exuberant pup fresh from his swim.

Gina removed a huge pair of sunglasses from a tiny sequined pouch and put them on. I took that to mean there was no need for renewing introductions.

Alex's affair with Gina Paloma was long over by the time of his gala at Tower Hill. A celluloid romance that was an unusual one because the roulette tables had turned on the fortunes of Alex-the-director, and his willing starlet.

In Rome, Alex had played the role of auteur: romantic, dashing and rich. Photos of Alex and Gina on the set of Danse du Sang told a story, in stills, that's almost cliché. Alex in leather jacket with flowing alpaca scarves squinting through cumbersome European cameras. Gina, clothed barely, barely clothed, laughing back at him provocative and indiscreet.

Gina began the relationship as starlet, Alex as Pygmalian. By the time of Alex's party, she'd become an international star praised for her screen luminosity. Alex had left Italy a hero, the artist who defied the church. But Italy meant nothing to Hollywood. Until Danse du Sang acquired box-office cachet in the States. Alex was just another Hollywood aspirant. And Gina was the reason the guest list that evening did not suffer from attrition, but swelled with the most desirable guests from both sides of the Atlantic.

Alex lifted Gina's hand to his lips with perfunctory grace. "Thank you for arriving."

"Avec plaisir," she demurred in the language they'd spoken together in Italy. Pauses more artful than phrases disguised the bitter vernacular of their estrangement. Alex was piqued he'd had to promise a queen's ransom to get her there. Gina Paloma, former ingenue, knew the value of her celebrity.

"Max," Alex detained me. "What time is the good time for our campaign?"

Gina rebuked me with her eyes and drifted off.

We agreed the trailer should be screened at midnight, the marketing campaign unveiled just before. The posters commissioned by Alex for its domestic opening were splendid—dazzling reproductions of Gina rising from a tub of eggshells in the meadow. And Gina was to address the guests with remarks that suggested her delighted association with a project at once so artistic and entertaining, a film destined to become an international classic, comparable to Fellini's 8½ or Truffaut's Day for Night. Finally, Alex was to introduce as buyer of the film, Trujillo, who would succumb to the enchantment of the occasion by announcing an early closing of the sale.

I glanced around. "Where's Trujillo? Point him out to me so I won't appear a fool when we're introduced." I pressed Alex, "What's he look like?"

Alex made a pretense of scanning the room, puffed up with excitement, "Not arrived yet—I'll find you immediately when he shows up." His interest had already drifted onto other, more exotic guests.

I realized Trujillo and Costa Brava were fictions of the DEA. But I had a plan to turn tables on the government. If I could get Costa Brava to put up its sting-money for

the "purchase" of Danse du Sang there was a good chance
the Justice Department would be forced to back off on its
charges against Irving and me. At least that's what I hoped.

As Alex excused himself and moved away I saw her.

Susie Grass was the only woman present wearing trousers.
A very mannish look. But the pale gabardine, styled by St.
Laurent, set off her saucy curves. Beneath her jacket, opaque
pleats of silk chiffon revealed every detail of her femininity.

As she floated toward me, I was aware she drew male
attention. That was not all. Several feet away Gina's cat-green
eyes turned black. Not entirely from appreciation.

It didn't worry me that sibling Grass was there too. Winton,
attired in white yachting trousers and double-breasted blazer,
nodded almost imperceptibly to me—that is, so slightly you
had to be staring to observe his gesture. And I was. The
fragile plantings which occasionally dotted Winton's scalp
like spruce seedlings, had matured, and wafted toward the
chandelier. Those pale eyes, the same as his sister's, fastened
on me with cool interest.

Susie tossed me a wan smile. I soon saw why. Ramòn
Brulée, that crude toad, brought up the rear.

The fiancé. I'm convinced he really was engaged to Susie,
despite her denial and Winton's phony good-chap claptrap.
Under the circumstances I wasn't anxious to meet him. But
he sought me out, Susie glassy-eyed beside him, enjoying the
rivalry and eager to see what would follow.

She was lovely through all her deceit. Her small lips parted
with just the suggestion of what she might do to me if we
were alone.

Brulée, aside from that trivial hairpiece, had a head like
a large boulder. His teeth were too small, tightly set, and his
cruel eyes flicked incessantly. Not terribly attractive as Alex

had said. Yet he wore power like his tailored tuxedo. It was easy to see how he could compel a woman's fascination.

"Rider," he said, biting my name with a kind of ferocity.

"Rider," he repeated, surveying the room as if he'd already lost interest. "Susie tells me you work in a bank."

I had a habit then, of remaining detached when people insulted me, I didn't reply.

"Fascinating group of people my fiancée's attracted to." He jabbed a milky nail at a skulking figure in black leathers. "I know that weasel. Rabbi turned biker. He was dealing an employee of mine who snorted coke. Cleaned up his act. Sperm donor now. They lock him up in a room with girlie magazines."

It's always an auditory shock, the way some Europeans adapt our vernacular. But I swear, on Humbert Humbert's grave, that's how he talked.

"I wouldn't want him as a father," I said.

Susie's ethereal gaze remained fixed on some inner perfection, "Completely unregulated," she said in her cultivated voice.

"What is?" I said in surprise.

"The sperm industry. They inquire whether a man's insane but if he answers no, he's accepted. Perfectly dreadful."

Brulée flicked his eyes over me. "Never heard from you."

"What do you mean?" I inquired politely.

"Several weeks ago. I offered to stake you on Filmland. Invited you to my ranch in Santa Barbara. Never heard from you."

I checked with Susie to see what effect this extraordinary grievance had on her. She tilted her head in a pose of languid interest.

"What would it have cost me?" I asked.

Brulée sniffed. "Ha! I could snap my fingers. Like this." He clicked his thumb and forefinger between us.

Brulée appeared to be working himself up. "Last Wednesday I was at Khasoggi's for dinner. Six guests," he lunged his bulky head, "not sixty."

"What are you trying to say?"

"I am a reasonable man, an idealist. You—you insult me." He jabbed his finger again, glowering darkly. I would have laughed at his intended menace but I felt curiously buoyed by it, confident of my intentions with Susie.

Instead, I shrugged. "I'm sorry you feel that way," I said.

Brulée's attention was caught by his glimpse of the matador with Marina Loge. With a scowl, he excused himself to Susie, "That fellow cheated me on a real estate deal," he said.

We were suddenly alone. Unless you count Winton, which I didn't. I brushed by him, guiding Susie toward a hall which I hoped led to the guest wing.

"What are you doing here with him?"

"Ramòn is a valuable friend. Don't be boring."

"He has no soul, remember?" I said callously.

"That's true."

"Then?"

"Ramòn's arranged for some very important people to see my paintings in Europe."

"What people?"

"Very good people."

"What has he done for the Inca Princess?"

"We no longer need him for that," she said slyly.

"You've bought the mine, is that it?"

"We close in January."

"Maybe you can strike the same consulting deal with

Brulée that your father had."

"Ramon has influence."

"And I don't."

"Maxwell, you can't ask me to choose. I choose both. Each of you attracts me in different ways."

"That's not good enough. You can't be friends with a man who claims to be your fiancé."

Her eyes grew opaque, "Darling Maxwell," she pressed herself against me. "After Danse du Sang is finished, let's travel in Europe. Vienna mornings, Paris nights. My friend Sunny Landeau married a prince, we can stay in Sintra, in their castle. It was built for kings. Fadoistas serenading in the courtyard, sunbathing in a private garden. Darling, let our affair begin. We've had our starts, but join me in Europe where we belong."

Her words stirred me, not so much with desire for Susie, right there in front of me but—I think now, almost cynically—with a false, pastoral image of Rider in Europe.

I moved her toward the white stone steps leading to the tower and Alex's Moorish bedroom.

Brulée burst in, fuming, "There you are!" Instinctively, I moved in front of Susie. But she stepped out to meet Brulée and turned quickly to me, putting her hand to her mouth to form an assignation: one o'clock, here, then she smiled at Brulée. "Let's mingle," she said.

I glimpsed Alex on the terrace. "This is a good time to meet Trujillo," I said.

Alex glanced around, "Oh, I think I saw him talking to Gina Paloma, that's a good sign."

I surveyed the room myself but the crowd was so thick Gina was hidden from me. I couldn't even locate Susie.

Christian joined me with a girl no more than 16 years old. She wore an air of startled fascination, and cherry red pumps that could have been her mother's. A precious little-girl quality inspired Christian to show off for her. He leapt lightly onto the narrow capstone that ringed the terrace eighty feet above the stone motor-court.

The guests crowded in to watch. It was astounding, and spellbinding. His Austrian good looks and dauntless grace expressed itself in a kind of vitality. After he teetered the whole length of the railing, he bowed deeply and jumped down, whereupon a spontaneous applause broke out.

I remained on the terrace with a stony-eyed butler delivering iced vodka in silver cups, and the dark quilt of Hollywood below, uncertain what our campaign—as Alex referred to launch of Danse du Sang—would produce.

Φ

Shortly before midnight we were gathered into the garden. This was not instantly accomplished. Alex employed two muscle-bound dunces, major domo à deux. Harry and Phil were a pair of guileless bookends whose intimidation derived solely from density. Within half an hour, they'd herded everyone onto the back lawn.

"Dearest Gina and dear guests," Alex began under the moonlight, "I would like to say thank you to all who attend this momentous event, this triumphant ending to the long saga of Danse du Sang that began in Rome with my selection of Ingmar Bergman's cinematographer and a charming starlet from the poor countryside of Calabria, our darling Gina Paloma.

"Realistically, the saga began centuries ago when my grandfathers—and grandmothers—bestowed their services on the rulers of Europe, which brought them rewards of land and nobility, allowing my family to avoid the humiliating exercise of scrabbling for money, and encouraging their cultivation in Art, Philosophy, and the higher disciplines of Civilization. All of which predicted my success in Rome, and impelled me to this Mexican market town of Los Angeles that, for me, has become a Mecca of film, an Athens of the twentieth century. And swept our beautiful Gina Paloma, our darling, to universal admiration and acclaim, all from her charming beginning in Danse du Sang."

Alex paused to accept a glass of champagne. "The journey of Danse du Sang to this historic moment in Hollywood was not without affliction. I leave to my good friend Maxwell Rider the toilsome task of explaining the freezing abyss in which we found ourselves during darkest moments of this enterprise. I am delighted to say only that I have triumphed over that infirm genie called Fate and," he paused again to beam in Gina's direction, "would not have done so without the lovely apparition of Gina Paloma."

I had my doubts that Gina was enjoying Alex's tribute.

"Fortune smiles to welcome among my guests the buyer of Danse du Sang, who will guide my vision to a fantastic commercial success in the United States and worldwide, envisioned by me even as I suffered the perversities of creativity in Rome."

Alex squinted into the throng of guests, packed among ice swans and candelabra, while I scanned every face for Trujillo.

"Ah," Alex spoke, "we will respect his wish for discretion!

"Tomorrow, I film the final scene of Danse du Sang, depicting the random brutality of Fate in an original and compelling way. My friend Christian Ruhl will meet the rigorous demands of the role, a poor drifter destroyed by Fate's cruel spontaneity. And," Alex smiled irresistibly, "this is something I can only confess publicly, I am still writing the final scene!"

One of Alex's dunces, Harry or Phil, wrestled a spotlight onto Christian, whose lifted brow and unsmiling lips reflected my own growing skepticism.

There exist in the film lore of Hollywood mythical stories of directors writing a script on the very day of shooting, or even shooting sans script. But they are, as I say, only stories, embellished after the film's success. I've known very few projects to benefit from chaotic rewriting on the set—I would not have predicted Danse du Sang to be one of them.

Alex frowned at Phil, or Harry, who refilled his champagne, "I want now to end by toasting my friend Maxwell Rider, without whose stoic generosity Danse du Sang would have languished like an aging coquette." Here, Gina's eyes blackened into stones.

"I delight you now with the marketing trailer of Danse du Sang!"

With that, the candles were extinguished, the screen illuminated with our brief montage of scenes from Danse du Sang.

Φ

Alex's vision was enchanting: Lovely Gina in an ancient square swilling Campari among surly Italian youths, a Catholic priest glowering comically in the background.

The editor I hired had won an Oscar for "Jaws." I had learned a lesson from the painful screenings I'd attended, and the trailer sparkled from the editor's skill. She had transformed an incoherent art film into a polished continental farce, rich with exquisite out-takes of Tuscany's countryside.

The bullfight scene was breathless, cutting back and forth between Gina in the stands, a single button detaining her effusive breasts—and the flashing cape in the bull ring. As a portrayal of passion it was brilliant. Close-ups of Gina's luminous skin and swollen lips were rapidly intercut with the beast's foaming nostrils. Jerky shots from cameras unwisely mounted on the bull's trunk enhanced a sense of impending climax.

Audience murmurs confirmed its effect. Even as I submitted to its spell, I became aware of a low rumbling in the crowd, a discreet rustling of elbows.

"He's biting her throat."

"What are they doing? I can't see."

"Oh, my God."

Like slow ripples forming into swells, heads turned to a point ten degrees from the screen. Gina and a dark young man, Marina's matador, struggled erotically on the fringe of the audience. Her head was thrown back, exposing her throat and one breast, released of its torn netting. The matador's oiled hair swept across Gina's upper body like marsh grass as he dove at her chest.

From the screen to the scene off-side, Alex's guests were driven to whip their heads from front to shoulder to catch the nuances of each performance. No less ravishing in person than her younger self, Gina demonstrated considerably more appetite.

I pushed my way to the lovers. "Why don't you go to Alex's rooms?" But they were beyond noticing me. The only dignity I could salvage was Marina's, who stood stiffly near, her fragile hand trembling with its cigarette. "Champagne?" I asked.

When the lights went on again, I stashed Marina with

Countess and set off to meet Susie, briefly pausing to interrogate Alex on the subject of his guest of honor, Trujillo.

Alex affected puzzlement. "I remember distinctly inviting him at lunch. And he said he might come. I explained we would be previewing the film and unveiling a marketing campaign. Bad luck he was tied up." He glanced around absently. "This party's rather an expensive act to encore."

I was furious with Alex. And with myself, for not personally assuring Trujillo's attendance. "Call him up immediately," I said. "Get him over here—we'll screen it again if we need to."

"That's it," Alex agreed. "I'll ring him up immediately. There's no reason he can't come by. And if he's unavailable, he can come tomorrow for the final scene. I have fabulous plans for it. It's going to be so realistic. Nothing like it has ever been done. In fact, I'm inviting you, Max. You must come."

"I have to attend anyway, Alex. Thanks to you, my deal with the federal prosecutors requires me to supervise the set as executive producer."

"Well, that's settled. I'll call Trujillo immediately."

I detached myself from Alex in disgust. It was minutes before one. I pushed through the crowd to the vestibule where Susie and I had met earlier in the night, and mounted the stone stairs that led to the tower. Through openings along the stair, I could see the courtyard below, with the valets running back and forth to fetch the cars against the distant lights of Hollywood.

Alex had transformed the tower room into a romantic retreat. A 17th century Spanish bed dominated its center with carved pillars of dark mahogany and white linen canopy. Elevated with an over-filled down mattress, the bed offered commanding views through casement windows in the turret wall.

The moonlight scattered magic upon the scene. Like an Ingres painting, I imagined Susie, her hair spread against the pillows and her skin tawny against the sheets. But she wasn't there. I waited restlessly. At one-thirty, I returned to the party. It had thinned out. I looked around for Susie, without success. A crowd had gathered in the parking court. I saw Brulée waiting for his car, and decided to join him.

The tiny lift was packed, its pulleys wheezing under the strain of departing guests. I descended eight floors by foot until I reached the plank door, made my way to the parking court and the night air.

"You are children, playing at business." I heard Brulée's sneering voice, and caught Susie and Winton fixed in his fierce glare.

"I don't give money to buy love, my dear." He twisted his huge head toward Susie. "I will buy your interest in the mine and I will control the mine. But I do not pay rich children to play at business."

Winton drew his shoulders back. I could see he was beside himself with emotion, but his words, and his speech, were like something out of a bad English play.

"This is an outrage!" he said, "You insult our friendship, you betray my sister's affections. The Inca Princess is our destiny. You will not have it!"

Brulée drew me toward them with angry words, "Here is the man who seduces my fiancée on the bare floor of a public art show."

"Lurking in the galleries, Ramòn?" I asked.

"I have the tape." He pronounced the hard syllable with a joyless tight-lipped smile. "Yes. I have the tape." Brulée skewed his hard mouth into a smirk, "Two times, two times to bring the lady her pleasure. You Americans are adolescent. Too eager, like dogs rushing to urinate."

"You're disgusting."

"Oh, yes. Sure. But I have the tape of it. And I study my rival."

"Buzz off, Brulée."

"No, no." He turned gleeful with fury and his toupée rose as if to snatch at the night air. "Fock you!"

"Come Susie, we leave now," Brulée turned toward the waiting Corniche, ghostly in the moonlight.

I swung at Brulée, caught his ear. His hairpiece lifted as in a sudden breeze, then pounced back down at a roguish tilt. He snapped his fingers in some command. Before I could launch another blow, Brulée's bodyguard twisted my arms and smashed me into the hood.

I heard the click of torn cartilage. My famous Gallic nose released an exquisite ribbon of scarlet on the pearl white car, coursing across the hood like brush strokes on a Pollock canvas. It beaded into garnet drops—testimony to a good hand-rubbed wax job at Galbraith's on Sunset.

I raised myself with great effort, checked my teeth. They were all there. My tuxedo shirt, French tucked, had a smear like strawberry jam. But I felt gratified.

Susie slipped her arm under my elbow, guided me to her own waiting limousine. "Spend the night with me, Maxwell," she said, smirking toward Brulée.

"I'll be back for the XKE," I said to the smiling valet, "take good care of it." I slipped him fifty bucks.

30.

Filming in Malibu

The following day we shot the last sequence of Danse du Sang. My throat felt dry, my head hurt. The membranes of my nose throbbed violently from a too-emphatic embrace of Brulée's Rolls Royce. Nine dainty stitches mended the tear along my nostril but ached as if fashioned from bailing wire. Despite this, I'd seen Susie off at dawn, TWA to Brussels. And I was not the better for it.

I've heard people rave that Malibu is like the Italian Riviera. Tiled roofs above the glistening surf and all that. It might appear that way in films. But that's illusion—most of LA's coastline is a jaundiced strip of tacky dwellings crammed together on skinny lots. Currents of treated sewage surge onto the sand from open drains with the flush of Santa Monica's toilets. It goes without saying you can't swim there—though an occasional tourist braves the risk of infection.

Just south of County Line, there's a long lick of sand that's secluded between canyon and sea, accessible only by foot and four-wheel drive. That's where Alex planned to shoot the film's final sequence.

The crew trucked out early. Crew, cameras and equipment caravanned north, passing more populated beaches with public access.

I arrived late, picked my way down a steep canyon from the road. Touch and go in deck shoes—a poor choice—30 vertical feet of snaggle-peak rock and spiny brush from the highway to the sea.

I found Alex in fine form, bristling with self-important

vitality. Christian Ruhl reposed uncomfortably on the sand while an assistant director's nervous fingers placed a giant stag's antler against his cheek, the barb of one tine resting upon his closed eyelid.

The events of that day remain scripted in my mind.

Φ

RIDER joins the film crew, sweat glistening along his temples. A bandage marks his nose, obvious casualty of a recent fracas, and there is a slightly bruised quality about his ego as well, the climb, the heat having enhanced his anxiety at being late. He addresses ALEX as if he has no expectation of being taken seriously.

RIDER
Where's MAKEUP? You're going to poke Christian's eye out with that thing.

ALEX, the DIRECTOR, ignores RIDER, adjusting placement of the sharp tines of the antler to rest on CHRISTIAN's eyelid.

RIDER
(Apprehensively)
What's the truck-crane doing here?

ALEX
(Accent: British public school)
It was in my dream last night.

RIDER

If your dream involves an action sequence, I'm getting a stunt actor.

ALEX
You must be serious, Max. Christian represented Austria in the `72 luge races. Of course we must have him. Authenticity is critical.

RIDER
I'm calling the Screen Actor's Guild to send over a stuntman.

ALEX
(waves a demonstrative arm at the
seclusion of their surroundings)
By all means, how will he join us—from the heavens?

CHRISTIAN rises, shakes off clinging sand with the graceful gestures of a young man.

CHRISTIAN
(pumps Rider's hand)

Rider, good to see you. A bit worse for wear I see—did you get the girl at least?

RIDER
(softened by this greeting, can't hide a boyish smile of victory)

Stuff it, Christian. I'm required to attend. I was lucky to get word of Alex's location change.

CHRISTIAN consults his wrist watch. He draws RIDER to one side.

CHRISTIAN
I'm missing a big day of limo tips, let's just get this scene wrapped. Don't worry about me—

(CHRISTIAN winks at RIDER)
If I can elude the angry dads of these charming girls who seduce me, ha! They want to spank me—naughty girls.
(The actor throws back his head, clearly
enjoying the memory of his seductions.)

Alex resumed filming what were to be the film's final images. The idea was to capture Christian, symbol of Truth, felled by cruel Fate. This would linger on the screen as final credits rolled. The difficult part was the montage of action-shots that preceded the final scene—the part where the stag's antler rappels toward Christian, striking his eye and blinding him. For that, we had dissected one of the stag's points and attached it to an invisible line.

Christian lay so still he seemed asleep, while Alex stirred over him, charged with ambition to master the scene. The strange yellow haze of the beach shut out all light like the inside of a helmet. The glare stung our eyes. At the same time, we had to use lamps to get the right effect. After twelve takes, I became frustrated and strolled away. Things went on in the same way for two hours more.

When Alex called a break, three assistants rushed Christian like pit mechanics at the Indy 500. The Assistant Director plunged a beach umbrella into the sand beside the toga-clad actor, raising him up and offering chilled juice from a thermos. The makeup woman mopped his face and chest, applied new body makeup and dusted Christian with powder. The man from wardrobe brushed sand from his toga, dried his sweating temples with a hairdryer.

I looked over to see Alex sketching furiously, a Leonardo da Vinci of filmmaking.

When the Assistant Director announced: "Ready Mr. des Prairies," Alex marched to the set and raised his hand dramatically. "Reload the cameras! We'll shoot in black and white."

At Alex's words, Ingmar Bergman's cinematographer moved slowly and dangerously from his camera, his eyes cold as an alpine frost. He turned on his heel—a difficult thing to carry off in the sand—and stumped down to the flat waves where he glared at the horizon as if he was planning to swim back to Stockholm.

I followed him.

"What am I doing here?" he asked. "This shabby beach in LA, with this—this madman. He demands close-ups. Soft focus. Gritty shots. Now black and white. I am gasping, dying in this desolate hole of Los Angeles."

"How long will it take you to reload?" I asked.

"How long? It will take a lifetime. It will take my spirit, my soul before he's through. That's all."

"There's an end to this, Gunnar," I said, wondering if it was the truth. "We have to wrap by tomorrow. This shoot will end today, I promise you."

The Scandinavian lowered his eyelids to half mast and turned—easier this time, the sand was wet. Then he stalked back to reload the cameras.

The day wore on. The dollars escalated like the heat rising from the sand. We couldn't pay the crew time and a half. But we had to pay for time on the set. Five hours. Six. That was before lunch.

I argued with Alex over technique. Safety. And argued overtime with the crew. I was assailed by malcontents. And dragged away repeatedly by the Assistant Director. Alex waved us away. He was completely focused on the two or three members of the crew essential to the shot, and oblivious to the others.

Grips, boom operators, camera technicians. I tried to avert a mutiny.

There was a girl on the set. Besides those among the crew, I mean. An actress, Sharmayne Lafont, whose nude arms and trunk had been cast for random shots of body parts floating among the final credits. Alex commanded that Sharmayne wear nothing but a robe so as to avoid the imprint of bra or panties on her skin. She was a constant presence on the beach, barefoot, impatient, a girl of twenty with the disgruntled temperament of a crone. I believe the grumbling began with her.

ACTRESS glances at her watch which flops loosely on her wrist. She's been on the set since dawn waiting for her scene. ACTRESS glowers at RIDER, then flounces over to ASSISTANT DIRECTOR and we feel the intensity of her reproach.

FIRST CAMERAMAN approaches RIDER.

We're leaving. We were told it would be a three-hour shoot. It's now going on seven hours. We've just been informed it's not a union shoot and we're not going to get our time and a half. (Indicates Sharmayne Lafont) Poor girl's been sitting in a robe since five a.m.

RIDER regards ACTRESS
This isn't a union situation, there's no money for overtime. This film was over budget before we started shooting today. If she's professional enough to stay, will you?

RIDER's guessed right. FIRST CAMERAMAN shrugs. His real interest is in the girl.

RIDER
I'll talk to her.

RIDER approaches ACTRESS in blue terrycloth robe; she's scuffing at the sand with a day-glo polished big toe.

ACTRESS
(sulky, Australian accent)
I've been on this bleeping set over six hours. No trailers. It's hot as the bleeping Outback out here.

RIDER
(calmly)
This is the industry, Miss Lafont. Who knows what your scene will lead to?

ACTRESS
Balls!

RIDER Think about Marilyn Monroe. How many scenes can you remember with Monroe in a robe? She's an icon. I'm sorry. There's no money for overtime. You must stay for your scene.

ACTRESS is unmoved, RIDER caught with inspiration, summons FIRST CAMERAMAN over to them.

RIDER
Can you take a couple shots of Miss— (RIDER smiles his most charming smile)
Hepburn—for her portfolio? She may as well have a memento—something to show Variety when they call—

ACTRESS
(grudgingly mollified, for now)
Give me a minute with Makeup. I could use a couple of new shots—hard-working actress on the set, all that.
(defiant)
A couple head shots too.

FIRST CAMERAMAN obliges, as RIDER signals MAKEUP GIRL to come over.

Disaster averted, I glanced over to where Alex was filming in black and white. He clasped the air in a victory clasp. It was a wrap. At last we could move on to the final principal shot. As he strolled over to gloat his satisfaction to me, I was aware of some commotion in the sand.

"Oh, God," the Assistant Director swore. "It's buried now. We've lost the goddamned antler point."

He hunkered down to fumble in the sand for the spear of the antler. "We've got to reattach the goddamned thing for the next shot. Oh, damn—all!"

I excused myself from Alex, strode to where the stag's horn reposed, rising from the beach like the skeleton of a giant crab. "Give me the damned thing!"

I seized the horn, turned it tines down and raked the sand firmly. After a frustrating few seconds, the fragment appeared and the Assistant Director bent down to lift the sand-encrusted tip victoriously.

Re-gluing the barb to the antler was another issue. Waiting for the adhesive to dry was the equivalent of desert torture. But the worst thing was, the adhesives we had didn't work. The tip kept falling off into the sand. Relentless raking, repeated recoveries. More glue.

I stalked over to one of the grips and snatched up his drill. I drilled a small hole in the blunt end of the antler and a small hole in the spear and joined them over a headless nail with airplane adhesive. I regarded the thing suspiciously for several minutes, but it held, and we called the lunch break before anything else could go wrong.

Our meal was anything but light-hearted. Alex's chef furnished the food, much of it left over from the party at Tower Hill. The meal should have been well received, but the grousing of the crew had grown ceaseless.

Christian moved about restlessly during the break. I think his insouciance was mere bravado. But he was none the worse for his sufferings as Truth. His skin glowed from a week in Aspen. And his energy was high. Half an hour before we resumed shooting, Christian tore off his toga, and charged into the sea. He splashed back and forth in the turgid waves, lifting his long legs high like a mustang in the surf.

"Rider, join me. It's fabulous!"

It was a measure of the crew's gloom that no one glanced up, or joined Christian galloping nude in the flat surf. "Ah, free at last!" he whooped joyfully.

The Assistant Director raised his palms in frustration,

"Jesus Christ! Makeup! You've got to do him all over again.".

Alex experimented with the technical aspects of the scene during lunch, while I kept my eye on things. We couldn't film the scene in a single take as Alex wanted. Neither Alex nor I had been to film school. But we were educated in the greats of film. Charles Chaplin, particularly, we admired. I strolled over to Alex with an inspiration.

"Ah—Chaplin," Alex replied to my suggestion. "Yes, I see. We could film the scene in reverse time."Alex was referring to Chaplin's famous scene where a building crumbles around him. I helped Christian to his feet, held the antler to his cheek then quickly drew it away. When the action was reversed, it would appear to be rappelling toward him.

"Yes. Yes. I see," Alex said again and I thought I had averted another costly delay.

While Alex was setting up after lunch, the Assistant Director detained me. It was the girl again. Sharmayne LaFont. The same issues we'd been over before. She meant to talk to her agent as soon as she got back to civilization. And file a claim with the Screen Actor's Guild. It was hazardous out here, no medics available, the heat, lack of shade—a production out of control.

I shared her concerns, silently. But she was all bluster. I knew she hadn't enough speaking credits to qualify for SAG membership. I listened politely.

After lunch the wind had come up. The stag's horn was attached by wench to a guy line at the end of the boom fastened to a truck-crane Alex had hauled to the beach. The boom formed a forty-five degree-angle to the sand. The figure of Christian, arms stretched to the sky, created the third side of a triangle.

It seemed to work well with the truck twelve feet or so

from Christian. But Alex saw the cable in the shot. A thinner wire was rigged. Then Alex saw too much of the boom in the shot.

The sounds of the crew and silence between takes informed me of the progress of the scene, and I glanced up when I heard the truck Alex had rented move closer to Christian.

The truck stopped on a shelf of hard beach. The sunlight glinted off the metal wench which Alex had rigged to propel the antler downward whereupon Christian would fake a fall. And then I saw it. Alex had placed weights at the top of the guy wire.

Ten pounds inside to slow the swing.

I was suddenly aware of our solitary effort on the empty beach, imprisoned by the steep cliff on one side, the laconic tide on the other. At the first crunch of wet sand giving way, it crossed my mind that something very bad was going to happen.

The fragile shelf of beach beneath the crane started to shift. Alex's head whipped up from its position behind the viewer. "Stop! Stop the boom!"

I watched the sand give way and the crane lurch forward. Christian arched backward, his arms raised, the boom descending upon him like a giant praying mantis. I lunged toward Christian and, too late, fell kneeling in the sand. With the crisp whip-crack of sound, the stag's points spiraled downward as if flung by demons. Swept forward in the sudden velocity of the wind, the boom of the crane crashed down upon Christian. And I knew then everything had changed.

FADE OUT.

31

Christian at St. John's

I remember the rest of that day, and the night, and the next day, only as an endless drill of doctors, nurses, photographers and news journalists.

That evening I waited at St. John's Hospital in Santa Monica while procedures were implemented to save Christian's sight. I concealed it from the cameraman and boom operator who waited with me, but I was beside myself with anxiety.

Around two a.m. the doctor emerged and I approached her expectantly.

"A blood clot has lodged in the brain," she said. "We've put him on the respirator."

"Can I talk to him?" I asked.

She looked at me as if in sympathy for my flawed intelligence. "He's in a coma."

I summoned what I knew of medical argot. "What's the prognosis?"

The doctor met my eyes, "He'll recover spontaneously, or he'll decline." She didn't know how, when, or whether, he would come out of it. A trauma like that was very serious. In Christian's case, it had created an embolism in the brain.

"What can be done?" I asked.

She smiled a ghost smile. "There's an experimental procedure—we call it experimental even though it's been done since the 1960s." She reflected, "Your friend's German?"

"Austrian. The procedure?"

She described the gamma-knife process, a treatment developed at the University of Geneva. Despite my anxiety

I was intrigued by her description. The physicist plots the location of the embolism, then puts the patient in a helmet with tiny holes through which the surgeon blasts the site with gamma rays. The beams dispel the clot, which dissolves into the body.

"It's not approved yet in this country. And," she glanced toward Christian's room, "it must be performed within the next ten days. After that the chances of success diminish radically."

"Arrange it immediately," I said.

"It's very expensive—only four such procedures were performed last year." She answered my silent query. "The last one came in around $400,000."

The figure set me back. I had no idea how quickly the film's insurance carrier could issue a check. "Thank you," I said, with bleak grace.

It was midnight when I tried to reach Alex at Tower Hill. There was no answer. I stole once more into Christian's room. He lay covered in white sheets and bed clothes, a fretful knitting of his brows on his bronze face. His toga hung in an open closet by the door, and the sight of it impressed me with the urgency of things in a way the doctor's cold terminology had not.

It was already the next day in Europe, and when I returned to my apartment I placed a call to Geneva. I spoke in tourist French to the surgeon in charge. Yes, he had performed the process. No, they wouldn't bring the equipment here. No, it couldn't be arranged on credit, they required proof of payment before they would begin. And it should be scheduled immediately. The power of his resistance drained me. I hung up, and flung myself into a fretful sleep. I didn't waken until noon the next day.

32

Alex on the Italian Riviera

I was questioned by the Santa Monica police several times after the accident. They were friendly examinations, as to my identity, my observations and so forth. At the first of these, as I waited upon Christian at the hospital, not much interest in me was asserted. They focused on Alex. Where did he live? Was he an American citizen? If not, had he a visa? However, the next day I was brought before a deputy district attorney for a written statement and I felt she eyed me with distinct curiosity.

She inquired if I had chosen a lawyer to advise me. I answered no, I hadn't thought of it and asked her if I needed one.

"Haven't you considered your position?" she said.

I replied that I regarded the case as very simple. As an officer of Filmland Credit I was on the set to see that the filming proceeded efficiently. Surely, bank officers were not accountable without some evidence of active negligence.

She smiled. "Well, it may seem that way to you. But you're the Executive Producer. The title alone conveys responsibility. And it appears the director, Mr. des Prairies, has fled our jurisdiction."

I didn't believe her on the last point. Alex could be difficult to reach. But he would not leave Tower Hill. And about the rest I was too concerned for Christian to take her quite seriously.

The room in which she interviewed me was like the interrogation room of a TV soundstage. She was attractive, with the strong calves of a dancer, and I fancifully imagined her, age eight, pirouetting with a scowl of concentration. Upon leaving, I very nearly offered my hand. Just in time I realized she'd said "criminal negligence. "

The perceptions of the District Attorney seemed remote and inessential. I found myself on Christian's side and alone. From the moment I telephoned news of the catastrophe to his family in Salzburg, every practical question was referred to me. At first I was surprised; then as he lay in his bed and didn't move or speak, hour upon hour, I felt as if it was my spirit lying there helpless. It grew upon me that I was in charge of Christian's destiny, because no one else conceded responsibility.

After leaving the DA's office downtown, I drove to the news stand in lower Westwood. From the headlines, it was clear the trades were already hustling the story, "Actor in Coma After Dance with Danse."

It made good copy. The writer plunged straight into speculation whether Christian's injuries would stall the picture's release date. Likewise, they fretted over the impact on industry standards for location shooting—based on the paramedics' delay before Christian was lifted from the set.

"Medical standby, if required on location shooting, would add several points to below-the-line costs. 'Financial concerns cannot be weighed against the value of an actor's life,' Reiger Dan, President of the Screen Actors Guild responded heatedly."

Variety's headline screamed:
"SAG URGES SUIT FOR SORDID SNAFU."
I called Ms. Vaughn from the phone booth in the lobby.

"I may need a criminal lawyer," I began. "The Santa Monica Police have questioned me. They're considering filing charges."

"I can't advise you, Rider. But you're in serious trouble. The Screen Actors Guild has the clout to press charges on behalf of its members."

"But Alex is the director, isn't he responsible?"

"If you're lucky, a judge might think so."

She broke my silence, "You have no litigation experience, have you?"

"You know how it is," I replied, "first years out of law school with a big firm. I was a glorified clerk, with a salary too small to get rich, and too large to quit."

"Let me give you some advice on criminal law," she said, "They'll indict you. Politically, they can't afford not to. This is Hollywood, after all, and the film business is a highly visible industry. Options? Get the best industry insider you can to represent you. Bertram Fields, Greg Bautzer. And put together as much money as you can to compensate the actor. Then, pray to God, Buddha, or Swami Sivananda, that Christian Ruhl is up and walking in six months when your case goes to trial."

I was shaken by her remarks, and the limited choices available to me. When I spoke to thank her, a change had taken place, not only in my spirit but in my voice.

"Good luck." She sounded almost wistful. I realized she meant it. The phone clicked its disconnect.

I telephoned Alex's haunts and houses. The Carlyle in New York. His apartment in Brussels. James Goldsmith's villa in Careyes—"Who? Don't know the fellow." The rich, the really rich, form an intimate circle. And when ranks close they do so neatly. I'd known that. It's almost a platitude. But the experience of being shut out by Alex's friends revived in me an ancient wound.

The following day I drove to Tower Hill. The wind was up and there was silence. A single automobile was in the parking court, its trunk lifted and crammed with luxuries from Alex's pantry. The entry had been left ajar and I ran up eight flights of stairs to the kitchen where I caught the chef and his wife the maid, packing their bags with Alex's food. Their new Pacer, a kind of flying wedge, was stuffed with cases of caviar, tins of truffles, canned pâté, hams from Denmark.

"Where's Alex?" I asked.

"I don't know but he owes me six weeks pay."

I was about to challenge the man as to five cases of Alex's wine, when the wheezing of the lift announced another visitor.

"Who's that?" I asked. But the couple had fled down the stairs—without the Mouton-Rothschilds.

A red-faced Englishman blustered into the room, fastened his watery gaze on me.

"I'll take charge of the wine," he said, eyeing me suspiciously.

"Who are you?"

He proffered a card. Sotheby's Estate Auctioneers, New York. Alex had consigned the whole of Tower Hill to Sotheby's for sale.

The agent glanced around in a proprietary way, "Looks like you've done an excellent job of packing up. Thanks."

I showed him through the house—not so much to be helpful as to check out such clues as might exist to Alex's whereabouts.

I looked at the exquisite things in the empty rooms. My thoughts returned to the party and Christian's tight-rope act along the balcony railing.

I paused before the pearwood secretary in the study. The draft of a letter in Alex's handwriting lay on the leather blotter. Under the agent's beady gaze, I managed to conceal the letter while he examined Alex's 17th century Castilian bed. Clumsily, I folded the gray airmail bond with one hand, and slipped it into my pocket for later study.

At the motor court the Sotheby's man installed a heavy chain across the blue door and a metal box over the lock. "I'll arrange a twenty-four-hour guard," he said. "Don't concern yourself about it."

"Oh," I said casually. "We've some royalties to forward to Count des Prairies. May I ask the address and telephone number you have for him?"

He studied the inventory on his clipboard. "Villa Teresino, Rapallo, Italy. Here's the telephone number." And he reeled off a number on the Italian Riviera.

Φ

For months, Mona and Lainie had hovered on the periphery of my life like spirits while I pursued the business of Filmland. It shouldn't have been that way. For when it came down to it, I had no one else.

Mona reacted strongly when I told her about Christian. She didn't break down, but tears came into her eyes. And the tears through her pale lashes made her look beautiful. She didn't know Christian. I'd never introduced her to my friends. But I told her Christian's story and she felt sad.

"You've got to help him, Maxwell."

I was trying. But I'd received no word from the film's liability company. And Christian's family was titled, but broke.

They owned a castle, some jewels, and cars. Nothing liquid.

"What about Alex?" she asked. So I related the story of Sotheby's, the guard, the chain, the chef.

"There must be some way to get the money," she said.

At midnight I called Villa Teresino near Rapallo. It was ten o'clock in the morning in Italy. I asked for Alex. And I was surprised when Gina Paloma identified herself.

"Don't you want to speak to me? I thought you admired me—it seemed so in LA." Her Gernreich gown with its torn netting came floating back to me.

"Let me speak to Alex," I said.

"It hurts me to speak English. Can't you speak Italian?"

"I can but I won't. I need to speak to him. It's urgent."

"You're being so tiresome. You have no gallantry. Where women are concerned, you Americans are only romantic about your Westerns. In fact, you know, Paramount is putting me in a Western. I will wear rawhide, with fringes, and look very beautiful. And they have even given me my own Stetson and my own horse. I suppose I am to be a Western star, an Amy Oakley."

"Annie Oakley," I said. "That suits you, but may I speak with Alex?" I grew impatient with her flirtation as I thought of Christian and the embolus lurking in his brain.

Her voice grew sharp, the aural equivalent of stamping her foot. "Why do you speak so rudely to me?" Just then Alex came on the line.

"Is it you Max? What a good surprise! Are you calling from the States?"

"Alex, things are bad. It's a debacle. Christian is near death, and we need $400,000 for surgery. I can't get hold of any cash at Filmland—especially at Filmland. When are you coming back?"

"Impossible. I can't be involved. I saw a lawyer before I left the States. He told me to drive immediately to the airport. I left my Bentley at LAX—perhaps you could recover it?" he added wistfully.

"Alex, you have to come back. They propose to charge me criminally."

"What? Americans. You use the law as a crucible to convert the heretic."

I interrupted him. "I don't have time for philosophy. Who insured the beach scene? Film Guarantee hasn't returned my calls. I need cash immediately for Christian's treatment."

"Well, you know, Max, it's terribly difficult actually. Not the most fortunate news. I simply let the insurance fall away."

"You let the policy lapse?"

"Yes. It fell away. And I placed the money in another investment."

"Where did the money go?"

"I—I, really can't say," he said sadly. "It is not something I fastened my eyes on."

"Let me guess. You invested in the Inca Princess?"

"Not the most fortunate choice I'm afraid. But if it's any help, you can have my position."

"I can't forgive this," I said, determined to speak for Christian. "You've not even asked about Christian's condition. But I'll tell you—it's very serious. He's in a coma. If he's not able to pay for an experimental technique in Geneva, he will remain in a coma, he may die."

"Oh, that is terrible, Max. That is awful news."

"But the millions we lent you. Where did the money go?"

"You're the best one to help Christian, Max. What can I do? I'm pulled up short," he had lowered his voice, apparently to conceal his words from Gina. "I have nothing. You have no idea how I regret this tangle of worms."

I did too. But I cut him off by putting down the phone.

Φ

I think it was on the third day that the manager of the Chateau Marmont called me out of the blue. I was surprised he even knew my name, despite the many times I'd called for Alex there.

"I'm sorry to bother you," he said, with diffidence. He understood that Count des Prairies had left the country. There had been, before the Count's move to Tower Hill, a dispute over the bill. It seemed the Chateau Marmont was holding some personal belongings which they hoped Alex would redeem by payment of his account.

"What sort of things?"

"Clothing, riding boots, rather expensive luggage, framed photos, a silver-handled shaving brush and, oh, yes, some shares of stock which he placed in the vault."

"Shares of stock?"

"Yes," the manager said. While Alex was in the country, the hotel staff felt they had—well—his consent to store these things pending the outcome of the dispute. But, being as he was—well—gone, they wanted my guidance; they understood I was—a lawyer. And, well, it came down to this: what should they do with Alex's things and—the manager paused for emphasis—they would be glad to turn them over to me for payment on the account.

"What's the name on the shares?" I asked.

"I beg your pardon?"

"Please identify the shares of stock."

"Oh, yes, I'm looking at them now. All the shares bear the

same company name."

"Yes?"

"Ahem. Ten thousand shares, apparently."

"Yes?"

"The Inca Princess Mining Corporation."

"And what is the amount of Mr. des Prairie's bill?"

"Well it is—$30,000."

"Thirty thousand dollars? How long did he stay with you?"

"This only represents the last three months. The Count was a very demanding guest."

"What do you mean?"

"We stocked his own reserve. And we employed a part-time chef for the Count's exclusive use. There are several singular charges. The bill is completely itemized, if you'd like to see it."

"If I'm able to arrange payment I'm sure you'd accept a discounted figure."

"That's impossible, Mr. Rider."

I allowed a long uncomfortable pause. "I'll see what I can do."

The manager sounded uncertain. "We will store these items until we hear from you."

"Of course."

"When can we expect—"

"I don't know that you can," I said.

33

Mona at Patisserie

My arrest this time was a simple affair. Without ceremony. No one would think I'd be prosecuted criminally. But sometimes events take us farther than anyone could anticipate. They asked me to come down to the police department in Santa Monica. And they informed me, quite casually there, that I was under arrest.

"I had nothing to do with the decisions," I said, though it sounded lame, even as I said it. "It was out of my control."

"You're not helping yourself, Rider," the male officer said. He'd looked me up and down when I arrived. I felt conspicuous, and I'd quickly come to regret my French cuffs and Gucci loafers. The assistant district attorney just smiled a smile that seemed pathological. She read the complaint:

Count one: Failure to adequately supervise stunts and special effects. Count two: Failure to maintain medical assistance on the set or within reasonable proximity to the set. Count three: Failure to operate and use equipment in a reasonably safe manner. Count Four: Conspiring to act with negligent disregard for human life—

Ten felony counts in all. I found it ludicrous, a Kafkaesque joke. How could I have supervised Alex?

The effect of being charged with criminal negligence was further diluted by my concern for Christian. After I learned Alex had fled to Europe, I began to have a feeling of defiance, of scornful solidarity linking Christian and me against them all.

Following my tête à tête with the manager at the Chateau

Marmont, I'd been submerged in efforts to redeem the Inca Princess shares. I thought I could persuade Winton to buy them back—$400,000 was less than half the price Alex had given for them—and I instructed Christian's doctor to make arrangements with Geneva for the gamma-knife treatment.

I submitted to the reading of the charges and the taking down of my statement as if it were a play. I even corrected the spelling and grammar and edited the thing. I declined a criminal lawyer—I hadn't the money to spare for his retainer. All the time my attention drifted away from these proceedings to Christian, wondering how things could be the same again.

After two hours, I understood I was to be released into my own custody. I was about to stumble out of Santa Monica's mundane courthouse when the prosecutor's words stabbed through my dream state, "We reserve the right to amend the charges to— negligent homicide."

I had about four thousand dollars in my checking account. I could get another twenty-five for the Jaguar, if I advertised two weeks, and $15,000 immediately. But it came down to this: I was far short of the sum necessary to redeem Alex's Inca Princess stock.

On Saturday it poured. I drove to Santa Monica for my visit with Lainie. But it was Mona's comfort I required. I asked her to meet me at a café in Brentwood. I couldn't stand the close quarters of her bungalow.

I arrived first and chose a table by the paned windows. It was a dark day and the coral trees along San Vicente Boulevard sparkled with tiny lights reflected onto the panes.

The proprietors were French, and made a fuss over Lainie. Her Gallic-American precocity delighted them. They led her to the kitchen where a fat baker made cookie houses. Mona and I were alone.

Mona was dressed in a soft voile frock, gathered under her bust princess style. She wore a ribbon around her throat like a demure country girl.

She spoke first in suppressed excitement, "Maxwell, I've done something. You'll be glad."

I could not remove my eyes from her. For all her girlishness of dress and manner, Mona had matured in some attractive way. Her face was thinner, revealing the strong shape of her bones. And expression lines fanned softly from her eyes.

With hesitant joy she tendered a check for $250,000, drawn on the account of Sotheby's, New York.

"It's an advance on Alex's heirlooms. I phoned the curator handling the sale of Tower Hill. I explained that the antiques—the ones I'm storing for Alex—should be included in the auction. Well—he sent me a check!"

Mona leaned forward with her dancer's body. "This is ten percent of the auction floor they expect to get at the sale."

I was dumbfounded. My remarkable ex-wife had made a call, and achieved results.

"Mona," I began. I wanted to put things back together. "We're your family, Max," she had told me. I felt struck by the compelling simplicity of that idea. Mona, Lainie and me. I closed her strong dancer's hand in my own. I studied her, and with the instinct one has for loss, I sensed wariness in her.

Lainie came dancing into the room like a blonde dervish. Drunk with attention, she twirled furiously, glancing off pastry cases and a patron's legs. I realized how dexterous she was. As she twirled, she tumbled in her fingers a ginger-bread cookie, an iced dandy whose arms and legs tumbled round and round like a falling star. Approaching us, she picked up speed, and came to a bumping halt against our table, sending waves of cappuccino into our saucers. The impact of her arrival snapped the dandy's head off, and left him grinning foolishly from the table top.

Lainie wore a stricken look. Her mother smiled. "He's still laughing," Mona said.

The moment of our intimacy had passed. I dismissed the brief impression that Mona had moved away from me. There would be time to mend our relationship when Christian's recovery was assured.

Mona considered that she had "borrowed" Alex's proceeds to aid Christian. And there was an ethical logic to that approach. But I knew better. By accepting Sotheby's draft, I subjected myself to disbarment proceedings. Yet with the plenary allegations against me, what was one more?

As I left the café to reclaim my car, the twinkle-lights among the coral trees of San Vicente Boulevard seemed to be flashing my good luck. I would get Alex's Inca Princess shares from the Chateau Marmont, and wrangle Winton Grass into buying them back. I felt my fortunes had changed.

34.

Rider at the Chateau Marmont

I drove immediately from meeting Mona to the Chateau Marmont to get the stock. The Manager would be more likely to accept Sotheby's business check than my own. Less than a year had passed since I first met Alex at the hotel, although it seemed like decades. The sun and warmth I remembered from that time were as different from January's dark rain as Rome from Pittsburgh.

If you've tried to find the Chateau Marmont, you know that billboards as large as cruise ships conceal the slender thread of driveway and shabby crest on its iron post. Old, quaint, forgotten. That's the impression I felt when I pulled off Sunset Boulevard that chill day to pay Alex's debt and redeem his shares in Suzy's gold mine.

I entered the lobby from the stairs. The year had not been kind to the Marmont. Or perhaps I had changed. With its high gothic windows, an air of gloom prevailed.

The pea-headed man was still at the desk. This time he was occupied with a pimpled skinhead bleating in Cockney English, "Say, mon, we're here for a gig—we got to practice, haven't we? Ya don't get it, d'ya mon?"

He turned to engage me in the dispute. "Tryin' to pitch us out!"

I stood to one side, impatient for the concierge's attention, and looked for some resemblance to the man I spoke to on the phone. But there was clearly none. I regarded hopefully a door behind him which could have been a small office, but it was firmly closed. I began to think I recognized the pimpled musician from large posters outside The Troubadour, a club on Sunset. An actor's voice asserted itself from the tiny lounge around the corner from the desk, "Quiet! Bloody limey. I'm studying a script!"

I glanced involuntarily at the public phone in its dark cubicle across the room from the desk, and considered the first time I had come there to meet Alex. My car took fire, Alex had announced then, and I thought remarkable his casual dispatch of the useless vehicle. I reflected on the dazzling but failed party at Tower Hill, his chaotic filming on the beach, which brought me again to Christian, and the urgency of my errand.

Alex had not changed. But I had. The magical illumination I'd imparted to this hotel, and our acquaintance, had dimmed. Its wattage had ebbed rapidly it seemed, until the candle was extinguished by Christian's tragedy.

The elevator pulleys made a haunted sound like a wind-flute and I turned, half expecting to see Alex stride toward me, hand outstretched to clasp me into his exotic world.

Instead a young woman of sly and self-possessed affect approached, dressed in the crisp white shirt, dark trousers and vest of the hotel chauffeur.

"Damon," I said, barely recognizing Susie's prurient driver.

"Need a lift?" she asked provocatively.

It seemed preposterous to be addressing a girl I'd imagined as a man. And my thoughts kept returning to the drab uniform she used to wear, and the dissolute hairs marking her upper lip.

"You used to have a moustache," I said tactlessly.

"Steroids."

I could still see faint dark hair along her upper lip and in the hollow forming her chin. I inquired why she'd not gone abroad with Susie and what she was doing at the hotel.

Damon regarded me shrewdly. "Susie's not coming back.

I work here now." She collapsed against the pillar in a bored fashion, biting her cuticle.

Susie's not coming back. I strolled outside, paused on the steps of the hotel. Rain slicked off the roof tiles into gutters, and plopped in noisy puddles at my feet. The trees of the lawn formed dark sodden shapes, while beyond the hotel on Sunset Boulevard the sun broke through with the gaping grin of an ancient crone. With its palm trees and billboards—hawking sex, films and Bruce Springsteen—I could almost taste, again, the fragrant promise of LA.

I stepped back inside reluctantly. The pea-headed man stopped talking, turned away. But the skin-head musician turned up the volume on his raucous twang. "Ya' can't throw us out. Would ya'? Would ya'? Ar take it then!"

He flung his room key at the clerk's back and stormed toward the door, signaling to Damon. Damon peeled herself from her post and offered me a small stub-nailed wave and a last lascivious smile.

As I strode to the desk where the clerk had retreated into chilly hauteur, the lobby phone rang abruptly, insistently. Like an urgent call to arms, it served to remind me: my time to help Christian was running out.

35

Winton and Rider at the Inca Princess

The transaction at the Chateau Marmont consumed forty minutes. After a round of intellectual bullying I signed over Mona's check, received the balance in bank notes, and left the hotel with a sheaf of stock certificates titled Inca Princess Mining Corporation. Then, having palmed off the Jaguar on Bunker Dodge for cash, I steered Irving's bucking Caddy toward Bakersfield and the Inca princess gold mine. I arranged to meet Winton there, though I hadn't told him yet of the opportunity I planned to offer him.

Two and a half hours east of Bakersfield, the land reverts to vast desert. The road is dry and desolate. No cars. No other sounds. Only the click of tumbleweeds along the naked dirt. I had the map, souvenir of Alex's and my adventures. And I recalled our trip that day in February, long ago, when we were friends.

The guard kiosk was empty this time. The road to the mine, deserted. It was Tuesday. And I assumed the yard would be a bustling hub of mine activity. Instead, the weathered structures were boarded up like the stage set of a western town. A lone dusty black Cherokee was parked outside the shack that appeared to be the office.

I walked in on Winton Grass and was immediately struck by the incongruity. Grass had risen at the sound of my entrance, still wearing his yacht club blazer and white bucks among the dust and desolation.

"What's up, Winton?" I greeted him.

"Oh—it's you."

"I've got Alex's shares," I said. "I thought I'd give you and Susie a chance to buy them back."

"I say, Rider," he said with that British affectation of his. For a young man, he moved stiffly, with an affected dignity like Laurence Olivier in King Lear.

"That's terribly decent of you after all that's happened." He had a crazy glint that belied the old school tie persona. I had to keep reminding myself he was an American.

Winton stopped before a Biedermeier bar, incongruously placed in this desert shed, and poured two scotches into crystal tumblers.

"Sorry," he said, holding up a bottle of Glenfiddich, "It's all we have out here in our little—outpost."

I wasn't a scotch drinker but my curiosity was aroused by this theatrical gesture. I accepted the tumbler, "Cheers, then," I offered, tossing it back.

Still holding the scotch, Grass moved close to me. Too close, his pale fanatical eyes five or so inches from mine.

"It doesn't matter a damn what you do about the stock," he said. "There's no gold."

I remember the moment for its silence. A far-off buzzing in the desert—dune buggy or roadrunner, creature or machine—only served to intensify the soundlessness. The faucet in the bar started a slow drip that cast a kind of hopelessness over the place, over us.

I stared at Grass, not knowing what to say. He looked like a madman. Outrageous and weak.

Winton slumped suddenly and I saw how narrow his shoulders were. He lowered himself into his chair and placed his head on the support of his hand. "I don't know how it could have come to this.

"We were never taught to ask for money, it was something

unclean. I remember First Communion. My grandmother gave us each an envelope, embossed with her initials and sealed with a wax cross. 'Open it privately,' she said. We already knew—money was a dirty thing. All the money, you know—it came from my grandfather. My father never made a penny. We lived on my grandfather's wealth. And now, it's gone."

Winton passed an elegant hand through the pale forest of his hair. "I never even asked to see the production records."

Susie and Winton had immersed themselves in the heroic struggle. They'd dreamed of vindication, and never focused on the realities. That fool Ridgely. Their so-called expert had merely interviewed Winton's father. There were no pan samples. No producing strains. No Placer ore.

"You have won control of the mine, haven't you?" I asked.

"Oh, yes. Rider. We've won. Susie and I. We've won the mine."

Winton raised his index finger dramatically. His voice rose in a strained and girlish castrato, "We've been deceived. There's no gold. And Brulée's pulled his contracts. We've been bilked by my father over a worthless mine."

"Winton," I said, after a pause. "How could you not carry out due diligence—how could you fail to conduct your own evaluation of the mine?"

He drew himself up ridiculously, smiling a tight, false little smile, "We were educated at Oxford, Rider, not Harvard. We understand perfectly the theoretical."

His dramatic tone made it all the more incredible. I couldn't take it in, the scotch, the desert, his yachting outfit. No gold.

The news numbed me. I sank back onto a desk as Winton's incoherent rantings swept over me. I couldn't help Christian. Couldn't buy my freedom with great good deeds.

My legal mind raced through other consequences as well. Filmland's partnerships. We'd sold them on the strength of gold collateral. Our prospectus described the plan with an auditor's detail. Only there was no gold bullion. So that was fraud. Securities violations and all the other white-collar criminal acts I'd studied at Yale. People go to jail for that.

There was something else. I wouldn't be hearing from Susie. Filmland's offering, tied to the Inca Princess, implied complicity. A charge like that—conspiracy to violate securities laws of the United States—made a compelling reason to live abroad. Winton Grass and his sister would be sipping Glenlivet in first class, British Airways non-stop to London as soon as Winton recovered his senses.

I forced myself back into the present and the cramped headquarters of the Inca Princess mine. Winton began to rave against his father's "patri-fraud." He'd force his father to return the money and take the worthless mine back. Sure. But I wasn't listening. I broke away. With the tumbler still in my hand and the stock shares sticking to my palm from sweat, I lurched from the mine office.

Flinging the crystal tumbler in the sand, I slammed myself into Irving's unwieldy Cadillac convertible and gunned it. Shoved the stick far left of the steering column and spun the car backward along the road, unfurling columns of choking dust until I reached the highway. With a touch of power steering, Irving's Detroit dinosaur thrashed one hundred and eighty degrees, spitting sand from its rear wheels, and leaped forward through the desert toward LA.

Φ

By the time I reached St. John's Hospital, fairy lights

illuminated the oil rigs off Santa Monica bay, and a pretty nurse cautioned me I couldn't stay. Christian had not improved. He couldn't speak. Couldn't move. But I needed to share my panicked thoughts with someone.

When the nurse returned to the night desk, I slipped into the darkened room. Christian's appearance haunted me, his form a heap of clothes under a smooth blanket. He didn't stir. His eyes were closed. I stole closer and checked his pulse, laying the fine hairs of my wrist against his nostril. Thank God, he was still alive. But I imagined him speaking, and his protest assailed my harried brain, Rider, you have to get the money, you've got to try hard, man. I can't end up a cripple in America.

36

Countess at Il Giardino

All of Christian's friends were gone or on their way back to Europe, save one. The next day I set out to find Countess. I sought her first in the leaf-dappled sunshine at Port's, and prepared myself to see her there, writing in her black and white lesson book, with ditto-spotted Mister D gloomy and contented by her side.

Brown-eyed valets still swarmed the curb at Port's. And Ruben, the maitre d', still greeted me warmly. I explained I'd only come to look for someone. While we both knew it was Countess, Ruben led me formally to the garden patio to see for myself.

Tables were pleasantly set in white linen. Versailles urns flowed with blossoms like burnt tissue. Dark, elegant faces blew smoke from Gauloise cigarettes. And young women regarded me briefly, then shifted their legs with insolent grace. I felt it acutely: my summer had passed.

Waiters jostled by with trays of mussel soup. The plump green shells tipped the broth like seals in a foamy sea. An aromatic parmesan loaf recalled me to the first afternoons I spent in the company of Alex, languorous with rare wines and grand soliloquies. So you might say Port's hadn't changed. But for me, it had. And to cap it—I was almost relieved— Countess wasn't there.

There was another patio restaurant not far from the Melrose galleries. A new place which seemed old. It wasn't easy to find. Indeed, its only marker was a frail parking stand obscured by a gang of car rustlers.

Il Giardino was not a dining room at all, but a bucolic garden ruled by the surliest waiters in the Western world. Each one a Sicilian god unjustly burdened by the petty claims of the restaurant's customers.

There were more waiters than diners. They dominated the bar. And they swirled chaotically among the tables, like corralled mustangs, slapping plates of insalata pomodori, mozzarella di bufala, sharply under the chins of timorous diners. Or they glared, defiant, while delicate handmade raviolis carciofi hardened into rubber sponges under the chef's heat bar.

I'd been there with Alex a couple months before. His fierce, autocratic command of peasant Italian was the only means to bend the natives to our service. On that occasion, we watched a Milanese customer throw down his napkin at a waiter's feet, waving away the osso bucco with flamboyant gestures of indignation while the waiter spat Italian at him contemptuously.

"This dish is cold," the customer averred.

"Ridiculous."

"You say ridiculous. Enough. It is your job to bring the meal while it is hot, not loiter with your friends ridiculing the guests."

"I know my job. If you don't like the service, go away."

"What! Such insolence! Where is the owner?"

"He's off today. Anyway, he will take my side. He is my cousin."

And so on.

Curiously, this contretemps energized both sides. After ten minutes, the waiter retreated, bowing petulantly. The customer resumed his chair, giving his napkin a shake of satisfaction.

Alex shrugged off their rude behavior, "What do you expect? These waiters are from Naples."

In January 1980, Il Giardino was still popular, especially among movie people. By the time I found the place it was two o'clock. Countess sat alone at a distant table beneath a bougainvillea vine. My heart flew up to see her, grateful for synchronicity. Yet suddenly, I felt hesitant to approach her. She was my last resort.

Countess saw me and signaled with her gloved hand. Her dalmation Mister D rose uncertainly, slightly worried. He was a dog who needed constant reassurance. He seemed not to know he was huge and handsome, and well able to look after himself.

As I proceeded to her table, Countess flashed a bold smile. I saw the vaguest outline of brisk brown eyes through the large tortoise framed sunglasses she wore. Her yellow hair was braided back tightly from her delicate skull, her mouth outlined dramatically in the same cherry mauve color I associated with her. I was surprised to notice her youth for I had always considered her a contemporary of Alex. But then, at twenty-six, I felt myself an old man.

"Maxwell Rider," she said in her amused way. She half-stood to offer me quick kisses on alternating cheeks. "What brings you here?"

"I came to see you Countess," I said. "I need your help about Christian."

Her expression grew serious, and sad. She'd been to see him. And she'd spoken with his family in Salzburg. Christian's mother had divorced from his father when Christian was very young. She'd bargained to keep her married title but had released all rights to his father's money, except for a sum of $7 million settled upon Christian on his twenty-first birthday.

"What's become of that?" I asked, hoping to hear it was tied up in trust in London, Geneva or New York, where it could be borrowed upon.

Countess patted Mister D's noble brow. "Gone," she said. She turned her gaze to study the box hedges that lined the patio, and related the sad news. Christian, like Alex, had invested the last of his money—what he hadn't squandered on lifestyle—in the Inca Princess.

I waved the waiter over for an espresso with steamed milk. He loped off again, insulted that I had ordered in English. Mister D regarded us anxiously. There was no need to relate my visit to the mine. Countess seemed already to know it was hopeless.

"Damn Alex!" I said, after I'd scalded my tongue on the espresso. "Countess, what can I do?" I explained the sliver of hope I held out for the gamma-knife process.

"You own a bank, Maxwell," she said.

"No," I said, reflecting on the simplistic inaccuracy of that remark, "I'm the has-been director of a defunct thrift. There's no way for me to get money from Filmland now."

It seemed she'd known that too. Countess tore a blank sheet from her lesson book, careful to conceal from me the last page she'd been writing upon. Her script was flamboyant; she spelled out for me to see, Ramòn Brulée.

"Impossible," I said, touching my nostril gingerly. The reptile having slammed my nose into the bleak metal of his Corniche, I could hardly shuffle along to his club to importune him for almost half a million dollars. "Impossible," I said again.

"You must try," Countess replied, her eyes looking wise behind the tinted plastic. A fragile blossom drifted onto the table between us. Its color matched the careful outline of her lips.

"I will arrange a meeting with Ramòn," she said firmly. "You will save Christian, Max."

At that moment I wished I had her faith.

As I rose to leave Countess, Mister D rose too, frisked along the stones after me as though to see me out. When he was confident of my departure, he returned briskly to Countess. She raised her gloved hand in a small sign and I could hear her speak to the dog,

"It's alright Mister D, nothing bad happened."

37

Rider in Montecito

The Saturday after meeting Countess, I headed up the coast toward Santa Barbara. Brulée owned a ranch there. He was already starting practice for the Pacific Coast Open, the most prestigious of West Coast matches at the Polo and Racquet Club.

I disdained Irving's irascible Caddy in favor of a zippy 3.4-litre Jaguar sedan Countess loaned me for the trip. "Ramòn sends his driver for me," she explained, "I won't need my car this weekend."

I'd driven many fine cars by that time—my Jaguar XKE of course, my father's Jensen Interceptor, the bathtub Porsche of my roommate at Yale. But I never appreciated such refinement as that morning I drove Countess' little bullet-gray Mark II.

Japanese autos might have eclipsed others after 1971, but the Mark II Jaguar sedan, made throughout the 1960s, is the car that most resembles a prowling feline. The engine purrs like one too. It's known as a lady's car. But I admired it. Fastidious and spare, it stole neatly up the grade at Paradise Cove that day like a stealthy cat.

I renounced Brulée's offer of accommodation; checked into the Miramar in Montecito, a blue-shuttered New England style compound of cottages on the beach. The hotel's charm consisted of its location between the railroad tracks and the sand. I took an upstairs apartment on the water, with a painted wood deck over a placid surf, and the rattle and roar of the Santa Barbara-Fullerton line ten feet behind.

I'd never smoked except on a dare—occasional marijuana, collegiate rite of passage. Rarely drank liquor before noon. After I found the room, I jogged to a liquor store on Olive Mill Road and bought a pack of Camels—I admired the stolid dignity of the animal—and the makings of a vodka tonic. Sliced a lime with fastidious care and a purloined plastic knife. Then thumped downstairs to a noisy ice machine concealed behind the bungalows to fetch ice in a tin bucket.

In the harsh breeze off the sea, I braced myself, smoking a Camel and tipping my cocktail, like William Powell on a backlot movie set.

I reflected on difficult encounters that had been forced upon me. Accepting help from Bunker Dodge, being interrogated by the Santa Monica Police, and appealing to the District Attorney Ms. Vaughn. But this cadging approach to Brulée seemed vastly more important. A genuine last resort. I knew it wasn't good to think that way. Always better to consider the worst in advance and imagine an alternative. So I tried to form the idea of another option. And I came up with—my father. It's not that he had that kind of money. He was after all, a gentleman at the end of his race. Yet he might have the means to secure four hundred thousand from his cronies in the City of London.

Curiously, this train of thought comforted me. Taking stock of my brief history, it struck me that my reputation as a failure rested mostly on my father's perception. Until now, I'd never really demonstrated the inadequacies he ascribed to me. And if I lay before him the facts of my present situation, it would be the first time my perceived deficiencies would be confirmed. This gave me a feeling of vast relief.

Taking out my Cartier memo book with its eighteen carat gold ballpoint, I wondered at the pleasure I'd taken in small luxuries. What were they worth to me now? I seated myself at the cramped faux-paneled desk, and scribbled urgently:

Dear Father,

I have made a serious mistake in my judgment of people and in my business affairs. I need your help in raising $400,000 to make things right. Please understand I intend to repay you. I believe, with my law degree from Yale and my work experience, I am a sound financial risk.

Respectfully,
Maxwell

I lifted an envelope embossed in bright blue letters reading Hotel Miramar, folded my letter within, sealed it and placed it in my pocket.

This terse correspondence revealed an unsuspected talent for skillful editing. I needed more than four hundred thousand dollars. I needed a miracle. Irving and I would surely be charged with fraud for marketing gold-backed partnerships through Filmland, when in fact the prospect of gold bullion was a sham. Ms. Vaughn had placed Filmland under federal conservatorship. And Irving's investment of $2 million would be lost. It wouldn't be long until they closed our operations. The government would call my note for $1 million. We were going to jail unless we could make good our promises.

In spite of all this, I had no intention of mailing the letter. Yet.

Φ

The match began at one o'clock. I arrived at the polo grounds at noon, tendered Brulée's name and was directed to Brulée's box, dead-center of the small grandstand.

The white-washed Montecito Polo Club is set upon ten acres of emerald lawn, ringed by eucalyptus trees. As I emerged from my car, the acrid smell of eucalyptus bark was borne to me by a brisk Pacific breeze. A few players were practicing on the field. I found a seat instead in the members-only section of the grandstand, an enclosure with the nostalgic intimacy of high school bleachers.

There's a California dynasty in polo, from the early 1960s. The Walker family calls their team Long Beach and that name's synonymous with the Walkers to anyone who knows polo in the States. A few of the team's players were warming up.

Polo is more than sport, it's a way of life. Winter in Palm Springs, summer in Argentina, a few months in Santa Barbara or down in Playa Blanca. Among those who pursue the sport, it must be high goal. Low and medium goal is for amateurs. And if you have to ask about the financial commitment, you can't afford it.

To form a high goal team as Brulée had done, you must employ at least three professional players. And the high goal game is so much faster and more demanding that just any string of eight ponies won't do. Argentina has the best stock. And, always, one of the best players in the world must travel with you, for a second opinion. And then it's the gypsy life: West Palm Beach, Calcutta, Careyes, Sydney. I was no tyro to the game. I'd played a little myself. With Reggie Ludwig in Palm Springs. But I'd never owned eight ponies. So I couldn't play on a team.

Ten minutes before the match Countess arrived and

signaled me to join her in the box. Mister D clicked in behind her. He sniffed me dubiously. It struck me as odd that Mister D should be there, as dogs are excluded from polo matches.

But Mister D was not about to run anywhere. He regarded the match with the same anxious concern he suffered at Port's. I'm sure his trepidation was as painful for him as mine was for me. But my risks were real. Brulée and his thugs had bloodied my nose. Despite Countess' assurances, I couldn't help doubting his good will. But I didn't doubt his greed. If I could get his attention sufficiently to offer a benefit to him, there might be something in it for Christian. I wrote a figure on the back of the program.

Out of his tuxedo Brulée had one of those curiously disproportionate bodies, large torso and head, weak bandy legs. As if all his power of personality were concentrated in the forty inches above his crotch.

A cut-throat player, I could feel his appetite for winning from thirty feet away. There was no doubt in my mind Brulée would kill his horse or teammate to improve the odds. The terrifying velocity with which he smacked his mallet to the ball made me wince in memory.

At the break, I asked the Countess: "What exactly is Brulée's business?"

Countess' look was one of sly amusement. "Ramòn consults to governments."

"I thought he owned a racetrack."

"His portfolio cloaks a variety of business interests."

Just then play started again. The horses pounded toward the stands, Brulée striking the ball with the precision of a steel drill. He didn't give a damn for any player or player's horse.

There was a girl on his team, an auburn ponytail swept

along the back of an emerald jersey. Her riding was more cautious than the men. Her shots were light, graceful taps, but her timing was excellent. Each time she spun the ball back toward the goal, seven panting male players reigned their horses sharply, turned and thundered back the other way.

After the match, I strolled downfield to the open paddock where the ponies were led immediately following their chukker. Exquisite in their sweat and wildness, they flicked white foam over the long-bladed grass and anyone standing nearby.

"Well played," I said. Brulée's black hairpiece lay matted with sweat beneath his small helmet.

Instead of answering, he barked at his South American grooms. "Raoul! Get the blanket on that pony. Jose, put the two chestnuts in the trailer, the others will stay for tomorrow's match. What is it Rider?"

I refused to play along with his pretense that I wasn't expected. "You know why I'm here. I have a business proposition for you."

"You and everyone else," he replied. "Jose! Not the bay. The mare." Brulée wrenched the saddle from his pony. "What is it?"

Before I could reply, Brulée lunged for the reins of the two mares. The groom Jose had looped the reins loosely— too loosely, over a hitching post. I sprang for the leads and got caught in a trot which threatened to split me in half. In a lucky dive, I recovered the reins and led the mares back, securing them to the post.

Drawing inspiration from chaos, I said, "Ramòn, it's Filmland, I'm authorized to offer it for sale. All its assets."

He whirled toward me, his heavy torso like a column of

stones. "Why would I want that empty shell?"

I didn't miss the interest that flickered in his dark eyes.

"Banking buys influence," I said.

"I've got plenty of influence."

"Tax loss." I dodged to avoid the spirited steed led by the obtuse Jose. "You can set off our potential loss against profit from your other ventures. It could save you millions."

"Too much regulation," Brulée said, wrestling the blankets from his pony to the ground.

"You wouldn't have the problems we had," I said. "Someone turned us in. If you operate discreetly, low profile…"

Brulée allowed a tight smile. "Problems, eh? Too bad." He shrugged dismissively. "I'm not terribly interested. What do you have in mind?"

I plunged ahead, playing the game as well as anyone. "If we cut away our initial investment, $2 million cash to Irving, cancel my note for $1 million, it's all yours. We ask only a small premium of –say, $500,000 to sweeten the deal."

"What about the liabilities? Alex's film alone is a $4 million nag."

"It's true it's over-budget, but if you've got the cash reserves you could turn a profit—eventually."

"Ha! Eventually."

I laid out for him the difficulties to be expected with the partnerships. Brulée waved them away. "The SEC—bah! Small tigers."

I was tired of dodging frothing nostrils and wrangling Latin grooms, "Can we discuss this sitting down, after you've finished here?"

"Impossible," he said. "I've got plans this afternoon. I only invite you for Countess."

My face was sweating when I addressed the man's harsh profile again. "I was told you have ready cash. If you do, then make your decision. The bank is in conservatorship. If we don't close a deal today, the opportunity will be lost."

He proceeded along his line of ponies, inspecting each with a rough gesture. "Now what about this half-a-million-dollar 'sweetener?' Why should I pay anything more than your investment—if I consider your proposal at all?"

I had regrets about beginning negotiations too near my bottom line. It was imperative he pay enough for Christian's medical procedure. Otherwise, Irving and I were made whole but little else was gained by the sale to Brulée.

I thought a moment. "The cash is for Christian. He was your driver, for Christ's sake."

He turned abruptly, met my eyes with shrewd appraisal. "Off the hook, eh? So, if I make this deal with you— Christian will be saved and the criminal charges against you will be reduced."

"Yes," I said, though I hadn't thought of it that way.

He stood facing me, his large hands resting lightly at the belt loops of his jodhpurs. "I personally wouldn't lift my finger to aid you, Rider, but my partners, they want Filmland. So I do it. We have a deal. Just as we discussed. Don't try to vary the terms Rider, I warn you."He turned away without shaking my hand. "Oh—and not more than $400,000 cash," he said shrewdly.

I remained on the field. The ponies brushed by me, one by one, on their way to the stables. I hadn't negotiated for my own self-interest. But Brulée was right. Christian's recovery would put an end to cries for my prosecution, especially if it were I who'd brought it about.

At the edge of the polo field I turned back and caught up

with Brulée, an impulse that was to determine my life beyond the mere events of that day.

"What now?"

"It must be in cash," I said.

"Two and a half million dollars in cash? You must be crazy."He thrust his large head, "I call you in a couple days."

"Cash," I said. For all I knew Ramòn intended to draw on the Rapunzel account Father Tim had turned up, an unsavory connection to the Inca Princess that I had to avoid.

Suddenly, the redhead in the emerald jersey ran up. "You dropped this, Mr. Rider." She handed me an envelope with blue script reading Hotel Miramar. I recognized her clipped English phrasing. I turned and found myself face to face with Filmland's receptionist.

"You," I said. "Darleen—how do you know Brulée?"

"Well—" she said coyly, "That's an interesting story, actually." Her tony accent was the reason Irving had hired her to preside with sexy confidence over Filmland's reception lobby.

"I've always worked for Ramòn," she said with false jauntiness. "He hired me to keep an eye on Filmland."

"Well, good luck," I replied coldly. "If our negotiations go through, Brulée may give you back your job."

I left the polo field a free man and a puzzled one. Who were these partners Brulée alluded to?

38

Rider at Filmland

Two days passed before Brulée called. I passed the time fixed to my chair at Filmland, tensing each time a light pulsed on my telephone. I'd left Montecito relieved and optimistic. But now, tethered in the daily swamp of my difficulties, I feared Brulée's reneging on our deal.

In the morning I received another call that was both unexpected and unwanted. Mona and Lainie were moving to Marin with a physician Mona called her fiancé. The subject touched some locus of despair in me, though I'd seen it coming: the good doctor's Volvo parked in front of Mona's house; his name, Philip, tripping innocently from Lainie's lips.

Would I be over to say goodbye? What arrangements would suit me regarding visits to Lainie? Sick at heart, I became perversely helpful. I would help Mona load her furniture.

"That's not necessary Maxwell, we plan to buy new things up north. Lainie's finally forgotten the bean-bag chair. Don't you think it's best to leave it behind?"

"Yes," I said. What could I say? My child, my wife, were leaving.

Conditions at Filmland were equally depressing. The government had thrown the bank into conservatorship. Our executive suite buzzed with G-13s assigned to run Filmland like the post office.

These vandals of the spirit plundered our offices in the Hollywood Roosevelt Building, a 1920s original Irving and I had gracefully restored. Lounging around our marble reception console, the new team slopped coffee on Tibetan carpets, while earnestly debating the subject of suburban crab grass. The scent of "Brute" aftershave clung to the interiors of our private elevator, and the impressive lobby waterfall went dry. Our conference room of Moroccan rosewood was now littered with files, and calculators lurked like armadillos upon each hand-lacquered desk.

Head of operations was Bob Badoo, an obsequious Texan who typed his own memos: "Messur (sic) Maxwell Rider, Vice Chairman, Filmland Credit of Los Angeles, a Federally Chartered Savings & Loan Association."

At first I suspected him of tongue-in-cheek, but he honestly believed in this curious formality.

Badoo convinced himself he knew something about the film business. But his ineptness was appalling. Badoo did not care, for instance, about a film's provenance, the reputation of its director, or the status of its stars at box office. He scarcely looked at the films in which we'd invested millions of dollars. Rather, he would stroll into my office fifteen times a day holding up a thin file.

"Where's the appraisal?"

"We don't use appraisals for films. Look at Irving's budget projections."

"Okay."

Three minutes later.

"There's no appraisal in this file."

"That's because there's no bloody appraisal." And so on.

Badoo was in my office when Brulée called, just before three o'clock. "It's for me," I said, depressing the speaker control.

Badoo stood there stupidly with one of our files.

"This doesn't concern you, Bob," I said firmly. "Close the

door on your way out."

The dull-witted Texan bridled at my tone. I glanced pointedly at the Florentine clock I'd picked up along the Ponte Vecchio.

"Don't worry," I said. "I'll know where to find you."

Sullenly, he turned on the heel of his size twelve Florsheims and lumbered toward the coffee room. He pulled the door closed after him. Brulée got right to the point.

"You said $2 million."

"And four hundred thousand."

"There's a private airstrip called the Imperial Runway about one half mile east of LAX. Be there at five o'clock. Watch for my party's arrival. They won't deplane so be there to meet it—alone."

"Never heard of that terminal. Where is it?"

"Take Sepulveda to Imperial Highway. It's not marked. Just plunge off to the right when you see a paved drive."

"If it's not marked, how will I find it?"

"You want the money, you'll be there."

"Five o'clock," I said.

"That's it. And Rider, we'll process the government's approval for the sale. If we need you, we'll ask. Otherwise, you and Irving Fain are deposed. When you take the money, you're out for good. Understand?"

I swept every paper off my desk into the wastebasket of hand-rubbed Pretorian zebrawood. All this. All of Filmland, finished. I felt like a pilot forced to eject from his plane. Things had gone too far to pull Filmland out of its spin.

I wandered into Irving's opulent suite for the last time. He was of course on the phone, reclined in his Italian leather chair, and squinting at the city of Los Angeles laid out brilliantly below Sunset Boulevard. The mahogany panels were swung open and a film played on the screen behind him. French Connection. The actors moved their mouths soundlessly while the stereo system played Mahler. Typical. Irving doing three things at once.

He was attired impeccably. That's something Irving picked up during our association. Conservative navy gabardine. But double-breasted. Pink shirt, dark tie. His nails were buffed to linoleum sheen and the large fleshy features of his Russian-Jewish grandparents were beginning to assert a mature distinction. Irving had come a long way from the Bronx.

He motioned me in. Creased his face into a smile and raised his eyebrows to embellish his end of the conversation. "Christ! These bozos are just window dressing. Deliver your voucher, I'll get it handled. Can't miss summer box office. Get the voucher over here. Yeah. Yeah. Best to Melina."

He waved a hand at the call he disconnected. "Niko. Got some re-shoot. He's under budget with Swirling Cameras. But those assholes down the hall—"

"Irving. Good news and bad news," I said, dropped into the chrome chair across from Irving. I spoke succinctly. It wasn't necessary to elaborate, Irving and I had discussed our options many times.

We were finished. Our dream for Filmland was over. Eleven months from the night we forged our partnership at Le Dôme.

Irving lowered his chin. He took some seconds to explore the inside of his jowl with his tongue. Then he swung around to the wall safe behind his desk. "Licorice?"

"No thanks."

Irving snapped off a chaw of cherry licorice like a Kodiak with a trout. I sat glumly as he chewed reflectively.

Once, he smiled. And the hairline gap between his front

teeth was Kool-aid red with licorice scum.

"Shit! No big deal. You make it once, you can do it again. We were the biggest players in this friggin' town."

Behind the smile, his eyes shone dark and inscrutable as the marbles we called Puries in the 1950s in the Bronx, before my mother's post with the Linens, before we moved to Greenwich.

"It's not a helluva lot of consolation, but you got my money back. Played Vegas for free. That ain't so bad, my friend?"

Behind the bold words, the brash show, we both knew the big one only comes once. There wouldn't be another Filmland. "Irving, you're a great partner." My voice broke.

"Me?" he said. "It was a good ride. It was class. Fricking short, but fricking good."

He didn't have to say that. And I felt some truth in it, although behind his smile, his eyes were hard with determination. He'd already begun to think about making it again. People say a lot of things about Irving Fain. Even now. Especially now that he's on top again. "When the contract's signed that's when Irving starts negotiating."

And all that. But then, in January 1980, he didn't have to prop me up like that. In his own way he's a gentleman. And for that, I was grateful.

Abruptly the present had become the past. Gone were my dreams for Filmland, a life with Mona, and a second chance with my child. Like another Ryder before me, I felt homeless, childless, loveless. I hoped it was not past tense for Christian too.

39

Rider at Imperial Runway

At five o'clock, already dusk, I arrived at a deserted airstrip enclosed by a chain link fence. Posted on the fence were signs of warning: No Access, Road Closed. Trespassers Will be Prosecuted.

A process of elimination had brought me there. For half an hour I'd circled the desolate maze of industry that forms the transportation complex for LAX, third largest international airport in the world. As Brulée predicted, a lucky plunge onto a paved drive thickly obscured by oleander trees brought me to the vacant strip.

Inside the wire fence, a low metal building of prefab construction served two narrow runways rising from weeds and dried grass. The field was not well lit. Faint yellow lamps barely illuminated the strip.

Despite its air of abandonment, I noticed the terminal appeared new, one of those modern shells of windowless aluminum with a flat corrugated roof. The skeletal structure of a steel tower rose from the fog like a mirage. A short flagpole added to the effect of a distant outpost, and an American flag, half-raised, played in the wind.

I'd enlarged upon Brulée's instructions, minimal as they were, by bringing an empty Mark Cross briefcase in green leather which had been my father's.

I left the car in the darkness and prowled along the chain-link seeking an entry point. I entertained the idea of scrambling up the fence and easing my way over two rows of barbed wire at the top. Before I could embark on this misadventure, I saw a limousine pull off the roadway and proceed slowly toward a gate marked Field No. 1-No Access. Its lights were off. When it reached the gate, it paused in front. A hand emerged from the driver's side and tapped the keypad on a short pole I hadn't seen before. The gate parted along its track and the limo proceeded inside to the grassy shoulder of the runway. Just before it closed again, I slipped inside.

A metal catwalk ran along the front of the terminal. I clanged up the metal stairs to a ramp where a door appeared. I was surprised to find myself buzzed inside. I proceeded down a long hall, quickly taking in the signs on the doors: Linguistic Monitoring. Surveillance Operations. Security. The words gave me a feeling of foreboding: who was watching me?

At the end of the hall a door to a control room stood partly ajar. Two men in khaki jumpsuits were seated before banks of pulsing lights and transmitters, observing various gauges and chatting between themselves. They looked up casually as I entered.

"I'm meeting a plane at five o'clock," I said.

They exchanged a glance and shrugged. "No flight plan's been filed," one offered.

He wore a buzz haircut and his eyes flicked erratically when he spoke.

"Nothing for five o'clock? I'm meeting someone scheduled to arrive on that flight."

The buzz-cut studied me with an air of cruel certitude, "No flight plan. No request for landing. We're not expecting anyone." He turned back to his companion.

"If you want to wait, there's a snack bar back down the hall," the other man said.

I proceeded back the way I'd come until a swinging door on the airfield side of the building gave way to a cramped lounge with vending machines. To my surprise a man waited there. Dark, impeccably dressed, in a style Americans rarely achieve, and he was reading La Opinión, which was published in Buenos Aires at the time. He allowed his eyes to sweep me briefly, then returned to his account of a coup in Argentina.

The snack bar was spare and modern, with that relentless gloom that frequently settles on office canteens. From a metal vendor, I prepared a cup of thin coffee, watched the cup drop unsteadily onto the chrome drain, while boiling water, then black liquid, sputtered into the cup. I pressed the button for light and a weak blond substance finished the creation.

I stepped outside through metal-framed sliding doors which led to the airfield. A strong wind gusted the yellow-orange wind sock and kept up a relentless flutter of my hair and tie, flapping the light wool of my trousers against my legs. But I preferred the irritating wind to the gloom of the canteen.

I glanced in at the South American. His presence recalled to me the draft letter I'd taken from Alex's escritoire at Tower Hill. I removed it from my billfold and reviewed Alex's Spencerian script one more time.

Dear Jorge,

I'm extremely irritated with your refusal to come through on the purchase of Danse du Sang. Your failure to attend the preview was malicious and irresponsible and you have jeopardized our friendship. I told you a hundred times, this is America and you cannot get away with insulting business colleagues. You must call your bank in Santiago immediately (if, in fact, that is really your banking liaison) and ask them to pay the amount we agreed into my account in Brussels. Had I known how insufferable this transaction would be, I would have cut off my hand instead of agreeing to sell you my film. (And it is more an act of charity than a business transaction.) In any case, after I have confirmed the money is in my account, go to see Maxwell Rider at Filmland Credit (on Sunset Boulevard) and ask him to deliver you the prints. Do not try to get the film until you have paid the money!

Sincerely,
Alex des Prairies

There were quite a few crossings-out and inserts, but that was the gist of Alex's letter. No one had come to see me at Filmland claiming the prints. I'd secured them in the vault. They were Brulée's baby now. If our plan went through, that is.

I consulted my watch. Five forty-five. I checked again with the controllers. No flight plan. No request for landing. Nothing had changed. Except for Buzz-cut's curiosity, which had mildly increased.

I returned to the snack bar, my own curiosity roused by the idea of the South American and myself waiting at an apparently deserted airfield. He had finished La Opinión and immersed himself in the most recent Spanish language edition of Newsweek. I took a seat in a leather chair resembling a spaceship, and flipped through the dog-eared pages of Soldier of Fortune and Artillery, tossed disconsolately on the wood-grained formica table. The writing stirred me to a feeling of adventure and a pleasurable tension concerning this waystation and the assignation which I hoped would take place.

I left the room and stepped softly down the hall to try the other rooms. Two were locked but the third, identified as Security by a name-plate, looked as if someone had recently stepped out. A mug of hot coffee sat on the green metal desk and a telephone line pulsed impatiently. On one beige wall a calendar was tacked, promoting the eighty-second airborne division of the U.S. Army. Combat photos of men in camouflage and helmets hastening through what looked like the Vietnam brush were arranged on a low table. I quickly closed the door and retreated through the snack bar to wait outside. A light marine layer drifted in.

At six-fifteen, the sun had descended to the horizon. A blaze of red and yellow lit the sky only seconds from being sucked down into the bottom of the world. Just before the barren airport's descent into darkness, I felt a sudden instinct of activity.

A fuel truck materialized out of the fog and rolled silently toward the farthest end of the airfield. Two men with small machine guns stepped outside on either side of me, and speakers mounted along the outside of the building crackled with urgent voices:

"This airport restricted. Identify yourself. Identify yourself immediately."

There was a long frightening pause. Then, faintly—

"Rapunzel two. Request instructions for landing."

I felt the snipers tense.

"Request confirmed. Permission to land granted, runway two."

Though I felt alarmed by the two guards with their paramilitary weapons, I started walking. Far off, in the distance, in the dark, I heard the plane touch down on the runway. Vaguely, I could make out its form from lights flickering at each wing and the tip of its vertical tail. It was a large corporate jet with radar, which I knew was unusual. It taxied in and waited at least two football fields away. I kept walking toward it, my heart thumping in fear. At the darkening landscape, the young men with their guns, and the purposeful quiet of the plane.

As I drew closer, I realized the plane's motor had not shut off. At the end of the field, a limo proceeded slowly toward the boarding ramp. What if someone, the man who'd brought our money, got in the limo and drove away? I almost broke into a run.

I reached the plane first. The limo parked in darkness at the edge of the tarmac. The fuel truck pulled up and the driver jumped down to hook up the line.

"If you've got business on the plane, you'd better get going. You've got five minutes of refueling time."

The pilot shone a light down on me from the cockpit, and someone opened the door and lowered a ramp. I couldn't see anyone, and boarded in the harsh glare from the cockpit. My shadow danced below me. A man wearing chinos and dockers, with a revolver strapped over his Izod golf shirt, greeted me in silence. He parted a curtain to the cabin and I walked back to where Brulée sat comfortably before a tray on which there was a bottle of Campari and a silver dish of cashews. He gestured for me to sit opposite him and summoned another glass.

Fear forced my aggression, "What's this all about, Ramòn, what's Operation Rapunzel?"

Ramòn raised his brow reflecting his surprise. "Once upon a time there was a young princess—"

"So?"

"I spin gold into gold, if you will."

"The Inca Princess," I said. "You had an arrangement with Tom Grass to launder money there."

Ramòn flashed his too-small teeth. "It's interesting how quickly a man's honor becomes tarnished when the money runs out."

"And now you need Filmland."

"Where else does one wash clothes but in a laundry?"

"Who's your client, Ramòn?"

"You don't want to know," he said.

"Where does the money come from—drugs? Guns?"

"You know, Rider, you should consider working for me. I could use someone around me with idealism."

"Let's get this over with," I said.

The preppy gunman returned with half a dozen fat, khaki pouches stenciled Property of the U.S. Government. From them, Brulée removed stacks of bills. He held them up tantalizingly before placing them in my open briefcase. I found myself too nervous to count the bills, although I quickly reckoned them in my head, sufficiently to estimate the money was all there, including Christian's $400,000.

As I moved to leave, something in Brulée's manner prompted me to ask, "Ramòn, this money is for Christian's surgery. Will you—can you fly him to Geneva for the operation?"

Brulée put out a hand to restrain his hard-eyed liege who was impatient to escort me from the plane. "Why not?" he said. "I am also an idealist."

It was a long walk back. For a time, I could hear the hum of the idling plane, and feel the lights of the limo at my back. But I didn't turn around. When the limo started to move toward the plane, I knew someone would board who I wasn't supposed to see. I kept walking, almost trudging with weariness now that my part in the adventure was over.

The plane was airborne before I reached the terminal. The limo receded from the field. I found myself in darkness and alone. The building was locked. The crew was gone. I walked around the building but the chain link fence was a heavy-duty one, and secure, and I finally had to scale the fence, awkward with my case, and drop down the other side. When I reached my car, I had torn my trousers but my father's briefcase wasn't marred.

I have no recollection of starting my car or leaving the airfield. But as I pulled onto the Imperial Highway I looked back. The terminal and airstrip were invisible, as if already they had ceased to exist.

40

Rider at the Federal Courthouse

There was one thing to be done to restore order to my life, an awkward unpleasant thing that defied conventional wisdom in criminal defense. I had made up my mind to offer a plea in exchange for Irving's freedom.

At nine-thirty the next morning I announced myself at the office of Ms. Vaughn. A curious secretary led me to the same drab conference room where Irving and I met the prosecutor in May.

"This is a good time to see her," her secretary confided. "She blitzed opposing counsel in court this morning."

The girl withdrew, and the silence called back doubts that had prevented sleep the night before. Under federal law at that time, my voluntary plea would be a basis for leniency. I'd prepared myself to accept two years. With time off for good behavior, I reckoned I would be eligible for release in sixteen months. Now I vacillated whether my odds could be improved at trial. I began to strategize a defense on technical grounds, working to rebut each element of the prosecution's case.

The term "men's rea," meaning criminal intent, drifted back from law school. I wondered how Vaughn intended to prove intent, when it occurred to me it could be inferred from Irving's and my casual disregard of banking laws.

Panicked thoughts crashed through my studied calm like hounds after a vanishing fox. If we lost at trial, a harsher sentence could be handed down. Three years—or six—was a long time in my daughter's life. Irving—I could see the impression he'd make upon a jury. And my thin defense of government misconduct at Costa Brava—well—too late I remembered I hadn't gone back to recover the DEA's files.

The futility of this debate returned me to the reason I had come: the certainty in saying, "Irving, I cleared it, you're free."

Vaughn appeared in crisp white blouse and olive suit. Her tawny hair was pulled into a clip at her nape, exposing silver crescents in her ears. She brushed by me, leaving my extended hand unclasped.

"I want to discuss the charges," I said.

She lifted a pale brow in mild surprise, "Where's your lawyer?"

"A luxury I can't afford," I replied grimly.

A man followed her into the room, his presence raising my apprehension. She introduced him as her boss, Frank Leck. He was sour and dark, with an incipient dusky shadow along his cheeks only two hours into the work day. He wore the look of a man about to pat a woman's fanny affectionately. I caught Vaughn's movement, cold and deliberate, rebuffing him.

He seated himself opposite me, with Vaughn between us at the head of the conference table.

"Proceed," he said. He twisted his wedding band impatiently and I quickly surmised an office affair with Vaughan had been called off by her—not him.

I catalogued the charges against Irving and me, to make sure we were talking about the same thing. There were twelve counts on the federal slate, from negligent management practices to fraud in soliciting investments. As I read from my notes the tedium of the government's claims assailed me. We had been careless—and foolish. But had we done anything criminal?

When I'd completed my recitation, Vaughn simply nodded.

"I've reviewed your charges," I said, "and they all come down to one thing—money." I smiled into her icy gaze.

"What is the amount of Filmland's loss?" I inquired.

"What do you mean?"

"What are the damages the government's alleging?"

"There are several loans at risk. Mr. des Prairies' for one."

"You once conceded we can't value Danse du Sang until it's sold. None of the other films have sold domestic yet either, so—" I spread my palms, "no loss."

Vaughn exchanged a glance with Leck. He flapped his hand.

I drew a fortifying breath, "Irving Fain, the money partner, he'll be acquitted. He had little responsibility for the transactions you're concerned about."

She smiled shrewdly, "That's not exactly right. Fain is a director of the bank, a principal. He's accountable. And he's far from lily white."

"If I save you the risk and expense of trial—"

Leck interrupted me, "Trials don't bother us. We like litigation, don't we, Nancy? That's what prosecutors do—try cases."

"What information are you trading?" the female prosecutor asked in a flat, disinterested voice.

"Information? I don't have any evidence of criminal conduct, if that's what you mean."

Vaughn studied me. "Let's talk about Irving Fain. Where did his money come from in the first place? How did he finance Hot Dawg?" She left out the surfer enunciation which had made Irving's film a cult classic. "You could check into it," she went on coolly.

I was shaking my head before she finished speaking. The idea was to get Irving off, not implicate him further.

"Bunker Dodge," she said. "What's he up to these days?"

I sat silent. Bunker wasn't one I counted as a friend. Yet I couldn't betray his candor. Everything Dodge had told me, well, I couldn't repeat it. He'd admitted to being a market shill. And they could have put him away for that.

Leck broke in. "We'll try the damn case—with pleasure."

He avoided my eyes, speaking with cruel precision. Why should they cut a deal to avoid a trial? Why let one miscreant off just to assure conviction of the other. Nobody settled winners, and this case was a winner. The Justice Department took special pleasure in prosecuting spoiled rich kids. Leck continued like that, argumentative and childish, showing off for his junior colleague.

I asked if I might have a glass of water. One was brought to me by the secretary Maria, whose eyes flickered encouragement, keep your nerve.

I pressed Vaughn. "The point is there's no loss yet. And no hard evidence of any." I shrugged, dismissing their audit with a flick of its pages, "This demonstrates nothing—only fiscal casualness."

Abruptly Leck rose, "Maria—where are the writs I prepared this morning?"

Maria started when she saw my pallor. She handed Leck a sheaf of federal forms, neatly typed. Leck tossed them across to me, one by one, looking at me with flat dead eyes.

"Here's the petition for proceedings to revoke your bar license to practice law."

I was determined not to show any fear, although I cursed myself for not anticipating the government's ruthlessness.

"So? You'll get out of prison and have no meal ticket." Leck smirked in satisfaction. "Ex-felon? You'll have one helluva fight with the State Bar to restore your privileges."

He nudged a second paper across to me. "Here's the freeze order on your bank accounts." I refused to look at it. "You know as felons, you can't vote?" he asked rhetorically. He turned to Vaughn, "Do they teach you that in law school?"

Leck flipped the last paper in front of me. Almost blind in disbelief, I struggled to read it—an order of attachment for Mona's assets.

"What's this?"

"The government is entitled to ill-gotten gains."

"What ill-gotten gains? I took a salary."

"Read your government code. We're entitled to protect against any loss at Filmland."

"What loss?"

"Prospective loss."

"But we're divorced. Mona's assets are her separate property."

"A common ploy—that's how defendants attempt to hide assets."

"Mona's engaged to someone else. She's moved away."

"We know where Mona is."

I appealed to Vaughn, "She doesn't have anything. I could barely make child support."

Leck answered, "When we slap this on her bank accounts, we'll see what she has."

I struggled for composure. "You're insane. How dare you pursue my family—"

"Ah ha! An admission."

Leck was turning backflips for his comely subordinate. "Divorce of financial convenience, attempt to avoid criminal prosecution."

Leck bellowed out through the closed door, "Maria, get these ready for Judge Tyra."

I stood abruptly, my hands trembling on the table, "You lunatic asshole," I said.

Leck stood too, enraged. "You're going up for ten years my friend, the maximum term." He twisted his ring more vigorously, his eyes flashed a kind of triumph. I saw it was no good then. Leck was psychotic.

I drew a deep breath, careful to mask the physical impact his words had made upon me. A storm had seized my gut. I dodged waves of nausea. This was my life and Irving's future Leck was ranting about. I saw months slip away. Pages of a calendar whipped by like the passage of time in a forties film. Months merged into years, and years into decades, behind bars. What about Mona—and Lainie?

"Let's break," Vaughn said crisply. Break? What for, it was no good. They left the room and I could hear them huddling in her office. She was doing most of the talking, loudly and rapidly. But muffled. I placed my head between my hands. I was sweating and I felt unwell. I'd come there prepared to go to prison. But not for ten years.

I staggered out into the hall and made my way to the men's lavatory. I lurched inside. Suddenly everything cracked. Supporting myself against the brushed chrome bar of the urinal, I retched helplessly.

All of the past day's lunch and dinner and all of my meager breakfast swirled past me. Great quantities of vomit sucked down the drain. I saw my guts disappear in the eddy, whirling toward the sewers of LA.

Abruptly, the door swung open and a man walked to the urinal without looking at me. He carried a newspaper in a foreign language which he propped under his arm. I supported myself on the bar and straightened my posture. I felt embarrassed at my reflection in the mirror. I cleaned the vomit from my lips and passed a wet paper towel over my face. I shaped my tie and tucked in my shirt. Then I allowed myself a glance to see whether the other man was staring at me.

I knew him. And as I debated what to do, whether to return to the room or leave the building, something clicked in my memory, I knew where I'd seen him—in the snack bar of the airfield on Imperial Highway.

Pausing outside the lavatory still weakened, I coaxed myself to walk away with a coward's logic—save the battle for trial. But I didn't believe it. I'd left my father's briefcase in the conference room. I knew I couldn't leave without it. Nor could I accept that my attempt on Irving's behalf should come to nothing.

I straightened my shoulders and practiced standing, beginning to sweat again with the thought of Leck pursuing my family. The cruel persecution of the man overwhelmed me. I struggled to press down fear, and discovered anger. Some inner resource had been restored to me, and I recognized my ally of recent weeks—defiance.

When I entered the conference room, Leck was collecting his papers.

"We're not finished," I said.

He registered surprise and paused uncertainly, but when he saw my face he gestured to Vaughn to take a chair. "What now?"

Instinctively I began to bait him, although I had no idea where it would lead.

"I ran into a mutual acquaintance in the bathroom."

"So?"

"He's working on the Rapunzel Project."

At first there was silence. "That's none of your concern."

"You've just confirmed it is."

I was on to something, feeling my way. The guy in the men's room had been at the airfield when Brulée's plane landed. Rapunzel II. And he was Latin, like Trujillo, Alex's elusive buyer of Danse du Sang.

"What do you know about it?" Leck demanded.

"Enough to fill a file."

"What are you talking about?"

"A DEA file, legal size, with a pink cellophane label and red stenciled letters, TOP SECRET—Restricted."

I hadn't the faintest notion what was in the files I'd concealed at Costa Brava three weeks before. The truth was I didn't actually know anything about Brulée's business, the Rapunzel Project, or anything else.

Rapidly, I clicked through flashcards of possibilities, pulling up clues like threads of an old sweater. Brulée schemes with the Arabs, Alex had said. Ramòn consults to governments. I recalled Brulée's boast at Tower Hill that he had dined at Khasoggi's— the arms dealer. And Susie at Café Chapeau: "Khasoggi's Park Avenue apartment was purchased with our gold."

Spinning gold into gold, Brulée had said. Or cash into gold bullion. I couldn't imagine why I hadn't thought of it before. Brulée laundered money for the Shah's friends through the Inca Princess.

It seemed a fairly simple idea. Fly the money in by courier, issue gold contracts, redeem them for bullion from outside sources—buy up Park Avenue.

Illegal, of course, a federal crime, in violation of the State Department's impound of Iranian assets. And the DEA's file—Rapunzel Project—meant the government knew about it. But so what? I'd gone about as far as I could go. I could feel myself running aground on conjecture.

"Get to the point," Leck said. A tic had started to twitch in the muscles of his jowl.

"I have the files," I croaked.

Ms. Vaughn stiffened. "What files?"

"Project Rapunzel."

Leck's eyes darted to my briefcase. I almost laughed at this comic gesture. "They're safe," I assured him, with more than a touch of irony.

"You have the DEA files," he said as if he couldn't grasp that our negotiations should have reached this absurd conclusion.

I nodded.

Vaughn rose abruptly. "We have to make some calls. And we have to see what you have. If you deliver the DEA's files to us, we'll talk about a deal."

"I need a commitment."

"Just show us the files." She studied me intensely before striding from the room.

41.

Beverly Place Redux

It's all very well to say you're going to break into an office on Beverly Place in the middle of the day to recover some papers, previously stolen and concealed in the draft of a faux fireplace, but it's quite another thing to carry it off without being caught or charged with unlawful entry.

My adventures—skulking the premises of what was formerly Costa Brava Films—consumed the afternoon, comprising another chapter in "The Accidental Crimes of Maxwell Rider."

I found Sharmayne Lafont, actress, through Extras' Casting. She feigned memory lapse, though just ten days before she'd flounced around the set of Danse du Sang, provocative in a blue robe.

She tried on one of her phony accents, "Of kawrse, I remember you, Mr. Rider." Her Ladyship with an Aussie twang.

"I hope you're not calling me for more still shots. I don't want anyone to see me in that bleeping turkey."

I recalled her from the beach set, petite, with red hair, and a petulant spirit which was not unattractive. She informed me with some pride that she was up for a part in a sit-com.

"British nanny," she said. "Spent every penny on the accent coach."

"I'd like to hire you for a day's work," I said. I explained what I wanted. A couple of hours that afternoon. It might be hazardous. It could be unlawful.

"No problem," she replied. "Piece of cake."

"I need an ingenue," I said, growing more dubious by the minute. "Seductive nymphet. Temptress."

She broke in aggressively. "That role's mine. Don't call anyone else. I'm into it. The Career Woman. Predatory but erotic. Knows what she wants and won't take (tyke) no for an answer. A bitch with a shopping bag."

"It's a cameo, Sharmayne," I said. Sharmayne LaFont, her real name (nyme)? "Don't go over the top with it."

Her zeal struck me as excessive for the hasty plan I had in mind. But there was no time to explore an alternative. I offered her $100 for the afternoon. And she countered. She wanted a speaking credit in Danse du Sang, to qualify for membership in the Screen Actor's Guild. I considered. It wouldn't be hard to dub her part before the final cut. What the hell, I was still executive producer.

"Deal," I said.

We agreed to meet at Beverly Place at one o'clock.

My plan was simplicity itself. A quick surveillance confirmed the address now belonged to an antique dealer. Sharmayne and I would pose as decorator and client. I intended to deploy her sexy hauteur to occupy the shop's owner, while I hovered furtively near the faux fireplace. When the time was right, I'd recover the files and make off with them in my briefcase. After we hung up I realized the owner could be impervious to female charm. Too late. Sharmayne's distracting presence would have to carry it off.

At one o'clock I found myself lurking in front of the former offices of Costa Brava. The facade had been transformed. Paned windows framed the Georgian door, which was newly painted. Its brass knocker and latch glowed from restoration. And above the door, the script-lettered sign, Gaybois' Antiques, To the Trade.

The new tenant had broken out the street wall of the room in which the boxes had been stored, and new paned windows allowed me to glance inside.

A chandelier lit the room. The glow of a fake log on the hearth gave rise to apprehension. What if the files were singed—or worse, cinders.

Down the street a car door slammed and I thought it might be Sharmayne. The driver stepped out and started toward me. I turned away. At the sound of high heels, I whipped around again, astonished to recognize Sharmayne behind the prim disguise of a schoolmarm.

She flashed a triumphant smile. "Told ya, didn't (dint) I?"

I stepped back to take it in. Her hair, rinsed a dull brown, was pinned up in a librarian's knot. A silk ascot lay at her throat, secured by a brooch in the shape of a bug. And the midi skirt bunched at her waist like a sack.

"This is the temptress?" I asked. "Where's the skin I remember so well?"

"Don't get your knickers twisted, lad." Her Cockney Uncle? "I know how to play it."

Stranger things had happened. It wasn't the femme fatale I had in mind, but who had a choice?

"What's that bug at your throat?"

"It's a scarab." She drew a mirror from her purse and checked herself. "An Egyptian relic—I found it at the flea market in Santa Monica."

Oh, good.

A bell chimed as we entered. It was Gaybois himself, I assumed, seated behind a colonial desk before the fireplace, neighing into the phone with a high, false laugh.

"Def-initely," he trilled into the receiver. "Yo quiero la margarita grandé!" He glanced up, and seeing Sharmayne and me, raised a pale brow. "Gotta boogie," he said to the receiver. "Cli-ents." He terminated his conversation and bounded over to greet us.

"Oh, what's this. Does she wear a scarab—is it real?"

The nomination goes to Sharmayne Lafont for quick adaptation in a non-screen role. She regarded Gaybois with her signature hauteur. "A gentleman doesn't fondle a lady's scarab without an invitation," she said.

I almost burst out laughing—the remark inspired Gaybois to fresh titillation.

"Ex-cuse me," he said.

She slipped into her repertoire of accents—from Eliza Doolittle to Margaret Thatcher—with the virtuosity of Mozart playing Chopsticks. For my money, not a penny paid to the voice coach was wasted.

"My client's budget is $100,000—for the den," she said. "We're talking ten thousand square feet, above Sunset." She moved imperiously about the shop. "French only. Louis Quinze. Nothing provincial, life's too short. And I despise eclectic."

"Okay, darling." Gaybois said. "I get it. But come, chickie, You have to see my scarab collection."

Sharmayne spun a dubious tale of her engagement to a screen star whose mother, in a death-bed scene straight from the soaps, pressed the broach on her, compelling Sharmayne's promise to marry her son, a commitment Sharmayne was forced to abandon when she learned he had murdered his first wife.

"His family knew," Sharmayne insisted. "Bloody ghouls."

"You're putting me on," Gaybois replied in a whisper.

He led Sharmayne into the back rooms of the shop. I waited a full minute. Then I wedged myself behind the desk, kneeling before the fireplace. There was a brass fender, circa 1865, with a row of finials along the top. The andirons were also solid brass and made for a hunting hall. A large set of Georgian tools lay along the hearth.

I fumbled onto the peat shovel and it sprung up and whacked my jaw. I caught the handle in my right hand and laid it gently to one side. Crawling into the grate, I banged my knee against the claw foot of one of the andirons. When the pain subsided, I reached up the shaft. And found nothing.

I withdrew my arm, with my jacket sleeve smoking from the flame of the gas log. I slapped the gabardine to put it out, and smoke billowed into the room. As I fanned the area, I caught a face peering in the window from outside, and waved the fool away. Why choose this moment to buy antiques?

My frantic efforts only produced more smoke, and the faint smell of burning wool. Gaybois' desk held a crystal port-jug half filled with water. I seized it and doused my arm over the metal waste-paper basket. The drops hit the can like thunder. I froze, my heart thumping grotesquely. I listened for thirty seconds, but I heard only Sharmayne's laughter, loud and artificial.

It took a minute to locate the switch for the gas log. Turning it down to a bare ember, I crouched again before the hearth, extending my hand into the flue as far as it would go. My hand brushed against the metal side of the firebox and I flinched from its heat. My elbow struck the brick. I realized then how difficult it is to be a spy. A profession that requires one to steal secret papers, conceal them and, especially, recover them, has been vastly under-rated. The physical demands alone are enough to part the wheat from the chaff. I felt a strong identification with the chaff.

Gingerly, I renewed my attempt. This time I touched

paper. The files had fanned out and filled the shaft. They unrolled noisily in my hand. As I drew them out, flakes of scorched folder drifted onto the log. The file cover was crisp as toast.

The job was done. The high bouncing voice of Gaybois still twittered from another room, while the click of the latches on my briefcase seemed as loud as a wrecking ball. I couldn't wait around for scene two of the Scarab and the Actress. I hauled myself up and out of Gaybois' Antiques without a backward glance. With Sharmayne's talent for improvisation, I figured she could look after herself.

When I reached the street, I felt exhilarated with my good luck. I stole across the avenue to Le Restaurant, a very tony venue for the time, and phoned the deputy prosecutor, asking her to wait in her office until six o'clock. It was urgent to return with the files. Yet I needed time to review what I had.

Φ

The first of the two files, labeled "Filmland," contained nothing save several photographs taken with a telephoto lens, grainy black and whites of Alex outside the Chateau Marmont. And standing with him, seemingly in conversation, was the man I knew from the airfield, the man I surmised to be Jorge Trujillo.

I turned to the file marked "Rapunzel Project." A newspaper clipping from the business section of the Los Angeles Times reported that Tom Grass, local geologist, had settled litigation with his family, which resulted in his relinquishing all interest in the Inca Princess Mining Corporation.

There were copies of Brulée's checks, like those Father

Rob produced in my offices at Filmland, and a typed surveillance transcript, perhaps thirty pages, of telephone conversations between Ramòn and Tom Grass. Although cryptic, they supported my assumption that Brulée used the Inca Princess to shield the wealth of Iran's elite.

Then—an exchange of memos so brief you wouldn't think they touched upon anything more significant than the lunch schedule for the clerical staff. But they revealed why the government was intent on getting the files back. The first, from J. Trujillo to Chief of Operations, Drug Enforcement Agency, Washington, D.C., reported as follows:

Subject: Operation Star Search
Suspect B's illegal activity confirmed by surveillance at Inca Princess Mining Corp. Wiretap suggests B is associated with an agency of the United States. Awaiting further instructions before proceeding.
J. Trujillo.

The reply was dated one day later, to Drug Enforcement Agency, Los Angeles, Attn: Acting Current Investigations Officer:

Subject: Operation Star Search
Terminate operation immediately. Do not apprehend suspect B.

In 1980, most people remained ignorant of the vast network of political skullduggery carried on under the aegis of the United States government. So my first instinct was to dismiss the significance of what I read. I sat there in the garden of Le Restaurant reviewing the pages of confidential, inter-agency memoranda with growing outrage, while the restaurant's parking attendant wrestled the valet stand to the curb. By the time limos were pulling up with patrons for a five o'clock tete-a-tete and $500 bottle of Cristalle, I knew what I had to do.

42

Rider at the Justice Department

Within half an hour I was seated again before Leck and Ms. Vaughn, at the beige table in the pea-green room.

"You should have called it "The Scorpion Project," I said, "for the government's uncanny ability to sting itself."

I sat with my hands lightly on the files, tracing the links between Trujillo—the government's gumshoe—and Brulée's board game of illegal activities.

Laying out the evidence of an astonishing bureaucratic bungle, I began to feel a mixture of elation and fear. Irving and I had faltered into a turf war among government agencies.

In its zeal to stop drug money from finding its way into film production budgets, the DEA initiated its four-year "Operation Star Search," to infiltrate the film community and identify money-laundering sources.

Trujillo, the man in charge of the project, came across Brulée's money pipeline between his Persian contacts and the Inca Princess gold mine.

At first, the DEA was euphoric to find Brulée, just as its undercover operation was beginning to look like an expensive boondoggle. But they didn't count on his connections to powerful friends of the Shah. Instead of indicting the arms dealer, the Agency was forced to fold its tent. Everything else followed from that failure. Cut off in the moment of triumph, Leck's fierce resentment fueled his determination to prosecute Irving and me.

"I think it's rotten, don't you?" I taunted him. "—the way one arm of government flaunts the law even as another pretends to enforce it?"

"Damn right. We spent four bleeping years and two million dollars on Star Search, and came up with butkus."

He waved his hand in anger. "Blanking thugs at Langley—what right do they have to tell us to back off?"

CIA? So Brulée—and the Shah's friends—were protected by U.S intelligence.

"You asshole," I said for the second time that day. "Were Irving and I your face-saving scheme?"

Leck was standing now, his hands clenched at his sides.

"Why shouldn't we—you smug son of a bitch? Dodge, Grass, Brulée. You sleep with dogs, you got to scratch the fleas, my friend."

"Why shouldn't you? You forget I'm an attorney, Leck. The evidence against Irving and me wouldn't fill a teacup."

I stood too. "Let me suggest this scenario. You bring your trial. I'll get a special referee appointed to investigate the source of your evidence. Scrutinize the government's motives. Wide-ranging discovery. That means all files—any links between the DEA and the Inca Princess. Ramòn Brulée. The CIA. I won't predict where this will go, Leck, but I suspect you know."

My words were coming fast and lucid.

"Preview of coming testimony: the DOJ allowed the Inca Princess to be used as a CIA front for friends of the Shah—to circumvent the federal freeze on Iranian assets. Quid pro quo, I suspect, for favors the Shah extended to the U.S. over the years. Your pet project, Star Search, was left to swing in the wind. The Department's prosecution against Filmland was initiated to cover up the failure of your undercover operation."

"You'll never prove it."

I pushed my face closer to Leck's. "Don't try to break the saber over me, friend," I said. "The dual edge will slice you."

Vaughn had already risen from her seat. Her eyes were daggers to Leck.

"Good going, Frank. He would have walked out of here with two years and a promise to cooperate with our investigation. It was all about ego, wasn't it?"

Rigid with anger, she jerked her head at him to indicate the door.

"You," she glared at me, "stay here."

It was ten minutes before they returned.

Vaughn strode in first. She sat on the edge of her chair without looking at me. Leck seated himself in silence. I watched her pretend to read from notes, although I felt sure she was the architect of what she was about to say.

"All charges, state and federal, will be dismissed with prejudice against Maxwell Rider and Irving Fain. Defendants are granted immunity from prosecution as to any incident arising from Filmland Credit of Los Angeles, including the filming of Danse du Sang. The government does require—"

She tossed her hair, stole a triumphant glance at me. "Defendant Maxwell Rider's United States passport shall be surrendered following immediate repatriation to France, his country of dual citizenship. For a period of two years from this date, said defendant shall be denied admission to the United States, its territories or principalities."

"I'm exiled?" I sat back in my chair, stunned.

"We want you out of circulation for a very long time." Ms. Vaughn smiled grimly. "This is not a negotiation, Rider, this is the deal."

I thought of Europe. Alex, Countess, Marina Loge were there. And Susie Grass. It's what I'd wanted, once, to live abroad. And it was a chance to leave my failures behind. But it grew on me I wouldn't see my daughter for years. I wouldn't see Mona. And there would be penalties to keep me there. I understood I was being offered a form of house arrest but it started to dawn on me that Europe was not my home.

Ms. Vaughn fixed her pale eyes on me in a question. "We're waiting."

I studied the table surface a few minutes longer. Then, in a strange gesture in the windowless room, I removed my sunglasses from my jacket and put them on.

"I accept."

43.

Rider in Paris

Within twenty-four hours, Christian was on one of Brulée's transports headed for Geneva. Mona and Lainie were in Marin, land of wine and honeysuckle. And I was in Paris, taxiing toward the concourse of Charles de Gaulle Airport. The weather was gray. A drizzle had started, perhaps reflecting my dejected future. I'd called Countess to set me up with Brulée. I had no other possibilities. I thought I'd ask him for a job—something legitimate. She arranged an interview at the Ritz Hotel. I feared Susie would be there. Yet I wanted it too. I knew there was something left to be done, something between us.

During these past weeks, dense with concern for Christian, something had altered irretrievably in me. Some romantic perception had shifted from its place in my soul and moved on. When I looked for it, it was gone. And I felt too old to ever look on Susie's flaws with the same tender regard as I had three weeks before.

I queued up at the taxi stand outside the terminal and allowed the drizzle to soak my hair and clothes. I hadn't thought of packing an umbrella; my things were being sent.

"Ritz Hotel," I said, glad at least to have a destination.

The Ritz exuded the dark suffocating charm I'd come to associate with European luxury. I'd stayed there with Irving six months before, in a high-living style, and the exhilaration of our designs for Filmland had imparted a glow to the experience entirely absent on this occasion.

Susie was there enjoying an absinthe in the bar. You could

still get absinthe in Europe at that time. I ordered one too, as they had the effect of making me a bit crazy. I kissed her circumspectly, then drew back to observe her exquisite poise for the last time. She crossed her ankles—they glimmered like mercury under the hosiery she wore. She looked very beautiful. My emotions surged up like tangled socks. And I began to have regrets.

"Max, darling," she said. "Ramòn's tied up but he's anxious to speak with you about your plans."

I pulled out a chair and we sat alone. I talked over and around what had happened to us together, and what had happened afterward to me, and she sat perfectly still, listening and sipping the cloudy liquid from a crystal tumbler. A harsh shadow moved over her face and she smiled with a brittleness I hadn't seen before.

"I can't expect you to know," she said. "Ramòn and I have set a date."

I doubted that, though she could have brought him to heel with the clap of her hands. But I pretended to be surprised. For just a minute I wondered if I wasn't making a mistake. Then I thought it all over again quickly and got up to say goodbye.

She detained me with a hand, "We've tried to reach you, Winton and I. We are willing to buy back your shares of the Inca Princess stock. Immediately. Out of friendship. Today."

For the second time in twenty-four hours I was stunned. What good was a gold mine with no gold? I'd left the shares with Irving, with my promise if anything ever came of them we'd share as partners. I swallowed hard. The warning prickle of intuition brought me up sharply, and I began to think I should call Irving for news of the mine.

"Excuse me," I said. I leaped up, strode to the magasin

off the lobby. The American publications were terribly out of date. I drew a day-old Variety from the racks, threw down five francs on the counter and began reading the inside column Just for Variety.

"Good morning! Producer Irving Fain called on his way to Le Dôme this morning. Apparently, he's back in the movie business. A gold mine owned by Fain and his partner, Maxwell Rider, is the site of discovery of a major oil-producing well. 'We'll be producing in no time. And then we'll be producing—ha, ha!' announced Fain. 'We're planning a slate of pictures on a Euro-American theme. My partner, Max Rider, is in Europe right now, lining up the best talent Europe has to offer.' This was good news to those of us who…"

I felt immediately joyful, charmed by an impulsive fate. I suddenly recalled the clay figurine I'd taken from the stones at Fiesole, and its message: Expect the Unexpected.

That seemed very long ago. I thought of my father's impatient gaze, and straightened instinctively. Unexpected tears stung my eyes. "Well done," I said aloud. It hit me then. I was free.

I returned to Susie in the bar, with a cock-eyed grin that wouldn't leave my face. I glanced up and saw Brulée moving toward me, his head lunged forward and his toupée pouncing discreetly. I rushed forward to clasp his hand and, to his astonishment, embraced him, lifting him off his feet.

"Congratulations, Ramòn," I said. "I'm glad to say we have nothing more to speak about. Apparently, I'm back in the movie business."

To Susie I tossed a salute. Then I charged from the Ritz Hotel to launch Irving's and my new venture—the Paris operations of Filmland Pictures.

EPILOGUE, 1996

Last year in late October I saw Alex. He was walking ahead of me on La Croisette in Cannes. Despite the years, I knew him. I was struck again by his irresistible jauntiness, which drew me toward him like the leaves tossing along the street. But the memory of our parting in LA restrained me. And I slowed up to avoid overtaking him. Just as I did so, he stopped to exchange pleasantries with the doorman outside the Majestic Hotel. When he saw me, he walked back holding out his hand.

"Max!" he exclaimed, genuinely glad to see me. "What a good surprise." Then he observed my reticence.

"What's the matter old man, do you object to shaking hands with me?"

"It's good to see you Alex," I stepped forward reluctantly. Resentments I'd thought long buried exhumed themselves. "It's just that—you never helped Christian. You left me holding the bag."

Alex stared at me in utter amazement. "Why, Christian's all right. He's forgiven me. We spent September at Rocco Gigli's on Capri."

Alex rubbed his palms together as if he were to be congratulated on Christian's recovery. "I had to leave, Max. I was flat. Pulling my pockets out."

I tried not to be charmed by him. My first admiration for my European friends seemed very long ago. I felt I'd heard it all before, and reached the limits of my patience—with the premise that deprivation is harder on the rich. I prepared to leave him, but he placed himself squarely before me and spoke with a candor I'd never seen in him before.

"European style, American practicality," he said soberly. "They haven't always made the best companions. But you know—there are times one is no good without the other.

"I couldn't help Christian, Max," Alex went on. "It was your intrepid spirit that pulled him through. I've always envied your resourcefulness, and I value your friendship more than you know."

His eyes were bright with emotion and I looked away to compose myself.

"If I'd have stayed things would have been a tangle," he went on with sincerity. "A legal nightmare. It would have made a colorful circus, but it was better for Christian that I should leave. And," he smiled shyly. "My Inca Princess shares gave you a start on Filmland again."

We both laughed in memory and relief.

Alex turned his attention to the fair autumn day and gestured appreciatively, as if he were responsible for its crisp beauty. "Let's take lunch."

"The Majestic terrace?" I asked rhetorically.

They say everyone returns to the scene of their time. And the riddle of our past always comes around again. I've often felt quite amazed at my younger self. How could I have believed the way I did?

There, on the terrace of the Majestic, I understood. For I saw Alex's actions were, by his code, entirely justified. It all had a careless, charming logic. And I saw I had a code too. An American code. During my time in LA I found it. And I saw, in that moment of forgiving Alex, I'd forgiven myself.

"You know I'm leaving for the States?" he said, as we entered the hotel.

"The States?"

"The new owners of Danse du Sang—they're releasing

the film at last. It seems Americans are into art films again. The terms are very generous. Spending tons of money. They've hired me to promote it! You'll help of course. We'll work together on it."

"My daughter Lainie's with me now," I said proudly. "Executive producer at Filmland. She'll have some ideas."

"Isn't America fantastic, Max? The land of opportunity!"

I see now that this has been an American story after all, for in the end, I am thoroughly American. Not of my father's world. That was never to be. And no amount of money, or style, or proximity to people like Alex could change that. My status was fixed at the moment of my birth. And the good thing to come of these events was my acceptance of it.

ABOUT THE AUTHOR

Kia McInerny is an author and former attorney whose colorful connections to the film business led to *Max in Filmland*.

Kia's other novels include *Bond Hunter*, a fast-paced international thriller currently available at Tecolote Book Shop, Montecito, and on Amazon.com. *Bond Hunter* is based on little known facts concerning Hitler's financial ties to Wall Street. Kia has also authored *Murder in Malibu*, a contemporary LA-noir tale of betrayal and murder, soon to be available on Amazon. Kia's short fiction has been featured on public radio and in literary magazines.

In non-fiction, Kia's wine and travel essays have appeared internationally in Singapore, Ireland and the U.K, as well as in the United States. She currently lives in Santa Barbara and Los Angeles with her husband.

For commentary and images regarding Kia's books, please check out Kia's Author Page on Amazon.com.

53577972R00175

Made in the USA
San Bernardino, CA
21 September 2017